Fantastically Flawed

Shonda,
Thank you so much
for sharing your family
with me.
Much Love
+
Many Blessings,
Wendy A. Wood

WENDY A WOOD

Fantastically Flawed

Editing by Kerry Genova of Writer's Resource Inc.
Cover by Wicked by Design
Formatting by Champagne Formats

ISBN-13: 978-1512163223
ISBN-10: 1512163228

Dedication

This book is dedicated to the two most amazing human beings to ever grace my life; my daughters,

Alexandra and *Samantha*

Although you are too young to read this book right now, know someday that you are the reason I believe in miracles and magic. I love you with all that I am.

Prologue

NICHOLE TWISTED ANXIOUSLY IN her chair awaiting the results of her daughter's latest battery of tests. Although it had been over a year since the operation was performed to close the hole in Hanna's heart, she approached each new visit with foreboding and dread, praying for the best, but expecting the worst. Life had taught her many cruel lessons, brought her to her knees more than once, yet never managed to completely break her.

She glanced over at her daughter as she played carelessly in the corner with her dolls. She laughed and played as any normal child of her tender age. While Hanna tenderly doted on her pretend child made of nylon and plastic, Nichole realized just how much she looked like her father; the same dark hair and beaming smile, the shape of her mouth and nose, all nearly an exact replica of the original. She became lost in her thoughts of how truly precious Hanna was to her. Never at anytime in her life did she believe she could love another human being so completely, so unconditionally. Yet, from the moment that tiny, helpless creature was placed in her arms her heart was transformed. It had been over two years, she thought to herself, but they were two very long years.

Lost in a world all her own, Nichole was startled as the office door opened bringing her back to the reality of her present time and place. As she watched Dr. Wellington enter the room she began to feel that all too familiar lump well in her throat followed by an uncontrollable churning in her stomach. His expression was unreadable as he placed himself in an oversized, worn leather chair. He carefully placed the papers he carried atop his antique style desk, folded his hands, and cracked a devilish smile.

"Nichole dear, could you please stop looking filled with gloom and doom every time you come in here? I'm starting to develop a complex." His tone was gruff yet reassuring. "I've told you before that these tests are a necessary precautionary measure. Hanna is perfect in every way. She's a beautiful and healthy, two-year-old little girl. Now stop worrying so much and enjoy her."

As the words registered in her mind she slumped in her chair, closed her eyes, and felt the nervous tension leaving her body. Her eyes stung as she fought to hold back the tears but it was pointless, they flowed against her will from between a mantel of wet lashes.

"Children are resilient," he continued, "They heal much faster than you or I. Her scar will fade with time and this will be nothing more than a distant memory to you both. The next thing you know she'll be driving you crazy with grades and boys."

"Let's not rush things, okay Doc?" She managed to laugh despite the whirlwind of emotions that were coursing through her.

He looked with compassion at the smile on her tear-stained face. Not only was James Wellington a doctor, but a true gentleman and friend. He saved the life of her daughter and her own sanity on more than one occasion. He was one of the few men on this planet that she trusted without question. Nichole's hands were shaking. He reached out to steady them. She looked at him with adoration in her eyes.

"There is nothing I could possibly do to repay you. You've done so much, been so patient and kind. You have no idea how grateful I am that you came into our lives."

He rose from his chair still holding her hand and looked down at her.

"All I want from you," he said, "is a promise that you will learn to relax and enjoy your daughter, enjoy your life. It's high time both of you became acquainted with a world not filled with doctors and hospitals and old coots like me."

A feeling of peace washed over her. She stood, kissed the old man on the cheek, and grasped her daughter tightly in her arms as she prepared to leave the hospital. Walking down the familiar pale blue corridor she said good-bye to the once nameless faces of the many doctors and nurses that had now become dear friends. When she stepped outside, the warmth of the sun beat down on her face. Its heat mixed with salty smell of the sea and the faint tingle of the crisp morning air mixed together to bring life back to her numbed senses, as the sound of the hospital doors closing behind her rang through her ears as a final farewell to years of unrelenting pain. She took a deep breath as she approached her car, opened her door, and placed her daughter tenderly in her car seat, securing it carefully as to not damage her precious cargo. She couldn't wait to tell Maxie the good news and left the hospital parking lot, destination McCallister's.

McCallister's was Nichole's second baby. She gave birth to it through her own blood, sweat, and tears. She had spent endless days and nights restoring it to its former grandeur, critiquing every detail until it reached perfection. Originally it was built as the home of a prominent English family that settled in America in the late 1700s. Six generations had been born and raised within its walls. Eventually ownership was transferred to residents outside the clan and had been most recently owned by a successful Yorktown attorney who considered it nothing more than an eyesore and left it vacant for nearly a decade. Time had not been kind to the structure and when Nichole made him an offer he jumped at the chance to unload his burden onto her shoulders.

When she first laid eyes on it she was immediately enchanted with the neglected Colonial Georgian style building. Despite its ram-shackled appearance she was determined to return it to the time and grace of its original construction. From its brass and crystal chandeliers to the Chippendale furniture made of mahogany, all details were intricate and fragile. Fresh flowers and candlelight adorned every table. She had managed to create a surrounding that overflowed with elegance, with a sophistication that was uncommon to the area.

McCallister's became an instant success. Locals and tourists alike filled the dining rooms throughout the year.

Nichole parked the car and took a long look at the building that brandished her name. Free from worry, she was able to appreciate all she had accomplished. A self-made woman raising a child alone was no easy task. It was the path she had chosen, paying a dear price for it along the way, yet now she was able to reap the rewards she deeply deserved. As she approached the renovated eighteenth century home the lunchtime hostess opened the door to greet her.

"Good afternoon, Ms. McCallister."

Nichole hurriedly returned her greeting and began looking around for Maxie, Hanna at her side.

"Where is Mr. Porter?" she asked.

"He is speaking with someone at the moment, but I was asked to give you a message," the girl replied.

Nichole disregarded her statement and walked through the entrance in search of her business partner and friend. As she neared her office another employee stopped her. A man whose name she struggled to remember.

"Ms. McCallister, there is a gentleman here to see you and from the look on Mr. Porter's face when he arrived, I'd say it's fairly important."

Nichole was in such high spirits that the last thing she wanted to do was deal with anything related to business.

"Yes, yes, all of that can wait. I'm sorry. I'm a bit distracted at the moment. Where exactly is Mr. Porter," she questioned, trying not to appear agitated.

It was then that Maxie, who was in the dining room, spotted Nichole. He kindly excused himself from the conversation that he was engaged in and rushed to her side. Grabbing her by the arm, Hanna trailing behind, he led them into her office in an attempt to divert her attention from the guests. Shutting the door behind them, they both began speaking simultaneously, neither hearing a word the other said.

"Maxie damn it will you listen to me." It was more a command than a question, she was almost yelling at that point. "You were right all along. I worried myself sick for no reason. The tests came back perfect, the EKG was flawless." She was practically beaming.

He hadn't seen Nichole this happy or excited about anything in a long time and he knew that attempting to dominate a conversation with her when the topic was her daughter was absolutely pointless. He yielded to her impatience to let her finish speaking and then began.

"I'm happy for you honey, for both of you, but there is something you need to know. Did Janey give you the message I left for you? It's a—." Nichole cut him off mid sentence.

"Yes, I know. There's someone important here to see me. Can't you handle it or tell him to come back later. I'm not in the mood to deal with any kind of problems today Maxwell. Whoever he is, he can wait."

The look on Maxie's face had gone from endearing to severe and she quieted. "Listen to me," he said and took her hands into his own. "The last thing I want to do is ruin this day for you, but you need to shut up and let me do the talking for a minute."

He rarely if ever spoke to her this way and she was momentarily stunned into silence.

"Nichole . . . Michael's here."

The room was suddenly a tomb of silence. The only sound to be heard was the ticking of the clock on the wall at the opposite side of the room. All expression left her face, a chill swept over her, and then the panic set in.

"Michael? You're sure it's Michael?" She struggled to maintain her composure as she asked the question.

"I'm positive. It's Michael Collier, the real estate mogul who owns half of the country, Michael Collier.

"I know who the hell he is," she began to shout as she paced the floor, "but what I want to know is why, in the name of all that's holy is he here and why now?"

Maxie shook his head. He had no answers despite his attempts to find out before Nichole had arrived.

"I don't know honey, but I don't think he plans on leaving until he speaks to you. I told him there was a good chance you wouldn't come in today, but he didn't seem to believe me."

She closed her eyes and began massaging her temples in a fruitless attempt to grasp the situation in her mind, but it was impossible for her to think clearly. So many memories, so much heartache, she couldn't possibly process this all right now. Frustration consumed her and she gave into the fact that the only thing she could do was face him and figure out for herself why he come after so long.

"Fine. I'm going to go and find out why he's here, but I need you to keep Hanna in here and keep her out of sight."

Maxie nodded in agreement and walked over behind Hanna who was scribbling at her mother's desk, oblivious to the conversation that was going on around her. Maxie looked down at her and then at Nichole.

"Are you going to tell him?" he asked flatly.

Nichole closed her eyes and drew in a deep breath in an attempt to stop her heart from racing.

"*No* . . . I mean . . . I don't know." Her words faltered as the tension grew inside her. "Please, one thing at a time. First I need to find out why he's here and I'll just have to make that decision when my head clears."

Nichole left her office dazed and confused. The day had started out perfectly. The hurricane that had passed through town had left them untouched. Hanna's final appointment with her pediatric cardiologist was all Nichole has hoped for. Why Michael? Why now? The main dining room was filled with the afternoon lunch crowd and busy employees rushing to and fro, catering to their every need. In the distance was the sound of a cork being released from its wine bottle prison. She scanned the room and within seconds her gaze was fixed on an all too familiar face seated at a table tucked neatly away in the corner against the opposite wall. His eyes, his face, his hands, all unchanged since the last time she had seen him nearly three years ago. She could never forget that day; the effects of it had changed the entire course of her life. The dozens of voices rising from the crowd gathered to reach her ears as an overwhelming buzzing noise. She began to feel light-headed and suddenly images of the past assaulted her senses. Falling back from sight she grabbed her head and leaned against the wall for support.

Chapter 1

MICHAEL WOKE WITH A jolt. He was not certain what the dream had been about this time, but he could guess. Although he had done his best to bury his past, built walls around him that no one could penetrate, his subconscious found it necessary to remind him now and again of a brutal, lonely childhood no man, nor beast should have to endure. His mother had died giving birth to him, a fact his father made certain he would never forget.

His father was all he had. Stephen Collier was a cold man and an emotionally unavailable parent. He never showed the slightest hint of interest in Michael. There was no affection or tenderness in his small world and those were the good times. When the old man got into one of his moods and took to the bottle Michael would try to hide, but Stephen always seemed to find him. A toy left out, what few there were, a dish left in the sink, he didn't need a reason, but it always ended the same; a new bruise, broken bone, or worse, much worse. Never properly treated of course and Michael learned he was always at fault. Deserving of the years of neglect and violent attacks at the hand of the one person in the world who was supposed to protect him above all else, the one person in the world he needed reassurance from the most.

By the age of six, Michael had taught himself how to cook basic, rudimentary meals. He did the dishes and knew how to use the washer and dryer. Each evening he would see to his bath or shower and put himself to bed, and he did it all out of necessity. It was about that same age that he learned it was best to hide his tears. By the age of nine, he had stopped crying altogether. He had no tears left and no one cared anyway.

Despite his living conditions at home he thrived at school. He excelled in sports and his grades were superior. He was popular among his classmates and even more popular among the girls. His achievements were never recognized by his father and that fueled the resentment he had for the old man. He focused on building strength in his mind and body and lived for the day he was old enough to escape the tormented world in which he existed.

Now here he sat, drenched in sweat, uncertain which memory dared to rouse him, but certain of one thing, his head ached. The sun was bright through the curtains and as he parted them to reveal the New York skyline it all came back to him. The deal had gone through and he had celebrated, bringing in his fortieth year with a blonde whose name he didn't remember and a bottle of brandy that lay empty on the floor. He was now the proud owner of yet another multi-million dollar commercial real estate property and that was one thing he took very seriously.

His business was his life. Slow starting at first, yet in less than two decades he had become one of the wealthiest men in the world and with wealth came women. Power, the world's most potent aphrodisiac. The nameless blond still unconscious in his bed was a testament to that. There had been many just like her over the years. So many he was almost too ashamed to count. Not only was Michael Collier powerful and wealthy, he was incredibly handsome. He stood at six feet two inches, with hair black as night, chiseled features, and a body no woman could resist. But it was his eyes that often caught people off guard. They were the palest shade of ice blue and in contrast to his dark features they created a contradiction of emotions when you first encountered him, inviting yet unapproachable, tempting yet menacing.

His cell phone began to dance across the nightstand and with the pounding in his head he was thankful he had the wits about him to turn it on vibrate the night before. The name on the display screen read

"Hogan." He wrapped a towel around his waist in an attempt to display some sense of decorum, should the young lady in his bed awaken. He flopped down on the sofa in the next room.

"Morning, Tom."

"Morning, Mike. You sound like shit."

"I feel like shit now that you mention it."

"I'm hoping that's a result of an overzealous birthday celebration and not a deal gone sour?" Tom inquired.

"The deal went through, we're good on this end. Where to next?" he asked, eager to move on to his next conquest.

"Mike, let me ask you a question. Are you hell bent on owning the world or just a major portion of North America?"

Michael chuckled. Tom was the one person in the world he allowed to give him a hard time. They had been friends since childhood and had seen each other through hell and back. Tom Hogan was the only part of Michael's past that he allowed into his future. He'd never once judged him or criticized him. Tom knew the demons that Michael carried and he respected him even more for not allowing a nightmarish childhood become an excuse to be a worthless adult. It was the opposite in fact. He used it as a catalyst to become a success. He'd made something of himself and made Tom a rich man in the process.

"North America will do, for now," he said with sarcastic humor in his voice.

"Well in that case you're headed for South Eastern Virginia. Your flight is set for Monday morning. I'll email you the itinerary."

"Don't we own something down there already?" Michael asked, trying to recall from memory what states he'd conquered was becoming increasingly difficult.

"Yeah. A small office type deal about thirty minutes drive from the new site. It's been run for the past five years by a woman . . . last name McCallister. Why?"

"Well if we already have someone in the area under our employ who knows the people, knows the area, she could be an asset. Find out all you can about her. Call me back when you know something."

Michael hung up with Tom and then called room service. He ordered coffee and an elaborate breakfast for two. He might not remember her name, but he could at least send her on her way with some nourishment in her. He headed for the shower and stopped to take a long look at himself in the bathroom mirror. He knew deep down why he did the things he did, but he would never admit it aloud to himself or to anyone else no matter their significance in his life.

Many years spent helpless and vulnerable had left their mark on his soul. Jaded and battle-hardened from birth, he prided himself in his ability to never depend on another living being, to never succumb or be made a fool of romantic notions. Any entanglements he had involved himself with over the years served one of two purposes, they either increased his power and wealth or satiated his physical needs.

Although Michael was never deliberately cruel or unkind to any woman, he made himself perfectly clear that he held no interest in the prospect of love and yet a multitude of broken hearts lay in his wake as he made his way around the country. Women of all ages were drawn to him, enthralled by his well-muscled body and the piercing blue of his eyes. His power and wealth and devilish good looks made him infinitely enticing and he reaped his rewards with an unrepentant arrogance and pride in the knowledge that his heart would never become victim to such folly.

Standing in front of the mirror he winced at his reflection. The image looking back at him bared an eerie resemblance to the man who fathered him, with burning bloodshot eyes and yellowish tinted skin. Perhaps the time had come when he needed to harness his enthusiasm for overindulgence. His stay in Virginia was to be exponentially longer than most, which would be as good a place as any to regroup, settle down, and focus on business alone.

Collier Real Estate of South Eastern Virginia was located off Jefferson Avenue in Newport News. It was a modest-sized building that was home to many professionals; psychiatrists, attorneys, an insurance company, and an architectural firm. According to Tom's email, Michael had owned the building for eleven years now. For the last five years, it had been run single-handedly by a young woman named Nichole McCallister. Trying to place the name with a face, he couldn't recall having met her.

Michael's stay in the area was to be an extensive one. Construction on the Collier Creative Arts Center was well under way and he was there to see the thing through. The Center encompassed a full city block, several smaller buildings already leased to multiple retailers surrounding the forty story Art Center was to be his crowning glory. It was being erected in the Towne Center area of Virginia Beach. Tom saw to it that a four-bedroom town house complete with all the amenities along the coast had been leased in Michael's name as well as a Jaguar XKA Victory Edition convertible.

Growing up with next to nothing led Michael to become and adult who enjoyed surrounding himself with the finer things that life had to offer. He sat on the balcony off the master bedroom suite. It faced the water, the sound of the waves relaxed him. He traveled extensively be it business or pleasure and he always preferred cities along the coastline. It didn't matter what coastline. No matter how far he had come in his life Michael never did find it easy to relax and unwind, but the sound of the waves repeatedly crashing the shore never failed to soothe him. It was hypnotic, he could stare for hours and not think of anything or anyone. However, it was Tom's latest email he stared at presently.

Mike,

I did some digging on the woman that we currently have employed as Director of Operations at CRC Newport News. Her name is Nichole McCallister, twenty-eight years old. From what I could find out she knows her shit. Started with us five years ago and has consistently increased the profit margin. I called around to some of the tenants there and they all seem to be fond of her, very professional, friendly, that sort of thing. Comes from a good family, single, no children. Oh and there is one more thing, she is a certified black belt and is licensed to carry concealed.

Regards,

Tom

Black belt? Licensed to carry concealed, what the hell was that about? Michael reached for his cell and hit speed dial.

"Hogan."

"The woman's licensed to carry a gun and certified in martial arts?" he questioned incredulously.

Michael's inquiry was half concern, half fascination. Most women that he had encountered, and there were many, were not so lethal. Twenty-eight and single to top it all off. She had to have a story. They all had a story and he wanted to know what hers was.

"Yeah, that one threw me a bit too. I stopped the search there. Thought you might want to investigate further on your own ole boy, but I can dig deeper if you want me to," Tom said trying not to laugh.

He knew that bit of information would get Michael's attention and thought he'd have some fun with him. The older Michael got the less he seemed to truly enjoy life despite his multitude of nefarious exploits. He rarely laughed and never smiled so Tom tried to throw him a curve ball every now and then to keep him on his toes, get a chuckle out of him to make sure he hadn't completely lost his sense of humor.

Tom was also aware that Michael's wounds ran deep and wounds that ran deep and that were left unattended would fester. That mixed with too much time on the road alone tended to take him into a dark place that was damn near impossible to bring him back from. The McCallister woman made it easy with this tidbit of information.

"As far as my investigation of her, I know what you were insinuating," Michael said dryly. "You know damn well my one rule is I never screw the women I work with directly and I'm going to be working closely with this one for the next six months at least. If you would be so kind as to extend your search a bit, I'd be interested to know what you find out."

When they had hung up, Tom laughed in spite of himself. Not because of Michael's comment, but because he had found out one more bit of information about the elusive Ms. McCallister. One he had failed to mention to Michael. Something that made her more lethal than the mere fact that she carried a gun, but all things in good time and Michael would be finding out for himself in a few short hours. He was due to meet with her in her office at three PM.

Chapter 2

"THIRTY MINUTES MY ASS," Michael said aloud to no one in particular.

The drive to Newport News had taken him over an hour and a half. Tom had forgotten to mention the Hampton Roads Bridge Tunnel and the construction from hell through the city of Hampton. He stepped from his car and spied the building before him. Not the most impressive structure, but well kept and lucrative for its size. It stood a mere six stories high, newly refurbished exterior, the landscaping was up to par. It was May in the area and all the spring flowers had bloomed. The air was warm with a slight breeze and the humidity had not yet set in. From the outside all seemed status quo, but he still wasn't exactly sure what to expect on the inside.

Most of the women Michael worked with tended to be less than fond of him. In the office he was strictly business, brash and intimidating. To Michael, his business was a reflection of himself, the man that he had made of himself in spite of the insurmountable odds he faced as a child. He did not go out of his way to be charming; there were no ulterior motives while he worked. Most women were completely enamored with him initially and as a result feelings got hurt. He hoped that wouldn't be the case with this woman.

Stepping into the lobby he took a moment to give the place a quick once-over. If a building displayed his name it had to be up to his standards and to his surprise it was, but then again why shouldn't it be, he undoubtedly paid for it all, leather furniture, shining tile, soft music barely audible yet welcoming. Whoever this gun-wielding woman turned out to be it was obvious she was earning her keep.

Michael was told that the director of operations office was down the hall and to the right. As he approached the cut-glass door, he paused to steal a glimpse of this already intriguing stranger. Her back was turned to him and she was obviously engrossed in a phone conversation that muted the sound of his light rap upon the door. Michael knew he was expected and entered with no further warning.

However, the reaction he received was not what he had been expecting, but then again neither was she. Nichole jerked her body around in a stiff defensive movement and stumbled back slightly, taken unawares at the presence in the room. That was when he caught his first glimpse of her. She stood about five feet seven inches he'd guessed, sable hair that she wore up, professional and strikingly beautiful. Although the weather was warm she donned a cream-colored business suit, slacks, and jacket that hugged her curves. He got the impression she was trying to hide herself somewhat, for what reason he could not begin to imagine. He wasn't sure if it was her emerald, almond-shaped, cat-like eyes or the fear that he saw in them that mesmerized him more. The fear was fleeting, but it was there. He recognized it, knew it all too well. He had seen it in his own reflection many times before, but he was younger then.

"I'm sorry. I didn't mean to frighten you," he said plainly in an attempt to conceal his surprise.

Nichole quickly hung up the phone and attempted a smile in an effort to thwart her unease. She met his stare and for several moments that seemed like a small eternity there hung a stunned silence between them. An unspoken recognition that defied explanation because although she had heard the many rumors she was certain she had never encountered the elusive Mr. Collier before. He appeared to be a man not easily forgotten. She broke the silence before it became awkward.

"Mr. Collier, I assume." She extended her hand in greeting. "I'm sorry. You merely startled me. Shall we sit?"

Nichole motioned to a small conference table where they could both be seated on equal footing. Michael was grateful for her gesture. He felt like he had smacked into a brick wall and had no idea what to make of it. When it came to business and women he had mastered the art of self-control and with a glance this beauty had rendered him speechless. She was beautiful there was no doubt about that, but there was something else, something evasive yet powerful about this woman that immediately fascinated him.

The phone rang again and she excused herself while she set the answering service to receive further calls. Nichole still wasn't certain why he was here. All the information she had received was that the man himself, Michael Collier was coming to town for an extended period and may require her assistance. Of the five years that she had been with the company the only thing she had ever seen of this man was his signature on her paychecks and that was a stamped mark, not the real thing and yet his notoriety preceded him.

She had been summoned to Houston for mandatory conferences several times during her tenure at CRC. Michael had been born and bred in Texas and the Collier main office building was located in the heart of downtown Houston. He never attended these conferences of course, he was always much too busy, but he had built quite a reputation for himself. The men always spoke of what a hard-ass he was, highly critical and overbearing. They said he was cold and cynical. "The bastard thinks the sun rises and sets for him alone," as one man from the Colorado office had put it. From their comments Nichole deduced that the men all appeared to be quite intimidated by him. The women, well that was something altogether different. She'd heard them talk at lunch and in the ladies' room. Michael Collier had become quite a celebrity in their eyes. Wickedly attractive, sinfully sensuous and they went on and on, all hoping to be the one to crack his code of fraternization among the ranks. Rumors of his libido and sex life had also reached tales of epic proportion. She'd heard it all, but never gave it a second thought, until now.

Now he stood a mere three feet away from her and it was more than obvious that the physical descriptions were accurate, he was wickedly handsome, but to her he appeared all business. He stood at the conference table and unloaded his briefcase. It was overflowing with blueprints, design plans, and charts of projected expenditures. He laid it all out and spoke to her simultaneously without bothering to look up. She felt slighted by this and it surprised her.

"Ms. McCallister, I have a proposition for you," he said dryly, still without bothering to make eye contact. "If you accept, it will mean a great deal more money for you, but along with that comes more responsibility and more hours."

He explained in detail that the new series of office buildings being erected in Virginia Beach, the newest addition to the Collier Dynasty was going to need someone to take control of the day-to-day operations. The new project was going to be a monster and he needed to be sure she was confident enough in her abilities to be able to handle the three towers that would ultimately occupy a full city block and literally hundreds of businesses. If she accepted, she would need to hire and train a replacement for herself in her present position immediately and spend time with him learning the ropes of running a major office complex. She would also have to be adept at drawing in new tenants, become comfortable with designating authority, hiring, firing, the good and the bad. Michael had presented it as more of a challenge than an opportunity and Nichole rarely passed up a challenge.

Being given little time to make such a life altering decision, her mind raced. She was hesitant at first, her thoughts bumping into one another at the onslaught of information presented to her by a man whose mere presence caused her to flush. Irritated slightly by the effect he was having upon her and never one to shirk responsibility, in the end Nichole had accepted.

It had become evident during the course of their meeting that Michael Collier was interested in her for solely business purposes appearing aloof and almost cold at times. Nichole rationalized that his approach was for the best. Despite the initial rush to her senses, Nichole had no interest in becoming another notch on this man's bedpost or in being the topic of water cooler conversation, besides he was twelve years her senior. What could they possibly have in common? For her first duties she would help him get acquainted with the area and its people. In return he was going to teach her everything he knew about running a multi-million dollar business complex.

Moments after leaving the building, Michael reached for his cell phone as he started his car.

"Hogan."

"Tom," Michael said. He sounded pissed off even to himself, but that was the effect he had been looking for. "When I hired you to help me run this monster of a company that I created, one thing that stood out about you was your attention to detail. You never miss a trick. Now is there something . . . anything at all that you forgot to tell me about Nichole McCallister?"

Michael quickly pulled the phone away from his ear as he received a steady, hearty laugh as his reply.

"You son of a bitch, you could have at least warned me."

"Mike, I thought it would come as a pleasant surprise. Maybe brighten up your day a bit. Besides she knows her stuff. Does it matter that she's a knockout?"

Michael closed his eyes and briefly imagined himself reaching through the phone and choking him. No, he couldn't actually kill him. Tom was his best friend, his only true friend, but he should have given him some indication of what he was about to get himself into.

Tom was well aware of Michael's only rule where women in the workplace were concerned; share their office, but never their bed. In all his years in the business game, he had never once crossed that line. He changed the subject instead.

"Have you found out anything else about her?

"No, nothing yet, but if there is anything to find, I'll find it."

As he drove down I64 he realized he it wasn't Tom that he was mad at. Something had been nagging at him since he laid eyes on her and it had nothing to do with the fact that he was physically attracted to her. It had been in the first fleeting moments when he had startled her and it vanished just as quickly, but there was no doubt it was real. It was the undeniable look of fear in those mesmerizing green eyes. Someone had hurt her, not merely emotionally, but physically as well.

For reasons he had not yet accepted, he had the urge to find the bastard that had done the evil deed and beat him to within an inch of his life. Michael had been guilty of breaking many hearts, but he never once raised a hand to a woman in anger and he would not tolerate anyone that would. No matter what people thought of him, he did maintain some semblance of decency about himself.

Hell, he half hated himself for being the cause behind bringing the fear to the surface for her, if it was only for a brief moment. He was sure she had been unaware of it, yet he struggled through every second of their meeting to remain as distant and uninterested as he possibly could. He knew next to nothing about her and yet he knew something she did not. They both had a secret they were determined to keep hidden from the world. They both wore a mask to hide the unspeakable. He understood her in ways she could never fathom. The next six months were going to be very complicated and take every ounce of self-restraint he could muster. The physical is one thing, but this raven-haired beauty had his mind spinning.

Chapter 3

THE WEEKS PASSED RATHER quickly. Michael had set up a temporary workstation in Nichole's office until construction at the new site had progressed enough that they would be capable of operating out of Virginia Beach. He had insisted they share her office space for the time being. She still had much to learn about the business and Michael was emphatic that she learn all there was to know directly from him.

He watched as the calls came in and issues added up and became increasingly impressed with her work, her ability to balance and handle the pressure of her old workload while training a replacement, mixed with the weight of taking on all of her new responsibilities. Her deftness in the boardroom and her flair for winning over seasoned veterans of the real estate world was unparalleled. Had she not been working for him, Michael himself would be concerned for his own assets.

As it were however, Michael found himself becoming increasing preoccupied with the assets of his young protégé. Many times since he had arrived in Virginia, he had caught himself cursing Tom under his breath; he had sent him into dangerous territory without so much as a warning or shield of resistance. He had been tempted more than once over the years with the desire to bed this secretary or that personal assistant, but he had always managed to resist those urges, knowing no possible good could come out of the situation.

In hindsight, those women barely held a candle to this brazen beauty who filled his days with her alluring presence. He longed to find a flaw, some chink in her armor that would alter his opinion of her and yet each day she appeared more enticing with a natural beauty that was unequalled, a passion for learning to matched his own and her effortless ability to command the attention and respect of Collier Reality's most hardened critics.

Each moment Michael spent in her presence he found it increasingly difficult to suppress the true thoughts he entertained in his troubled mind, with every smile or irresistibly enticing glare of frustration that Nichole sent in his direction, his need to discover more about her grew. Countless times each day he forced images from his mind of that same dazzling smile, same hypnotic eyes looking up at him from a tousled place in his bed. Never had a woman had such a bewitching effect on his hardened heart.

To Nichole, Michael Collier appeared to be a man of ever changing moods. Initially he had appeared to be predisposed to maintain a consistently foul temper when in the boardroom or engaging in an argument over this plot of land or another with a cell phone permanently attached to his ear, yet he presented at times an unexpected gentleness that gave Nichole pause. It was a side of himself that seemed as if he had it reserved specifically for her. If his voice was raised in anger and she walked into a room, his tone would immediately soften, his temper instantly pliable. She often found him irritating and frustrating and simultaneously charming and intriguing. He was truly a man to be reckoned with and possessed an invisible driving force that had catapulted him into a position of power.

Nichole felt it necessary to put in longer hours than were actually required of her although she was certain she had already proven herself a worthy choice for the new role that was suddenly thrust upon her. Working ten, or twelve hour days was not always easy, yet she was adjusting to the pace that was being set for her. Still, Michael's workdays seemed endless, arriving well before six in the morning, and staying late into the night. She'd oftentimes wondered if he slept at his desk. Yet each morning he donned a flawlessly pressed suit, was clean shaven and more often than not, in a somber mood.

Several times a week they drove the commute across the water, from the Peninsula to the Southside, a necessity Michael had hoped that would not be required of them for much longer. Summer was soon approaching and with summer came tourist season and hours of hellacious traffic. Thousands of visitors from all over the country coming to frolic in the warm waters of the Chesapeake Bay while simultaneously turning the highways and tunnels into an intricate maze of headlights and exhaust fumes that could remain at a standstill for hours on end.

Despite the tediousness of their daily trek they managed to put their time together to use wisely, Michael putting Nichole through an onslaught of question and answer sessions that he deemed necessary for her to be able to work confidently alongside him. Today however they rode in silence, Michael brooding inwardly over what he viewed as his weakness brought about by the rising temperatures and Nichole's nearness. Nichole sitting quiet and still with the window down, the breeze dancing across her face.

Although curious as to the cause behind Michael's sudden shift in mood Nichole was grateful for the respite and allowed her mind to wander, thankful that she was not the one behind the wheel this day. It had taken slightly over two hours to make their way through a backup caused by a semi that had overestimated his driving ability and jackknifed, blocking three lanes of Interstate 64.

By the time they had reached the Norfolk side of the tunnel, Nichole wandered closer to the side of sleep than consciousness. A curse from Michael directed to the driver directly in front of them jolted her awake as they passed the Pembroke exit. Nichole arched a brow and looked in his direction.

"Um, Mr. Collier?" she questioned.

Michael spied her out of the corner of his eye.

"Would you please stop calling me that," he demanded, a clear hint of irritation displayed in his voice.

Nichole sat tall in her seat, equally shocked by his request as by the tone it was delivered in.

"Well what exactly would you like me to call you or shall I simply address you as God from now on?"

He smiled unexpectedly, a welcome change from his usual dower expression. Never had he met woman or man that had the tenacity to stand up and confront him the way this woman did. Although he would never admit it he admired her all the more for it, wanted her all the more because of it.

"God's a bit over the top even for me. Michael will do just fine," he said.

"All right then, Michael, are you aware you just passed our exit?"

He turned to look at her, blinked twice, and then turned his attention back to the road.

"There is a property being sold as a foreclosure at the oceanfront. I wanted to take a look at it and would like your opinion of it as well."

This explanation seemed to satisfy Nichole for the time being, she settled back into her seat and continued viewing the landscape that passed by her window with little concern or interest as to their destination.

Michael stopped the car in the empty lot of an abandoned building on 26th Street. Stepping from the car Nichole was more confused than ever. The building itself a mere four stories, its appearance unimpressive and why anyone would stick and office building smack in the center of the tourist strip of t-shirt shops, bars and ice-cream parlors made no sense to her whatsoever.

She stepped up to the entrance, placed her hands upon her hips, and tilted her head skyward in an attempt to find one redeeming quality of the structure. She found none, but said nothing at first. Michael had walked up and stepped in closely behind her, too close. She was instantly aware of him, the scent of his cologne, the heat in his presence. Why did this man have to be so unnerving and worse yet why would her body eagerly betray her and respond to his nearness instantaneously?

Nichole felt a blush rise to her face and her heart beat slightly faster within her chest. Ugh, she thought to herself. Five more months, the man is going to be here, everyday by my side for five more months. She forced her focus away from the stirrings within her and back to the task at hand. One last surveying glance at the structure and stepping a safer distance from the man that was closely upon her, she turned to face him.

"You want to buy this?" she questioned incredulously, pointing at the worn building behind her.

Michael stood solid, his expression unreadable.

"I'm considering it."

She turned yet again to face the building, looking for something she may have missed, anything to give her some clue as to what would make a man as wealthy and powerful as Michael Collier consider purchasing such a tawdry and misplaced piece of property. She trudged her way to the far end of the building and spied the back lot, which if possible, was far worse than the front.

"Why?" she questioned. For all her efforts she could not find one redemptive quality of the building, the lot or the location. It was all wrong.

"You think it's a bad idea then I take it," he said, removing his jacket and tossing it casually over one shoulder.

Nichole was confused and becoming irritable. The afternoon sun beat down upon them mercilessly, nary a single cloud hovering overhead to lend the slightest promise of a reprieve from the scorching temperatures and here she stood discussing a building whose most promising future included a wrecking ball and a dozen construction workers. That's when it occurred to her.

"Yes, actually I do think it's a bad idea and if I'm correct so do you?"

Half a grin appeared on Michael's face that resembled a smirk more than a smile.

"What is this some sort of test?" Nichole demanded. "Did you drag me all the way down her in the middle of the afternoon, in this heat just to see if I knew a piece of shit property when I saw one?"

Michael's grin widened, yet he ignored her heated questions.

"Tell me why it's such a 'piece of shit property' as you so eloquently put it?"

Nichole drew in a deep breath and let out a long sigh. She was losing her patience with this man, his financial status and prestige quickly becoming a matter of inconsequence, now that her make-up was beginning to melt off. Twice now she had stumbled having caught her heel in the cracked pavement of the parking lot.

"Okay fine," she relented, "first the building itself is in horrible condition, you would practically have to rebuild it from the top down to get it up to code. It's too small to house enough business to even cover the rent in this area and most importantly the location is all wrong. For a bar, maybe a souvenir shop, this spot is perfect, but not an office building, which is more than likely why it sits empty as we speak."

Michael nodded and stalked his way back to the car, opening the door he spied Nichole unmoved as if set in stone, casting him a look of utter disgust.

"Well," he asked as he held open the passenger side door, "are you coming or not? We have work plenty of work to do today Nichole and time's wasting."

Nichole's hands balled into fists and she mumbled unintelligibly as trudged her way back to the car. Once inside she glared at him with beads of sweat lining her brow and forming in the folds of her cleavage.

"What?" he asked innocently as he pulled into traffic and maneuvered his way back to the interstate.

"Would you mind explaining to me why you wasted my time with this expedition of yours and why you chose to do it at the most miserable time of day?"

For several minutes Michael said nothing. He sat smiling to himself like a Cheshire cat. Stopping at a red light he turned to her.

"I knew you would know that that property was worthless. What I wanted to know is if you would give me your honest opinion of it despite what I may think."

A look of confusion replaced the flayed look of anger that was etched in her features.

"Of course I would and did? Why wouldn't I?" she said.

"You'd be surprised Nichole, how many people tell me what they think I want to hear instead of what I need to hear. It's difficult for me to find someone whose motives are genuine. To find someone who doesn't get caught up in the so-called status I hold. It's rare to find a man or woman who speaks their mind the way you do and boy do you."

Michael laughed aloud in spite of himself and in spite of the wicked glare being cast at him from the fathomless eyes of Nichole McCallister. She set her jaw and refused to speak to him looking ahead aimlessly, yet each time he turned his head in her direction she would cast him an irritated glance that spoke volumes and each time he erupted in a new fit of laughter.

Chapter 4

NICHOLE GAZED OUT THE window with dread; it was almost noon, yet by all appearances dusk had settled in. The sky was ominous and foreboding. The storm had not yet begun, but the wind was picking up and the clouds in the sky near black. The moisture in the air made her pale silk blouse stick to her skin and thin strands of hair had fallen out of the twist atop her head and danced along her cheek. She and Michael had been working up proposals for potential investors for the past three hours and she was due in Williamsburg in forty-five minutes to meet with a man named Phillips. Something Michael had set up for her, her first outing on her own as it were. A knock at the door drew her attention back to the present moment.

"Is Michael around?" the woman asked making herself welcome without invitation.

Nichole immediately recognized her as Melanie Anderson an attorney from the fourth floor. Not that anyone was likely to forget her, tall, blue eyes, red hair and stunning. She had never been shy about her flirtatiousness and it was said she had made her rounds through the Collier building. From the impression Nichole received she had planned to add Michael to her list of conquests.

Nichole stiffened at the inquiry, the manner in which the woman tossed Michael's name about with such coy familiarity, rousing an unexpected pang of possessiveness.

"He stepped out for a cup of coffee, he'll be right back," Nichole replied dryly and returned to reviewing to the papers she held in her hands.

Melanie let herself in and took a seat behind Michael's desk. "That's okay. I'll wait."

Leaning back leisurely in his chair, she propped her feet upon the desk as if she already owned not only the man, but the building itself.

Nichole continued to pack her briefcase and appeared to be totally disinterested. Inside she was fuming and she had no idea why. Nichole had no feelings for him, he was her boss, co-worker and that was where the relationship began and ended and if that were true than why should she care in the least bit what the man did with his free time? Fortunately it was time for her to head north and she left the office as quickly as possible. The door closed behind her as she stormed through the lobby. Focusing on a hasty retreat and oblivious to her surroundings her heal caught a loose piece of carpet and she bumped into Michael full force.

"Nichole, why the hurry?" he asked trying to avoid from spilling hot coffee on either of them.

Nichole stepped back and looked at him. This time she truly looked at him, through the eyes of all the Melanie Anderson's of the world. God he was impressive. He had discarded his tie, unbuttoned the first few buttons of his shirt and she could see fine dark hair peeking through the opening. His shoulders seemed broader than she had realized without his jacket on and she felt a flush rise in her cheeks.

"Mr. Collier you have a visitor. She has already made herself quite at home." Her hand struck out in the direction of their shared space. Her words were curt and to the point "I am on my way to Williamsburg, all I ask is that whatever plans you have for the rest of the afternoon, please have the decency to take them elsewhere. As far as I'm aware this is still my office and I would like it to be treated as such."

Smart, beautiful, refined, and feisty to boot, he thought to himself. Michael had no idea what she was referring to, but whatever it was it had lit a fire in her eyes and he found it irresistible. She had stormed off before he had the chance to question her, but when he stepped into his office, their office, the question answered itself. He closed his eyes and let out a sigh.

"Oh shit," he said quietly enough that Melanie hadn't heard.

Seeing the buxom redhead seated behind his desk upset him almost as much as it had upset Nichole, yet for different reasons. Melanie was a mere distraction for him. Daily he fought an increasing attraction to Nichole, an attraction he knew he must never act upon. It wasn't worth it to him to lose such a talented asset to his company for a fling that would last weeks, a few months at best. He resolved to focus his attention elsewhere. Elsewhere happened to be the attorney from the fourth floor. To flaunt the situation, made both appear tawdry and vulgar. Normally he wouldn't have given a rat's ass what anyone thought of him, but he respected Nichole, she was a lady and he had come to value her opinion and possess an unprecedented concern for her feelings. He needed to reign in control of the situation here and now.

As if her day hadn't been completely awful already, by the time Nichole's meeting had ended the skies had opened up releasing their furry in buckets of rain. No thunder or lightning or a sprinkle of warning, it was a hard steady downpour that showed no sign of waning anytime soon. By the time she had reached her car at the far side of the parking lot she was drenched from head to toe, her clothes stuck to her skin, her slender heals making a horrendous sloshing sound as she walked. The one thing she was grateful for was that her office appeared abandoned upon her return.

He saw her through the glass and thought twice about entering. He wasn't sure it was her at first. He had never seen Nichole with her hair down, he had no idea how long it was. As she stood with her back toward him, he could see that her sable locks extended the length of her back, her blouse practically see through clinging to her skin. Michael knew it was in his best interest to retreat to safer ground but his curiosity got the better of him. He turned the knob and approached with caution. Sending her on that meeting with that ass of a man had been an effort to save his sanity. He could imagine what she was thinking at this point and those thoughts made him cringe, especially after the brazenness of Melanie Anderson without any form of discretion as to her intentions.

Nichole had been sifting through papers on her desk when she heard the door open. Her hand flew in the air without her attempting to turn around. Michael was beginning to notice that she became quite animated when she was angry and Heaven help him he was beginning to find that attractive about her as well.

"Not one word," she shouted, "Not one or God help me I will not be held accountable for what I may do to you."

She had straightened, her body ridged and tense and despite the warning Michael approached with little concern for his safety. It was obvious she had no intention whatsoever in looking at him so he crossed the room to face her.

"It's not what you think Nikki," he said his voice sounding softer than usual.

She had been staring at the floor, her jaw locked, but when she heard him use her name with such familiarity, as if they had been lifelong friends, her eyes flew to meet his.

"How dare you," she hissed at him. You have absolutely no idea what I think and I can assure you, Mr. Collier, that at this moment in time you'd be much better off ending this conversation before it has a chance to begin.

There were definitely more sides to this woman than she liked to show the world. As he stood before her, he could not help but be amazed at her spirit. She was haughty and proud. A will of her own and that will was strong. No one stood up to him that way and he respected her for it. Seeing her this way with her fiery temper, completely disheveled from the storm, she was that much more enticing. Most women would be headed for hiding having been exposed to the elements as she was.

No woman he had encountered had ever been willing to let him see her with as much as a hair out of place. Yet, here Nichole stood, with long strands of dark wet hair clinging to her neck and shoulders, dancing across her cheek. All traces of make-up had been washed away, her lashes so full and long, her face flushed with anger. He was silently in awe over the creature standing before him.

"My God, woman will you silence yourself for one minute and listen?"

He reached to lower the hand she had been pointing in his face, a sudden movement with no volition behind his intent. She flinched and jerked away and for a fleeting moment he saw it there again. A slight semblance of horror in those beautiful eyes, revulsion at the thought of being touched. He knew it was there and this time she knew he had seen it too. A dead silence hung over the room, she looked away, but try as he might Michael could not force his attention from her. Inwardly she groaned

Michael took a few steps back and leaned against his desk. He spoke gently barely above a whisper, and there was tenderness to his voice she had never heard before.

"I owe you an explanation."

She glared at him, her eyes stinging with fought back tears. "You sir, owe me nothing." Her voice hissed.

She wanted to hate him, but the longer he held her stare the more compassion she saw in his eyes. She turned her head to look at the floor a vacant expression upon her face.

For some reason that he was not completely aware of her words stung. He never found himself to be overly concerned with the hurt feelings of any woman or the opinion that anyone held of him, yet this situation was different. Michael was patient. He knew he probably deserved the hell she was giving him and preceded to attempt to clear the air between them as professionally as he could. When all the while he fought the urge to take her in his arms and hold her close enough, make her feel safe enough that whatever horror she had endured that engrained such terror into her eyes would be erased from her mind forever.

"Yes, I do," he said. "Regardless of what you think, I do have at least as small sense of morality. Melanie was way out of line today. I invited the woman to lunch. That is all. She took it upon herself to make herself at home here and imply otherwise. She obviously has an extremely high opinion of herself, one that I do not share and it won't be happening again."

Nichole lifted her head. She was tired and frustrated, not to mention soaking wet.

"Why are you telling me all of this?"

"Because you are a professional and you're damn good at what you do. This is your space. I'm the intruder here."

The look she gave him was a suspicious one, as if she were searching for an ulterior motive behind his confession. He detected the doubt in her eyes.

"I'm guilty of many things Nichole, but I don't lie and I'm not lying to you now."

Her anger was beginning to wane. The man that stood a mere few feet away from her was one of the most powerful men in the country. He exuded charm and at times arrogance, was twelve years her senior and yet here he stood trying to justify himself to her and handling her with kid gloves. He could have easily replaced her with someone who would bow to his every whim without complaint. And as he was about to let the whole thing drop she remembered why she was soaked to the bone and the meeting she had come from.

"Okay, let's say I believe you, then why did you find it necessary to send me on a four hour excursion with a total twit of a man when a deal this big you would have usually handled yourself?"

Michael bit at his lower lip, there was no getting around this one, and he knew it. He held his hands up in mock surrender.

"Fine, I admit it. For that, I'm guilty of being a no good son of a bitch. I've known the man for a few years now and I cannot stand to be in the same room with him for more than ten minutes. I was sure you could handle it or I wouldn't have sent you and yes it was an attempt to spare myself the pain and suffering of his company, but I swear to you it had nothing to do with that woman coming in here earlier."

He fought back laughter. He knew J.B. Phillips was a pompous ass that could prattle on about himself for hours, but the money he would venture was too good to pass up. He sent Nichole to save his own sorry hide.

"Does he want space?" he asked.

"Does he want space? Yes, he wants space. He wants a whole damn floor and to his exact specifications. I spent the entire afternoon following him and his gaggle of ass kissing minions around writing down those specifications and listing to his relentless drivel about his superior standards and keeping his business running at top performance . . ."

That was all it took, he could hold back no longer. Michael burst out in a hearty laugh. The mental picture she created was too much, especially since he had been through the exact same scenario with the man a year before in Miami.

At the sound of his laughter Nichole wasn't sure if she wanted to scream at him or hurl something at his head, but when she looked up at him his smile caught her off guard. It was so genuine and made him much less intimidating, younger maybe, a boyish charm hidden behind the power suit and boardroom persona. She shook her head and fought off the urge to laugh herself.

The air conditioning had not stopped running since she had come in and the cool air had mixed with the dampness of her clothes. Now that her temper had settled and the adrenalin was wearing off she could feel a chill down to her bones. On her way back to her desk to retrieve all she needed for the trip home she caught a glimpse of herself in a mirror that hung on the wall by the door.

"Oh good Lord," she said aloud to no one in particular and her hands flew to her face to brush away a few stray locks of wet hair that were sticking to her cheek.

Michael was halfway out the door when he saw the defeated look upon her face.

"Nichole."

She turned to look at him.

"No other woman, having been through half of what you've been put through today could come out still looking quite so beautiful."

Chapter 5

All the windows and doors locked, the phone taken off the hook, secluded and surrounded by lavender candles and her vintage slipper clawfoot bathtub with a layer of bubbles so thick they carelessly spilled over the sides onto the floor. Nichole watched the steam float off the water and disappear into the room as the heat broke through and melted away the chill that had set in upon her. It was one of the few luxuries she allowed herself, her refuge, a respite at the end of a day that went on forever. Outside the storm was relentless. The wind had picked up and howled through the trees and she could hear the rain pounding mercilessly on the skylight above her. She let out a sigh and relaxed, safe and warm, protected from the elements.

This was one of the few times she allowed her mind to wander, to drift along carelessly wherever her thoughts would take her. For several years now her life had been all about control; control of her surroundings and her career. Control of the people she allowed to get close to her and their numbers were few. For Nichole as long as she felt as if she were in control she felt safe.

It hadn't always been this way. She thought back to the years before, how reckless and carefree she was. Spirited her father liked to call it. Beautiful and feisty, determined and capable yet she had such a playful nature about her. It made everyone that came in contact with her want to get closer, yet for Nichole remembrance was bittersweet. She allowed herself a nostalgic glimpse back at the girl she once was, but reckless and carefree were no longer a part of the description.

Everyone who knew and loved her saw the walls she had built around herself and they all had their share of advice to offer. She needed to get out more, learn to enjoy life, she needed to find that someone special. The advice, more often than not, fell on deaf ears. Nichole knew she was not the person she used to be, but she was content with her life, at least until recently.

Over the past few weeks, her contentment had been giving way ever slowly. Somewhere inside her stirred a restlessness she could not seem to shake. At twenty-eight, she was beautiful and successful, financially comfortable with a beautiful home yet her life lacked passion and purpose.

Gradually the bubbles had dissipated leaving a soapy film floating on the surface of the water. It was still clear enough however that she could see through to the few scars that remained, marring her otherwise perfect body. Time had caused them to fade into faint jagged lines but what remained was still a constant reminder. And after today she was certain he suspected something. What surprised her most was that she wasn't horrified by the notion. It was in the way he had instinctively stepped away from her and spoke in such a soothing tone, kind, not demeaning. She immediately relaxed, aside from being angry of course, but he knew what to do to put her at ease. Nichole knew that there was no possible way he could have known what exactly caused her reaction, somehow he understood it all the same and she smiled in the realization that they shared and unspoken understanding of one another.

In the few weeks she had known Michael Collier, she was made privy to a side of him that he kept hidden; a genuine kindness, a gentleness that he seemed to reserve for her alone. Although he could be undeniably charming when the situation called for it, he was more often than not demanding and intimidating in his dealings with people. He was a man used to power and comfortable with it and private, almost to the point of seeming cold.

Yet Nichole he handled with the grace of a true gentleman. He never once raised his voice or lost his patience. He considered all her ideas with earnestness and welcomed her myriad of questions. Oftentimes she thought she felt his gaze on her when she wasn't looking. Several times she met his unexpected glance, his eyes pierced her to the core, seizing something inside her long buried and resurrecting it to the surface. He was dignified yet ruthlessly handsome and Nichole couldn't help but wonder in spite of herself if he truly thought her beautiful.

By the time she had entered the building the next morning, a small crowd had already gathered a short distance from her office door. Michael's voice could be heard booming out in the hallway with the door closed, his dialog less than politically correct with his choice of expletives surely offending the faint of heart. Nichole drew in a deep breath and made her way through the spectators.

When she emerged into the room, the change in Michael's demeanor was immediate. Although he still wore a scowl upon his face he quieted, ended his conversation, and hung up the phone. His jacket hung over his chair, he wore no tie today and with a few buttons open at his neck Nichole could see faintly a thin patch of dark hair that covered his chest. It sent an unsuspected rush to her senses and she retreated to the safety of her desk to hide the blush that warmed her face. Propped against her monitor was a large manila envelope with the word *mandatory* written across the front in bold letters. She opened it to find a flyer done on pink paper with black printing. She held it in the air in Michael's direction questioningly.

"What's this?"

Michael inclined his head back and gave a sigh. "It's a company function. You need to be there."

"Umm . . . Michael . . . this says Bachelors Auction. In case you haven't noticed, I'm not a man."

His hands went to his head and he massaged his temples as if stress had rendered him mute. In reality, he knew he was about to take one hell of a ribbing from her and she was going to enjoy it, especially considering the afternoon he subjected her to the day before.

"No one in their right mind would ever accuse you of being anything but all woman my dear. I got myself suckered into going to this thing and you are going to help me out."

Nichole looked at the flyer again and then at Michael and let out a not so discrete chuckle. She bit at her bottom lip to control herself, but was unable to wipe the sarcastic little smile from her face. His story lacked a few details. She already knew she was going to thoroughly enjoy every minute of the telling.

"You're going to be auctioned off?" Her smile grew with every word.

"Yes."

"And how did this come about if you don't mind my asking?"

Michael sat back in his chair twirling a pen. "I went down to the site last night. A reporter from one of the local news stations was there doing a piece on the redevelopment of the area and I got caught in the crossfire. I answered a few questions and then she mentions this auction and how it is to benefit the Children's Hospital and one thing led to another . . ."

"And you're on the auction block," she said, unable to hide her delight in the irony of it all.

"Exactly."

"Okay, I've got that part, what I don't understand is why do I have to be there?"

"Because you're going to buy me."

Her words stuck in her throat. She fought back the urge to laugh out loud. "Bid on you, you mean."

"Bid, buy, whatever as long as your bid is the final one."

"Michael, there are a lot of lonely women in this area with fat pocketbooks. Chances are the price on your head could add a new wing to the hospital. I can't afford you."

She was taunting him now, playfully teasing him and he was actually enjoying it although he would sooner walk on hot coals than admit it.

"I'll be fronting you the money. I don't care how high the bidding goes. I will not be at the mercy of the whims of a woman I do not know, nor care to know. These women are lonely for a reason. You make certain you bid higher than anyone else, write the check and I'll transfer the money into your account."

Nichole relaxed in her seat and rhythmically tapped her French manicured nails atop her desk. She looked away from Michael feigning deep concentration. He shook his head waiting for whatever she was going to throw at him next. Somewhere over the past few weeks, gradually, the walls between them had started to crumble without either of them being aware it was happening. This was no longer president and owner of a major corporation dealing with an employee, this was a teasing game of cat and mouse. He had never seen this side of Nichole before. Her eyes were practically gleaming she was having entirely too much fun giving him such a hard time and he admired her for it. Few people he encountered in his lifetime possessed the prowess to confront him on anything.

"Let's say I agree to help you pull off this charade," she continued. "Where will you be taking me?"

"What do you mean?"

"The way this thing works is, you are part of a package deal. The woman who bids the highest gets you for a day along with whatever trip, dinner, carriage ride you offer to sweep her off her feet."

His brows knitted together, he hadn't thought that far ahead. "Where would you like to go, you want dinner in Rome, we'll fly to Rome, gambling in Monte Carlo, you'll play on the house all night long. Hell, if you want to go to the moon let me know and I'll call NASA."

Nichole did not doubt for one minute that he would do just that. He was a powerful man, capable and in control and she didn't dare joke about the NASA comment for fear she might find herself floating aimlessly aboard the MIR space station. She thought for a moment, searching for something that would bring him out of his comfort zone-no satin sheets, no servants rushing to his every whim.

"Do you know how to pitch a tent, build a fire?"

"Yes," he replied, a confused look upon his face.

She batted her eyes in his direction and gave a coy smile. Revenge was sweet she thought to herself and she hadn't sought it out. It fell right into her lap.

"Okay, if I decided to go through with this you can take me camping . . . in the mountains, complete with dinner over the campfire and champagne and if you could arrange fireworks at dusk that would be a nice added touch."

The giggle that escaped her lips was precious. He could not take his eyes off her. Never in his life had he encountered a woman that could pull off being as playful as a kitten and yet seem utterly exquisite in manner and beauty simultaneously.

"Done," he said plainly, "if that is your heart's desire my dear I will find a way to make it happen."

"Michael, I wasn't being serious." She blushed.

"I was." His tone had suddenly turned severe.

Nichole quieted. She looked in his direction and the gaze that she met was fueled by intensity. He had been studying her as she spoke. Committing to memory the perfect line of her jaw, her fiery green eyes flecked with amber and the way her face lit up when she smiled. A tempered silence hung in the air, words no longer necessary. A knowing smile crept across her face letting him know she shared his thoughts. She felt an immediate flutter in her stomach and could hear her own heart beating. She swallowed hard trying to remember to breathe.

Michael let out a sigh. This woman had the ability to completely undo him and she hadn't been trying. The situation was impossible at best, yet logic and reason could easily be pushed aside by fate. He knew he had to get out of there before he completely lost control of his senses and did more than merely look. He stood and put on his jacket, his height and broad shoulders blocking the stream of sunlight that filtered through the window.

"You'll come then?" he asked.

Nichole simply nodded. He walked over to where she was seated and struggled to maintain his composure when she looked up at him. He gently took her hand in his. The warmth of his touch sent sparks through her.

"My angel of mercy," he said, bringing her fingers to his lips, placing a soft gentle kiss that warmed her throughout.

As the door closed behind him she quickly grabbed for her cell phone. She needed to talk to Maxie, it was time to seek the advice of her partner in crime, the one person who knew her better than anyone else on the planet. Max Porter was her confidant and if anyone knew men it was Maxie.

Chapter 6

East Beach Gym and Fitness Center was filled with bright lights, loud music, and hopeful enthusiasts walking, running, and lifting their way to total body perfection. The Zumba class was filled to capacity. The weight room was being dominated by several men who were way too tan, had lost all appearance of ever having had a neck and insisted on chest bumping after completing each set, sending Max and Nichole in the direction of the elliptical machines.

Twenty minutes had past, then thirty and Nichole had yet to say a word. She focused instead on the blank wall in front of her, staring into nothingness yet a million miles away in her mind. Max was patient at first, she had called him the night before insisting he meet her at the gym as soon as it opened because she needed advice only he could give her. He ran on the machine beside her trying to keep up with her steady, driven pace, but when she kept going strong at the forty-five minute mark with no sign of slowing down he reached for his towel and retreated to the bench beside her.

"Nichole," he called out to no avail. "Nichole," he said stepping closer this time, but she was far away, lost in her thoughts. "Nikki," he yelled, frustrated and exhausted as he wound up his towel and popped her on the behind.

"Ouch, what did you do that for," she screeched rubbing a rising tender spot on her left butt cheek.

"You called me remember," he said pausing to take a sip of water, "dragged me down here at the crack of dawn to seek my wisdom and you have yet to say a word. What's up, Nikki? I can't help if I don't know what the problem is?"

Nichole slowed her pace, eventually coming to a complete stop. She wiped away the sweat that was dripping down her face and plopped down in the seat next to him.

"I think I have a problem," she said, attempting to catch her breath.

"With the way you were trying to kill yourself on that thing I assumed as much. Why don't you tell me what it is and I'll see if I can help."

Nichole reached for her bottle of water, draining half of it in three gulps. She squared her shoulders and took a deep breath.

"You know about my situation at work right?"

"Yes, the head honcho is in town and training you to run the big complex at the beach correct?"

"Correct," she said, "now, the problem is the head honcho."

A look of concern came over his face. Max had been very protective of Nichole in the years they had known each other. Fate had thrown them together in such a tragic way he couldn't help but feel apprehensive where she were concerned. She had become the little sister he never had as well as his closest confidant.

"What has he done?" he asked, his voice severe, his expression grave.

Nichole knew that look. Her hands flew up in defense. "Calm down, he hasn't done anything."

"Okay," he said visibly relaxing, "then what's the problem?"

"I think I might be falling for him . . . just a little . . . maybe."

Max smiled the boyish beaming smile that Nichole loved so much. "Just a little, maybe, huh?

"Yeah, maybe more than just a little," she said feeling a flush rise in her cheeks.

Two women had taken their now vacant spots on the elliptical machines. Nichole longed for privacy. It was near impossible for her to talk about her feelings. She often preferred to exist, numb, inside the walls she had built around herself, but with Max she felt safe. They retreated to a secluded corner in the juice bar where no one could overhear their conversation. Max grabbed a pineapple protein shake for himself, and acai detox tea for Nichole. Putting the drinks on the table he sat across from her and took her hands into his.

"Okay sweet girl, you have the hots for your boss, how does he feel about you?"

"I don't know, that's part of the problem," she sighed. "On the surface, in his dealings with people in general he's a real prick to be honest, but never with me. He's professional and he's driven with work, then there are times when he completely catches me off guard. He can be very gentle, soft spoken and charming. I've caught him staring at me several times when he thought I wasn't looking, he told me last week that he thought I was beautiful and now he wants me to bail him out of the Children's Hospital Bachelor Auction that he got himself suckered into. I honestly don't know what to think. There are so many mixed messages."

Max paused for a moment to evaluate the situation, many possibilities, many potential pitfalls. Sharing a man's boardroom and his bedroom is more often than not a recipe for disaster, but Nichole was the most sensible woman he had ever met, sensible and emotionally shut down. To see the slightest flicker of hope dancing within those big green eyes, the blush on her cheeks, her beaming smile, this could be exactly what she needed. Hell, he thought to himself, if she did decide that Michael Collier was the man that she wanted to unleash seven years' worth of stifled sexuality upon, the poor bastard wouldn't know what hit him.

"Do you want my honest opinion, Nik?"

She waded up a napkin and threw it at his nose. "You know I do or I wouldn't have considered risking the embarrassment of this conversation."

"What do you have to be embarrassed about?" He scoffed. The fact that you actually are capable of being turned on by some guy? God forbid you be human," he said rolling his eyes. "Nikki honey, I say you go for it. It sounds like he's into you, to what extent only he can say. Regardless you need to start living a whole life. You're beautiful, smart, and talented, but you have been shut down for many years. You need to take a chance, get laid a few good times if nothing else."

The slight pink blush that tinted her cheeks had now turned a fiery shade of red as she nervously twirled a loose strand of hair around her fingers.

"That's not what I meant, Maxie." She scowled.

"I know that's not what you meant, but it's what you should mean. Listen to me, he is the owner of a massive real estate conglomerate, and if I remember correctly he's only here for a few more months. He has no intention of staying in the area am I right?"

Nichole nodded, her smile fading. Maxie's words rang true, yet were surprisingly painful to hear.

Noticing the subtle change in her, he continued. "Nikki I say you get dressed to the nines, go the bachelor auction, and have fun. I know you are familiar with the meaning of the word, but you haven't let loose and had fun once since I've known you. Let Collier take the lead and go from there. Stop over analyzing everything, reach down, grab your inner sexy bitch, and let her out to play. Try living in the damn moment for once in your life and to hell with all of the what ifs."

Nichole slumped back in her seat considering all he had said and sipped at her tea. She could no longer deny that she felt something for Michael. Defining that something was going to be no easy task. They hadn't known each other for long yet whenever he was near her body seemed to warm all over. His smile had a dizzying effect upon her and despite her attempt to remain completely detached she was becoming increasing preoccupied with the idea of what it would be like to be kissed by such a powerful and intriguing man. Maybe she did need to get laid and get it out of her system. Most women her age did that kind of thing all the time right, at least most normal, undamaged women.

She drained the last few sips from her cup and stood to discard it in the trashcan. Maxie watched in amusement. He knew her thought process, knew her pattern. Right about now she was overanalyzing the fact that she should stop overanalyzing. He couldn't help but smile. As she made her way back to her seat, he grabbed her by the arm and pulled her onto his lap.

"Stop," he said.

"Stop what?"

"Stop thinking so damn much, woman."

Nichole rested back in his arms and smiled. "Actually I was thinking that you are right."

"Oh well, in that case, by all means carry on."

Nichole reached out and playfully mussed his blond hair. They shared a bond few people could comprehend. Max was her safety net, her sounding board and at times her only hope at sanity. He accepted her neurotic ways without judgment and never once tried to change her.

"I'm going to do my best to take this one day at a time, no expectations and maybe, maybe have some fun."

"Well thank God," he said with relief, "But you know I will be all up in your business as this thing plays out and I expect details. It's not everyday your twenty-eight-year-old bombshell best friend lands a forty-year-old billionaire as a plaything. Actually I think I'm jealous."

"I haven't landed . . . as you eloquently put it, anything yet. Remember no expectations," she reminded him.

"Good girl," he said. "You're learning quickly my little grasshopper. Now let's go hit the showers. We stink."

As the hot water beat down on her skin, Nichole was suddenly aware of how hard she had pushed herself during her workout. The muscles in her calves and thighs were already becoming stiff and sore, her feet ached and her shoulders and back longed for a hot stone massage. Steam filled the air and whirled around her as thick foamy layer of bubbles slid down her neck and across her full, perky breasts.

She looked at her hand, the hand Michael had placed a soft, gentle kiss on the night before. The man was an enigma, complicated and confusing, yet enticing. For years the mere thought of a man's touch caused her recoil in horror, sending her into the familiar darkness that had become a part of her lonely reality. It stole every chance she had at happiness, every hope and dream of future without fear until she stopped hoping and dreaming completely.

They all said a time would come when things would change, a time when she was healed enough, felt strong enough to let someone into her life and her heart, but she had scoffed at the idea time and time again. Michael's stay was only temporary and he had a well-known lecherous reputation yet for some reason she could not explain to herself Nichole knew somewhere inside that he was her first step out of the darkness.

Chapter 7

THE LAST PLACE MICHAEL wanted to be right now was in an overcrowded restaurant at the oceanfront surrounded by a dozen shareholders, discussing the future Collier Creative Arts Center income overview and potential internal rate of returns. It had seemed like a good idea at the time to schedule the luncheon for the end of June, two months prior to the building's grand opening, however with the Fourth of July around the corner the tourists had begun flocking into town early, jamming the freeways, and swarming upon eateries in droves along the strip. That faux pas he would attribute to poor timing. The matter that he overslept and almost missed the meeting completely he would attribute to the fact that his mind was anywhere but on business.

The previous night was a restless one, falling asleep before the dawn, his mind not filled with the usual barrage of facts and figures that preempted a meeting such as this, but focused on a solitary face, a solitary smile, and two of the most amazing eyes he had ever seen in his life. He had returned to his townhouse on Sandalwood Drive with the intent on spending no more than one hour preparing the briefing he was to give today and then spend the rest of the evening relaxing with nothing but a bottle of brandy and the sounds of the ocean outside his door.

It was unlike him to be easily distracted. The day he turned eighteen he walked out his father's front door, leaving his nightmare of a childhood behind him and set out on his own. He was driven by his inner demons to become the man Stephen Collier would never be, a man that commanded respect. He climbed the corporate ladder with arrogant ease and built a real estate dynasty that was topping out in over a billion dollars, the measure in which he valued himself. He defined his self-worth in his successes and took no deal, no matter how small, lightly.

And with a flash of Nichole's amazing smile it all suddenly seemed insignificant. Inside him raged a battle, a torrent of conflicting emotions. He was a man who took what he wanted and held on to it for as long as he wanted and he had never wanted a woman with such urgency as he wanted Nichole McCallister. He knew he wanted her the moment he laid eyes on her. It made him apprehensive, knowing that she had been hurt to a degree extreme enough to bring about reoccurring fear to her expression. It enraged him. Yet, to see her come out of her shell and laugh with abandon, playfully vexing him was his undoing.

The one-hour limit he had imposed upon himself quickly turned into four and then five. He retained nothing of what he read, his thoughts repeatedly retreating to her. He swore aloud at no one or perhaps at himself out of sheer frustration. In four decades no one woman had ever dominated his thoughts so completely. Naively he believed that a few stolen glances, could satisfy his curiosity, but that only led to him wanting more.

Well after midnight he pushed aside the mound of papers before him and opted for a run on the beach. Four miles, three brandies and one cold shower later he finally fell asleep shortly after five AM. And now she sat immediately to his right expertly discussing the demographics of his latest project.

She wore her hair down today, pulled back at the nape of her neck allowing long loose curls to cascade down her back, the odd tendril escaping to dance along her cheek as she spoke.

She had chosen a sleek, tight fitting pencil skirt and wrap jacket both the color of mink for today's meeting, surprising both herself and

Michael. She remained every bit the professional and was simultaneously every bit the temptress.

As she spoke, all eyes were upon her. Her unmistakable beauty was an asset with the male clients and she knew how to use it to her advantage with charm and dignity. In the same respect, her professionalism and growing knowledge of the inner workings of investment real estate won over the female clients. She outshined those who surrounded her and Michael sat back in silent awe, a faraway look in his eye.

"Michael . . . Michael," a voice called out from midway down the table.

Robert Ward, a textiles millionaire from central North Carolina, who was looking to expand his profile, was in attendance. He had repeated his question several times, however, Michael had been engrossed in his thoughts he had yet to acknowledge him. Nichole kicked him slightly under the chair; it startled him and brought his attention back to the table.

"I'm sorry, what was the question?" he asked openly uncertain whom to address.

Robert leaned back in his seat with a smirk upon his face as he tapped out his cigar. "I asked if you had prepared a Cost Segregation Study for today and if you did may I take a look at one?"

"Certainly," Michael replied, standing to retrieve a stack of individually bound reports from the table behind him. As she stood to meet him taking the papers from his hands, Nichole caught his eye with a questioning glance. He had seemed a bit off kilter to her since he had arrived and she was becoming concerned, a slight nod was his only response.

As she walked around the room passing out the information, her constituents received their first full glance at Nichole McCallister. She had been seated upon their arrival and had remained seated throughout lunch while she spoke. It was then that Mr. Ward was able to fully appreciate all there was of Nichole. Her skirt stopping above her knee exposed well-toned calves and accentuated all that they led to. He chuckled out loud looking directly at Michael.

As the meeting concluded, Michael for one could not get out of there fast enough. He still had to endure the tour of his newest property and answer and endless bombardment of questions sure to arise. As he and Nichole passed the potted palms and exited, he was stopped by the booming voice and pungent odor of Robert Ward and his cigar.

"Michael," he spoke, halting them both. "Ms. McCallister my dear, if you don't mind I'd like to have a quick word with Michael for a moment."

Nichole excused herself and began walking in the direction of her car. Michael looked at his watch and then at the man before him. They had been friends for years although Robert was well into his sixties with a full head of white hair, beard to match, a slightly protruding paunch, and a laugh that was gruff and hearty.

"What is it Bob?" he asked, hoping to get this over with as quickly as possible.

He nodded in Nichole's direction. "Tagged her yet?"

Michael drew in a breath, the muscles in his jaws tightened. Had it been any other woman he was referring to the comment would not have fazed him, but since it was directed at Nichole it irritated him to no end.

"It's not like that Robert," he paused, "not with this one."

The older man was momentarily rendered speechless as if it took more time than necessary to process the words he had heard. He scanned Michael's face for sincerity and found it immediately. He laughed in spite of himself, his face turning a shade of crimson. Michael took it in stride he knew he meant no disrespect. For that matter, Michael was equally as confounded by the whole situation as he was.

Bob slapped him hard on the shoulder. "My apologies dear boy. I was out of line but by God I do believe you are a man smitten. I never thought I'd live to see the day."

Michael combed his fingers through his hair and narrowed his eyes. "I honestly have no idea what the hell I am right now."

Nichole crossed the street a half a block away and stopped at the entrance of the parking garage. A man, tall and slender, with the build of a runner stepped out of the parking facility and into the light of the midafternoon sun. Robert Ward spied them out of the corner of his eye and seeing that Michael was unaware motioned with his cigar in their direction.

"You'd better watch out now Casanova, looks like you just might have yourself some competition."

Michael turned to see Nichole, smiling, almost giddy in the embrace of a handsome, blond-haired man he did not recognize. The familiarity with which they greeted each other grated on him and he tensed. The stranger in the black polo and tan slacks stepped back as he held her by the elbows, looked her up and down as if giving her a once-over then gently kissed the top of her head. Offering her his arm they disappeared within the darkness of the lot's lower level.

Daggers shot from Michael's eyes. His business associate and friend silently stood watching the scene unfold before him with unabashed amusement. Bob had known Michael since he was in his early twenties and in that time had seen the way women flocked to him and melted in his presence. He envied him somewhat, until now. Men like Michael did not fall for one woman that often, when they did they fell hard.

Bob puffed on his cigar. "You got it bad son," he said making his exit. His hearty chuckle heard as he strode away.

Michael said nothing, but his eyes smoldered with rage. He had laid no claim to her and yet felt an all-consuming possessiveness seeing her in another man's arms. An unsuspected pang of jealousy coursed through him. He was not used to the feeling of it and despised every second of it.

Located in the heart of Towne Center, between Virginia Beach Boulevard and Columbus Street stood forty stories of concrete and steel, strewn with mirrored glass windows that glistened like far away stars with the light of the afternoon sun shining upon them. It was an impressive structure. It was near completion, all of the external construction finished four weeks ahead of schedule. All that remained was interior cosmetic finalities. The painters crowded the lower floors, priming the newly plastered walls with a layer of white. Soon the decorators Michael had hired would be called in, the carpet laid and furniture ordered.

He drove on autopilot from Dante's Restaurant to the lot adjoining the edifice that bared his name. The first to arrive, he had exceeded the speed limit by ten miles an hour at least along the way. He was in a foul mood and the scowl upon his face looked as if it were etched in stone, but that did not alter his ruthless good looks. It merely added a dangerous quality to his icy blue orbs and chiseled features, his skin darkened by the sun. His phone chirped in the seat beside him before he had a chance to exit. He recognized the number as Tom's.

"Yeah," his voice boomed through to the opposite end.

"What's the matter with you?" Tom asked cautiously, not certain he wanted to know.

"Tom, if I told you, you would never believe me. Let's leave it at that and get down to why you called?"

Tom knew Michael's moods well. He knew when it was safe to push him and when it was best to back off. He proceeded warily.

"Is the meeting over?"

Michael's eyes rolled. If only it were he thought. "Not yet. I pulled up in front of the center. I'm waiting for the others to get here so I can get this damn day over with. Why?"

Now was not the time Tom decided. The information he had to share with Michael would likely make him snap and that was on a good day. There was no telling what he would do on a day such as this.

"Listen man," he said, "why don't you give me a call at home later tonight? This can wait."

He was becoming increasingly annoyed. Tom was trying to appease him and he knew it.

"Get to the point Tom. What's this about?"

Tom let out a sigh of resignation. There was no getting around it. When Michael wanted answers he got answers.

"You wanted me to dig, Mike, I found dirt and you're not going to like it. It's about Ms. McCallister."

"Nichole," he retorted.

An inner warning went off in Tom's head. They're on a first-name basis?

"Yes, Nichole McCallister. You need to hear this, but not now. Not while she's around. Trust me on this one."

"Shit," Michael swore.

Cars began filling in the spaces around him. They were arriving on time, Nichole among them. And it was his duty to see that they were assured the money they had invested rested safely with him.

"Listen to me," he fumed. "I have to go. I'm going to call you back in fifteen minutes. I'll make sure she's not around. You be damned sure you answer your phone because I want to know what the hell is going on and I'm not waiting until tonight." He slammed his phone shut and jammed it into his pocket.

Nichole sensed his tension immediately though he did an excellent job of trying to cover it up. Most people would never have noticed, but she could feel it. What confused her was that it seemed as if it was directed at her. He hadn't seemed himself all through lunch. Now they stood in the main lobby of the building, the vapors of fresh paint stinging the air. As he spoke the muscles in his face tightened and he completely averted her gaze when he announced, to Nichole's surprise, that it would be her showing them around the building instead of him.

Nichole proceeded as if the entire thing had been planned and headed toward the elevator cars, inviting those that followed her to feel free to ask any questions they may have. Michael headed down the hall. He had seen to it that there was one functional office prepared and completely furnished as soon as the electricians had finished their end of the work. No carpet had been laid and the walls remained an untouched white for the time being, but it was fitted with a desk, chair, computer, and fax machine. A one cup coffee pot yet to be used sat atop an empty filing cabinet. Not exactly warm and welcoming room, it served its purpose and nothing more. He waited for the computer to boot up; making certain Nichole was well on her way to the upper floors and then called Tom.

"All right, tell me," he demanded.

"Where is she?"

Michael was losing his patience's. His voice boomed through to the other end.

"She is in the process of taking the fortune five hundred on a tour through the building."

Make it quick, Tom thought to himself. Michael was going to blow, he was certain of it, best to get it over and done with.

"Pull up your email. It's all there and before you ask I checked and double-checked. The information is accurate."

Michael clicked on the link to his email account. There were two recent emails from Tom both marked confidential. He pulled up the first one and opened the attachment. He looked to see what appeared to be a scanned newspaper article. He placed his elbows on the armrests of his chair leaning forward. His brows knitted together. The words from the headline assaulted his eyes. *Local College Student Raped, Savagely Beaten.*

Perhaps it was shock or disbelief, his thoughts blurred in confusion, "What the . . . what the hell does this have to do with Nichole?" His voice was volatile.

Tom had had the same initial reaction when the private investigator he had hired presented him with the information. He had only seen Nichole McCallister on one occasion. It was six months ago at a conference in Houston. He never had the opportunity to speak with her beyond a brief introduction, but hers was a face not easily forgotten. The momentary rage he had experienced paled in comparison to what Michael was about to experience.

With regret in his voice, he spoke softly, "It was her Mike, seven years ago. Read the article."

Michael's eyes skirted through the text. There was a ringing in his ears and he began to feel nauseous. Phrases such as *left for dead* and *in critical condition* leaped out at him.

"There's no name here." His voice sounded weak. "How-how can you be sure this is her?"

He was grasping at straws, his mind still refusing to accept the truth despite the inner warnings he felt to the contrary.

"They don't publish the names of victims of sex crimes to protect their identity. Open the attachment on the second email. They caught the guy. It took them six months to do it, his name is Denton Walsh. Apparently he worked as a security guard on campus. When the police searched his apartment they found an entire room plastered with pictures of Nichole, candles, ropes, handcuffs, all kinds of sick shit. Apparently he had been stalking her for years, would send sick twisted letters to her house and her family and friends in these creepy scripted envelopes tied up in red bows. The case went to trial, he was given a life sentence. I sent you a copy of the court records. I knew you'd want proof so I pulled some strings. Her name is there."

For what seemed like an eternity Tom received nothing but silence on his end. He remained on the line waiting for Michael to process all he had read. He half regretted not flying out to Virginia and telling him in person. At least that way he could be certain Michael didn't go off the deep end or do something stupid to land himself in jail.

"Mike, you all right?" he finally asked.

"Uh-huh."

"I'm sorry man. I'm truly sorry."

Chapter 8

A 21-YEAR-OLD LOCAL UNIVERSITY student was found Thursday night clinging to life in a sparsely wooded area of Ghent three blocks from her home.

It is believed that the attack took place between the hours of nine and ten PM.

The woman had been hit from behind, stabbed multiple times, and sexually assaulted. She was rushed to Norfolk General and remains unconscious and in critical condition.

Police are encouraging anyone with information on this crime to contact your local authorities or call the crime line.

Michael could hear the pounding of his heart echoing relentlessly in his ears. His eyes were beginning to blur he had read the article so many times. It amazed him how reporters had the ability to string together words, forming sentences, creating short concise paragraphs that summed up horrific, life-altering events in one neat black and white package. He had tried, a dozen times at least, to logically reason away the fact that the woman in this article could not be Nichole. Tom had to have made some horrendous mistake.

Despite his attempts at denial, Michael knew without reading the court documents Tom had supplied him that all of it was true. On two separate occasions thus far he had already seen in her eyes the aftermath that that hellacious night had left upon her. Seven years had passed, yet no amount of time would be able to completely erase the sheer horror of the crime committed upon her long ago.

Decades had passed since Michael himself was but a small child, defenseless and vulnerable at the hands of a sadistic father. He knew all too well the feeling of total and utter worthlessness, almost welcoming death as a means to an end. To this day, the memories haunted him. He would never wish that hell on anyone and to know the vaguest of details of what Nichole had endured created vile mental images that he was unable to shake.

He had no idea how much time had passed. He hadn't heard the horde of affluent investors as they made their exit. He hadn't heard the door to his office open or close. He felt her there. There was an energy about her that was unmistakable. He recognized it whenever she was near.

Nichole took a seat opposite him, the only other chair available in the room. She said nothing. Michael closed his eyes and let out a long sigh. He knew his emotions were well written on his face at this point and the last thing he wanted to do was frighten her. He made a wasted effort at trying to clear the images from his mind and appear as casual as possible. He quickly closed his email account and met her gaze.

"I'm sorry. I didn't hear you come in." His voice was sullen.

Nichole crossed her long, shapely legs and relaxed in the chair. "I'm aware of that."

She had been growing increasingly concerned about Michael all day. He was not the type of man to be easily distracted, especially when the stakes were high. Until today, Nichole had been led to believe that this meeting was the single most important thing in Michael's world and yet the entire day he grew increasingly distracted and uninterested in finalizing his multimillion-dollar deal.

"Michael, is anything bothering you? You haven't been yourself today?"

For several moments he sat silently scanning her flawless features. At least the bastard didn't leave a mark on her face he thought to himself, a small consolation considering the circumstances. It took every ounce of restraint he could muster to stop himself from taking her into his arms right there. He wanted to hold her, to make her feel safe and protected. He wanted to erase all that was done to her so that she would never again flinch in fear. Yet he knew all too well she would be mortified to know that her darkest secret had flashed across his computer screen. It was her confidence to share if and when she was ready.

Michael stood and walked over to her, he leaned back resting on his desk. His jacket and tie he had discarded and Nichole could see the outline of taut muscles beneath his silk shirt. She felt a flutter in her stomach at his close proximity and the intense look on his face made her heart skip a beat.

"I'm sorry about today. I had no intention on putting this all off on you." His words were drawn out as if he were searching desperately for each syllable. "I've had a lot of . . . unexpected issues come up over the past twenty-four hours and I do appreciate you picking up the slack. I never doubted for a minute that you were up to the task."

"You don't have to apologize, Michael. I've never seen you like this. I was starting to get worried to be honest with you."

He reached down and lightly took her by the hands, lifting her up from the chair he pulled her closer to him. She tried to read his eyes, but saw only an unmistakable sadness that confused her. He took the back of his fingers and gently drew them down one cheek and up the other. Her head tilting instinctively toward his touch she closed her eyes to breathe in the scent of him. How could this be happening? This was one of the most powerful sought after men in the world, here with her. She was unable to resist his slightest touch. She was a grounded, sensible woman not given to flights of fancy and yet as he touched the skin of her cheek a warm heat surged through her that she could not deny.

"I have some things I need to take care of tomorrow. Do you think you can manage without me for a day?" he asked tauntingly.

Nichole could only nod in reply. Her ability to speak rendered mute by his touch.

Seeing her reaction to him brought Michael to his limit of self-control. He had to leave and he had to leave now. He wanted her more than he had ever wanted any woman in his lifetime, but it had to special, magical. He cupped her face in his hands and brought a brief, light kiss down on her lips then pulled her to him.

Her arms wrapped around him. Nichole knew office affairs were the worst kind of taboo, she knew Michael's reputation, but with his body pressed closely to hers, her ability to breathe, nevertheless think was rendered helpless. Michael held her there, his face buried in her hair, taking in the scent of jasmine, the softness of her skin.

He took a deep breath and stepped away. "I have to go."

She nodded, her eyes beaming, knowing the unspoken reason for his retreat. Nichole stood half light-headed; a myriad of emotions tangled inside her and watched him walk away.

Six o'clock in the morning and the traffic from Norfolk International Airport to the oceanfront was already gridlocked. It had taken Tom the better part of an hour to drive a mere ten miles. The Tidewater area is home to the world's largest naval installation. Men and women and their families from all over the country live here and are expected to report for duty bright and early every morning, often jamming the freeways and causing backups for miles.

He had been up most of the night trying to contact Michael to no avail, his phone calls went unanswered, and his emails received no reply. At 3:00 AM he abandoned all hope of sleep and called to have the corporate jet fueled and ready for takeoff within the hour. During the entire flight to Virginia Tom's mind raced anxiously, wondering what he would find when he arrived. Michael's temperament was consistent for the most part, yet certain things had the ability to pull him into a blackness, a somber, disparaging mood that was frightening and absolute in its hold on him. He would retreat inside himself, become withdrawn, violent to any man who was unfortunate enough to provoke him. Pulling him out of the darkness was a hellish task. Tom hung on desperately to the probability that Michael went on a bender to burn off some steam and hadn't landed himself in jail or anyone else in the hospital.

Years ago they were two kids growing up in a rough neighborhood, light-years away from suburbia. A lonely place, distant from all that was good and decent in the world. Theirs was a world filled with drug deals and prostitution, gangs, and never-ending violence. Flowers never grew there, holiday decorations were never hung. Hopelessness and despair festered like open wounds, draining the life from the dreams of the young, harboring bitterness among the old.

Michael was the older of the two. He was bigger, stronger, often preferring the streets to the hell that awaited him behind the closed doors of the ram shackled, rundown structure he would never call home. He knew the tricks of survival. Walk with your head up, meet every face straight in the eye head on, show no fear, and never smile. He had earned respect from the thugs in the neighborhood and was left alone.

Tom Hogan was a scrawny kid, freckled faced with straw colored hair. He was loved by his mother, but she was single and worked two jobs to give her son what little they had. His father had abandoned them both before Tom's second birthday.

He was eleven years old when he met Michael Collier. His mother had given him twenty dollars to go into town and buy himself a new pair of shoes, a pair that fit and did not have holes in them. Along the way, he decided to take a short cut through a back alley, unaware that a new crack house had been established among the layers of filth and stench of urine. He was accosted and was in the process of being beaten to within an inch of his life by a pair of drug addicts when Michael had heard his cry for help.

Michael was fifteen at the time and almost six feet tall. He was uncommonly strong for a boy his age and the one thing that made him quick to anger, driven to rage like a man possessed was to see anyone or any creature, man, woman, child or animal, helpless, demoralized at the hands of another. He paused briefly to size up the situation. One emaciated junkie he could handle with his eyes closed, two might actually make it entertaining. Neither of the men stood half a chance.

One lay moaning with a broken nose among a pile of empty liquor bottles, soiled diapers and cigarette butts, the other on the verge of unconsciousness, taking blow after blow from Michael's beefy fists. Years of pent up fury instilled by his father being released without regard for the consequences. It was the muffled cry of the kid with hair the color of wheat, screaming for him to stop that brought him back to his senses. Strung out junkie or not, had Michael continued he would have surely killed the man and been sent to juvie, lost to the system forever.

After that day, no one messed with Tommy Hogan again and he stuck to Michael like a second skin. To his surprise, Michael didn't mind. They got into some minor trouble together every now and then. Most days they spent daydreaming and planning their escape.

When he pulled up to the house, he was relieved to see Michael's Jag parked in the driveway. The street was lined with crape myrtles in bloom, the sun beating down on their pink and lavender petals. There was a cloudless sky and few passersby out for a morning stroll gave Tom an odd glance as he stood pounding on the front door for nearly twenty minutes.

As the door finally opened Michael quickly raised an arm to shield his bloodshot eyes from the sun. His unshaven face bristled with stubble and he squinted to block out the offending glare.

"Tom? What the hell are you doing here?"

He gave Michael a quick once-over. No stitches, his nose wasn't broken, no bloody knuckles, life was good. He walked in closing the door behind him.

"After not being able to get in touch with you last night I decided to fly out here to make sure you hadn't done anything stupid."

Michael flopped down on the black Italian leather sofa and ran his fingers through his hair. The Venetian blinds were pulled shut yet thin beams of sunlight poured through their slits giving an eerie glow to the room. Tom stood in silent amazement and took in the disarray that surrounded him. Tables had been turned over, mounds of paper strewn across the floor, shelves ripped from the walls, leaving gaping holes where they once were anchored. Tom was careful to step over several empty brandy bottles and shards of broken glass as he made his way to sit opposite Michael.

"Did you go anywhere last night?" Tom asked cautiously.

Michael shook his head no. A chill swept through Tom when he looked at Michael. He was a man dancing on the edge, his eyes vacant and hollow, empty inside. The demons he had buried for many decades rising to the surface in multitudes. Tom had come to Virginia in hopes of saving Michael from himself but in that instant he realized that only Michael would be able to pull himself out of a darkness this thick. He had to deal with his past or let it destroy him. Tom stood and paced the room searching for the right words.

"There is nothing you can do about this guy that hurt her, you know that right?"

Michael reached to the floor beside him where there sat a bottle of cognac and downed the remaining drops.

"I know. The fucker is in a supermax facility in northwestern Virginia, allowed to breathe the same air as all the decent people of the world. I thought about calling in a few favors, have a hit put on him. Death is too good for that bastard. He needs to suffer."

Draining the bottle dry he flung it to the opposite wall, it crashed sending a small explosion of glass fragments around the room. Tom jerked quickly and shielded his eyes. He loved Michael like a brother, but he'd be damned if he sat by and let him drown in self-pity. He needed to make him face the real issue.

"Mike you know what," his voice suddenly filled with indignation. "You can sit here in your self-imposed prison and destroy things, destroy yourself even for as long as you like. I don't deny that finding out what happened to Nichole McCallister isn't deplorable at best, but what this is really about is your old man. The sooner you deal with it and get on with your life the better."

Michael stood slowly and faced him. He spoke quietly, his eyes burned with rage.

"You don't know what the fuck you're talking about."

He had hoped to avoid this, but it was a necessary evil, he had to pull Michael out of himself. Tom screamed his reply.

"The hell I don't. I was there Mike. You couldn't have forgotten. I know I never will, the night he almost killed you."

"Shut up Tom," Michael's voice began to quiver, his hand were shaking.

Tom kept on. "The son of a bitch beat you till you couldn't stand and then kicked you over and over till the blood squirted from your mouth and he thought he had killed you. He ripped your shirt off Mike. I saw the burn marks. Exactly how many years had he been putting his smokes out on your back?"

Tom had expected it, but nothing could have prepared him for the force behind Michael's fist. He flew several feet to the wall behind him and landed in a limp pile on the floor. Michael swore out loud and went to get ice from the kitchen. After the ringing in his ears had stopped, Tom stood rubbing a rapidly swelling jaw.

They had sworn to never speak of that night, of the things Tom had witnessed. Michael had been Tom's hero, his savior and to be totally demoralized in the eyes of the one person on the planet that looked up to him was beyond humiliating.

Michael had figured out a few seconds too late, right before his fist met its target exactly what Tom was trying to do. He handed Tom the ice and both men sat in silence for quite some time.

Michael finally spoke. "It's not broken is it?"

"I don't think so."

Michael needed to be alone. There were too many emotions coming to the surface, too many memories. Thank God he told Nichole he wouldn't be in today he thought to himself. Then he remembered he had barely over twenty-four hours before he had to appear in all his glory at the damned Bachelors Auction.

"I appreciate what you tried to do," Michael held his head in his hand, eyes closed as he spoke, "and I'm sorry I hit you, but I need some sleep and I need to get my shit together on my own."

Tom nodded, he left without a word. Tomorrow it would be business as usual. This event would remain unspoken. He hoped he had gotten through to some small part of him, the part that would let him heal himself. Tom shook his head at the irony of it all, Nichole beautiful and engaging, Michael rich, powerful and every woman's dream brought together by fate yet bonded by a brokenness they both kept hidden from the world.

Chapter 9

NICHOLE CAUGHT THE FINAL notes of Fleur Elise emanating from her cell phone. She raced down the stairs to answer it, but missed the call. She paused for a moment, waiting for an indication of a message left on her voice mail. The number she recognized as Michael's mobile number.

She hadn't heard from him since her previous encounter with him two days before at the construction site. His increasingly odd behavior confused yet intrigued her. He was making it blatantly obvious in a slow, subtle way that he saw her as more than an associate and she let it be known without hesitation that she welcomed her new role, whatever that was.

Neither had spoken of the dramatic shift they both felt, emotions went un-discussed, there were no expectations. Yet, each time he left her with a gentle touch the feeling of him, the scent of him seared itself to her core. Much of him remained a mystery to her. Michael had secrets he guarded fiercely and sadness he struggled to suppress. She was nothing short of amazed to find herself desperate to break down his walls or be locked inside the fortress alongside him.

The message he left was brief and to the point. "Nichole, it's Michael, despite my lack of professionalism over the past few days I still expect you to be my angel of mercy this evening. I'll be sending a car around for you at six thirty. I have also reserved a suite in your name at the hotel. I don't want you traipsing back to the peninsula in the middle of the night, please don't argue with me about this one. I expect to see you there."

Nichole dashed back up her room to continue rifling through her closet for the perfect gown for the evening. After a few short minutes she accepted that it was hopeless. In the years before she was attacked her closet was lined from end to end with gorgeous silks and satins of the deepest reds, fresh corals, and airy blues. There were black velvets with rhinestones, silvers studded with pearls, all form fitting, alluring. After a long week of classes she would morph into a siren of the night bewitching every man that she encountered. But that was a lifetime ago. Shortly after being released from the hospital, she ripped from the hangers any and everything that resembled seduction, piled them in her backyard, dousing them with gasoline she set them aflame, eerily reminiscent of Savonarola's Bonfire of the Vanities.

Out of circumstance and necessity, Nichole sought new meaning and began to redefine herself. Her once lavish social life had given way to a cloistered existence. She created a regimented lifestyle that focused solely on a sense of safety and control. In an ever-shrinking world of self-imposed isolation, she found contentment.

After many long, often lonely years of merely existing, life had decided to throw her a curve ball in the form of Michael Collier. Michael made her feel alive. He made her want more. She laughed to herself at the dichotomy she found herself in. Once content, now restless, a recluse yearning for adventure, fearless and afraid. She was an undefined contradiction in terms, fantastically flawed and falling fast.

Michael had sent a sleek black limousine and as he had promised which arrived at exactly six thirty. Nichole had expected nothing less. After pouring through endless rows of gowns at every designer dress shop within fifty miles her best friend, Maxwell Porter had helped her find the perfect frock guaranteed to raise the pulse of every man in attendance. The gown she had chosen was the palest shade of coral. Made of silk it hugged every curve, with a dramatic plunging back that dipped down to the top of her derriere. Sparsely beaded throughout her body seemed to shimmer as she moved, elegant and graceful, Nichole had transformed from power suit to princess in under an hour.

She couldn't help but to smile at her reflection in the tinted glass of the limousine window. Her hair she left long in cascading curls that danced across her shoulders and bare back with drop diamond earrings that sparkled with the slightest hint of light. Her eyes were lined in black with thick lashes that fluttered and accented the spark in her catlike eyes. The contrast of light shades against darkened features created an air of the exotic, yet to every man that eyed her she was nothing short of erotic.

A subtle giggle escaped her lips. Years of living an emotionally stagnate life, devoid of love and laughter, a life she had created and learned to embrace was slipping out of her grasp and she was glad to see it go. No matter how long Nichole tried to deny her true self, the fire inside her, that passion that was Nichole McCallister lay in wait for almost a decade now raced to the surface screaming to get out. A mundane daily existence would no longer do. She was a survivor, a temptress, a woman in love with life.

As the chauffeur pulled up to the entrance of the La Cara Hotel Nichole vowed to leave behind all doubts, old fears, and her past. Tonight she would shine. Tonight she would live, not merely exist.

The door opened and a gloved hand extended to help her from the car. The sun was in its descent and a whiff of honeysuckle hung in the air. Women of all ages and social standings filtered through the revolving door of the grand hotel, dressed in their finery and dripping in jewels like proud peacocks strutting their feathers.

It was Nichole's wish, however, despite her mesmerizing appearance to remain discrete, at least for the time being. She thought it would do Michael some good to sweat it out a bit and not be entirely certain she would come to his rescue simply because he told her to. She grabbed a billet of the evening's events from the main desk clerk and pocketed the key to her suite.

Enchanted by her surroundings she gazed in wonder at the combination of gothic and medieval European decor. Sculptural wall mirrors ten foot in length topped by winged lions and ornate coats of arms were hung strategically throughout the lobby, finely carved furniture of mahogany and solid pine with candlelight dancing from sconces of filigree and dragons claws.

Outside its walls magnificent gardens as far as the eye could see. Pebble pathways led to scented arbors spilling over with honeysuckle and jasmine clinging to metal trellises, grass covered turf seats placed sparingly throughout a flowery mead.

Nichole not only looked the part of a princess, but in these surroundings she felt as if she had been transported in time to a land of dashing knights and their lady's fair. According to the lineup of events, Michael was not due on stage until nines. She chose to pass the time in the gardens. She gazed, lost in thought at a fountain surrounded by fairies and sprite-like statuettes hidden among the greenery. In a tranquil, almost dream-like state she gasped as a warm hand pressed against the middle of her bare back.

"Estelle" she exclaimed in sudden relief.

The look of delighted surprise in Nichole's eyes was equally reflected in the eyes of the handsome seventy-year-old woman before her. Nichole grew up living next door to George and Estelle Peterman and she was a woman Nichole admired and regarded as part of her extended family. One of the few who knew the secret she held inside, a feisty strong woman who remained vigilant in trying to coax Nichole back into life.

"Nikki . . . my God you look absolutely gorgeous."

She grabbed Nichole by the hands and took a step back to take a proper look at her. The silver-haired woman's heart swelled with pride.

"Well, well, well. Whoever he is he must be something pretty special," she replied with a spark in her faded blue eyes.

Nichole made a halfhearted attempt at trying to conceal what was clearly written all over her face.

"It's not what you think; I'm here for work, nothing more. Helping my boss out of a sticky situation."

"Of course dear." She cupped one of Nichole's hands in both of hers and gave a devilish little wink.

Suddenly aware of the two other older ladies glittering a few feet behind, Nichole stammered as she spoke.

"Estelle . . . are you . . . you're not here for the Bachelor Auction are you?"

Feigning insult Estelle let go of her hand and stepped back jutting her nose in the air.

"I most certainly am. I'm old honey not dead."

"You're also married, what does George think about this?"

"Huh," she scoffed. "George said as long as I pick one that will do the yard work and take out the trash I can spend as much as I like. It would serve him right if I spent our entire savings on a hunk of a male stripper that would take me to Vegas for the weekend."

"Estelle," Nichole said aloud, her eyes dancing with laughter. "I've never seen you like this. Have you been drinking?"

The old woman gave her a coy smile.

"Oh I've had a glass of wine and a gin and tonic or two, but the night is still young. The girls and I left the men home with their pizza and poker, thought maybe we deserved to live it up for a night."

Nichole let loose a hearty laugh. Estelle Peterman was a rare treasure. Despite all the struggles she had faced in her life, she never let the harshness of the world around her get the best of her. Ever present with a winning smile, a helpful hand, or a word of encouragement she blessed every life she touched. She was a strong and wise woman with an indomitable spirit that was infectious.

Nichole laced her arm through Estelle's and they walked the distance back to the hotel. She too would "live it up for the night," throw caution to the wind and give not a thought to the past or the future. She would live in the now because now was the only guarantee any of us truly have and what better company to share it with.

Chapter 10

At eight forty-five Nichole made her way to the ballroom. Three glasses of wine had lessened her apprehension and she was beginning to feel rather daring. She was certain Michael would be searching the crowd for her by now, abandoning the main entrance she chose a discrete side portal that opened into the shadows at the far right corner of the stage.

It was standing room only at this point in the evening. Most of the women in attendance had obviously arrived when the doors opened at seven and drank heavily throughout. Hoots and hollers echoed and ended in applause as the auctioneer slammed down his gavel on a closing bid of ten thousand dollars for a tall, bronzed, fair-haired cardiologist from Chesapeake General. He exited the stage to join the recently divorced Celia Matheson who had outbid all others with ease thanks to her ex-husband's alimony checks.

It wasn't difficult to remain hidden in a room full of women literally screaming to be noticed. Nichole remained in the background moving slowly, a ghostly silhouette working her way to the direct opposite of center stage. She bit at her bottom lip to keep from laughing aloud when she spied Estelle and her friends at a table in the center of the room. The dignified Mrs. Peterman appeared to have a glass of champagne in each hand as the woman to her left waved a hundred dollar bill in the air. Her smile was quickly replaced by a look of agitation when she caught sight of the flaming red locks of Melanie Anderson in the front row a mere few feet from the stage, her cleavage resting comfortably upon the table next to a bottle of Dom Perignon.

The lights dimmed signaling a new bachelor was about to take the stage and the master of ceremonies took to the microphone.

"Ladies, up next I have for you a special treat. A man of this caliber is so rare he should be on the endangered species list."

Cheers erupted throughout the room and he continued, "The gentleman I'm about to introduce to you is not only wealthy, but powerful, devilishly handsome, a man's man and a gentleman. He has graced the cover of Fortune Magazine, is listed in Forbes five hundred, and is soon to be the wealthiest man in America. He has traveled from his home state of Texas to grace Virginia with his real estate genius. Ladies, I introduce to you Mr. Michael Castus Collier."

The buildup was so great the estrogen filled room erupted with whistles and applause and Nichole enjoyed every second of the spectacle before her knowing that Michael was behind the red velvet curtain cringing and likely cursing under his breath. A mere few feet from the center isle still completely inconspicuous to those around her an inaudible gasp escaped her lips as Michael walked on stage. The spotlight followed him and his rakish good looks as he stalked his way forward. Nichole was almost breathless at the sight of him. His hair black as night, piercing ice-blue orbs that subtly scanned the crowd, chiseled features and darkened skin. He wore a black tuxedo with tails, he oozed masculinity, and every woman in the room wanted to be the woman to leave with him tonight.

The master of ceremonies was cut short not being given the chance to read the details of the romantic package that went along with the man.

"Five thousand dollars," was called out from across the room. "Seven thousand five hundred," was challenged immediately after. Bids were being cried out from all points in the ballroom and within minutes they had topped thirty thousand.

Michael stood and bared it all with a wicked grin and a gallant, stoic presence. He gave no inclination of being offended at the prospect of being treated as a piece of meat, a sacrificial lamb for a good cause. Almost within arm's reach of the stage sat Melanie Anderson, a smug glare upon her face she had been waiting for this moment all evening. A quick glance over each shoulder and she stood, intent on making a grandstanding offer and put an end to all competition.

"Fifty thousand dollars."

A collective gasp was heard around the room followed by stunned silence. The highest amount offered all evening by far for any man. Michael remained unwavering, his expression set in stone. He said nothing, he merely tipped his head chivalrously in the direction of the scantily clad, titan-haired beauty before him. A hush hung over the crowd as she leered at anyone that may dare to challenge her.

"Fifty thousand it is," replied the stunned auctioneer, "ladies do I hear fifty-one?"

No one challenged. He raised his gavel, "Fifty thousand going once . . ."

A streak of possessiveness had taken hold of Nichole. After regaining her composure from the initial awe-inspiring presence of seeing Michael take the stage, she was rather enjoying watching the women trip over themselves to be the winner of the grand prize. Now she was becoming annoyed with the direction the performance had taken. She sauntered forward out of the shadows, her head held high, candlelight reflecting like diamonds off her beaded gown.

"One hundred thousand dollars," she retorted doubling the previous offer.

Instantly stunned heads turned in the direction of the fairy tale like creature who had magically appeared out of the mist. Her gaze connected with Michael's and she flashed him a knowing smile and a subtle wink. She stood proudly. Daggers flashed from Melanie's eyes, in the distance Estelle had begun clapping and laughing hard enough that she almost fell out of her chair and on stage Michael breathed a hidden sigh of relief.

"Castus?"

"Nichole, please, haven't you tortured me enough for one evening?"

A childlike giggle escaped her lips, her fingers locked at the nape of his neck. He held her close to him as they danced.

The hospital board members had put together an elegant reception in the La Cara gardens following the auction and anyone who was anyone had made an appearance. Benefactors to the Children's Hospital, the affluent upper crust of southern Virginia and northern North Carolina never missed this annual event. It was their opportunity to rub elbows, dance till dawn and at the same time flaunt their generosity in the form of a tax-deductible donation.

There were dozens of satin and tulle net canopies sheltering rows of hors d'oeuvres, desserts and an endless supply of champagne and wines. The walkways were alight with twinkling fairy lights and brass hanging carriage lanterns were placed throughout. It was an enchanting, magical night and as soon as Michael had stepped down from that blasted stage he was intent on spending every possible moment with Nichole in his arms.

When she had stepped from the shadows to reveal herself it had taken every ounce of control for Michael to keep his feet planted firmly upon the stage. The sight of her was his undoing. From the glitter of her gown to the wicked gleam in her eye he became brutally aware that this woman held a power over him that was beyond his control. She was a fiery beacon in his darkened world. He wanted her in a way that frightened him. He yearned to know not only every intimate detail of her body, but of her mind, her soul. He wanted to keep her safe and protected and possess her, marking clearly for the world to see that she belonged to him alone.

"You're not angry with me are you Michael?" She lifted her head from the warmth of his chest and looked up at him with eyes filled with wonder.

He drew in a slow deep breath, completely dumbfounded at how this amazing creature had the ability to completely annihilate every ounce of restraint he could muster with a mere glance. Most women would take advantage of that kind of power, but he knew with Nichole it was pure. He loved this new playful side he had uncovered in her and he was totally aware that it was a part of her she shared with few.

"No, my lady, I'm not angry with you."

"Your lady? I thought I was an angel of mercy?"

"Showed a bit of your devilish side tonight did you not?"

Nichole jerked her head slightly to the side and stuck up her nose in mock offense.

"I don't know what you're talking about?"

It was Michael's turn to laugh. He laid a finger softly on her chin and turned her head gently so that her eyes met his.

"Oh really? Why is it that you arrived at the hotel shortly after seven, yet managed to stay tucked away until my head was literally on the chopping block? Not to mention that deliciously wicked smirk you had on your face when you pulled the rug out from under Melanie. Are you going to try and deny enjoying that?"

Nichole surrendered. "Okay maybe I did enjoy that last part. But you didn't look like you were suffering up there. As a matter of fact, you looked like you were enjoying yourself."

"Never let them see you sweat, my dear."

All eyes remained on them for most of the evening. The astounding amount that Michael had brought in for the hospital and the raven-haired beauty willing to pay such a price had piqued everyone's curiosity. Countless times over the hours that ensued Michael was forced to give up Nichole's hand to a CEO or company president who politely requested one dance. Left on his own he was approached again and again by women of all ages hoping to sway his interest in their direction.

Their attempts were fruitless and he laughed in spite of himself. He had never imagined a time in his life when only one woman mattered, but Nichole was all he could think about from the moment he laid eyes on her. And at one in the morning he had had his fill of being gallant and charming.

Nichole, who had been dodging J.B. Phillips all evening had finally agreed to a waltz. Phillips was drunk and becoming increasingly obnoxious and against her better judgment and against advice from Michael to tell the man to take a long walk off a short pier, she consented in hopes of preventing any damage to their business relationship. Michael had gone in search of two glasses of wine and Nichole was immediately regretting her decision.

The night had been everything she had dreamed it would be and more. She had let her guard down and felt a freedom she hadn't felt in years. The freedom to live, truly live life on her terms without fear. As they danced, she fought to keep a reasonable amount of distance between herself and the balding paunch bellied man that was her partner. She began to grow anxious when he forcefully pulled her closer to him again and again. His hand grabbed at her behind and she began to feel a rush of panic wash over her. She swallowed hard and looked frantically for Michael.

"Mr. Phillips please, that's quite enough."

He grabbed her by the arms, his fingers digging into her flesh.

"What's wrong sweetheart? You can walk around all night hanging on Collier's arm like some kind of wannabe trophy wife, but you're too good to dance with me."

Nichole tried to wriggle free of his grasp. She wanted to scream, but couldn't find her voice. She was dizzy, her heart pounded. Dear God, where was Michael? With Michael she felt safe, she need to feel safe.

His grip on her grew fierce. He lifted her off the ground to within inches of his face. His words slurred.

"I'll show you what it's like to be with a real man."

He brought his mouth down on hers. She jerked her head to the side. There was a ringing in her ears, the air stung with the smell of his cologne and sweat. He forced his mouth down on her neck and she managed a terror filled shrill scream.

"*No.*"

Michael turned in the direction of her cry for help. Both wine glasses shattered on the cobblestone walkway beneath his feet as he raced to the dance floor. An indefinable rage took control of him. Nichole was unaware of Michael's presence, her mind had turned in on itself back to that horrible night seven years ago. She was unaware of being released. In her mind, she was back at the university, helpless, alone and dying. She saw blood spatter the front of her dress and collapsed.

Chapter 11

HE COULDN'T GET TO her fast enough, couldn't hold her close enough. J.B. Phillips lay squealing on the ground bleeding profusely from the mouth and nose. Michael stepped over him without concern and rushed to Nichole.

He scooped her up as though she weighed not an ounce, her head and arms limp, her long dark hair cascading about him. He could not remember a time in his life when he had felt more helpless, not as a small boy at the hands of the monster that fathered him. The band had stopped playing, a multitude of onlookers had gathered. None dared utter a word. The only sounds heard were those emanating from J.B. and the waves of the ocean crashing in the distance.

Michael carried her from the dance floor, through a sea of stunned faces that parted before him and into the hotel. He kicked open the door to her suite and laid Nichole down gently on the massive four-poster bed. Sleeping beauty spattered with blood. It wasn't supposed to happen this way. He cursed under his breath, a furrow in his brow, his face sullen. She had suffered enough for one lifetime and Michael vowed to see to the professional ruin of the insipid bastard that dared to put his hands on her.

Lighting a small bedside lamp he retreated to the bathroom and wet a washcloth with lukewarm water. His mind was reeling. He tore off his tie and threw it to the floor, rushing back to Nichole. Getting the blood off her skin at least, before she woke up was a priority. He knew all too well the effect that trauma can have on an individual's mental faculties. Once the mind had been subjected to true terror, it develops a series of defense mechanisms to ensure its survival, a way to adapt to day-to-day living, holding the past barely under the surface. Problems arise when faced with similar situations in the future. The defenses are forgotten, your mind turns in on itself and panic takes control. Michael was concerned about Nichole still being unconscious but for her he was more apprehensive of what she faced upon waking.

A fifteen minutes had passed, her skin again flawless, he sat on the bed beside her lightly stroking the side of her face with his fingertips.

"Nichole, wake up baby."

He looked at her, peaceful, perfect. The defenses he had constructed to protect his heart from ever truly loving another human being finally failing him.

"My angel, please wake up. You're safe now."

She began to stir, squinting in the amber glow of the light upon her.

"Nichole."

He took her hand in his and pressed it to his lips. Nichole's eyes widened. She looked around the room frantically confused. She looked down at her arms, no blood. But it was there, on her dress. She ran her fingers through her hair, quickly she pulled her legs to her chest and covered each ear with her palms. In an upright fetal position, she began rocking back and forth.

"Dear God," Michael murmured.

He wanted to break something, hurt someone, anyone who dared to lay an unwelcome hand on any defenseless woman or child. Michael struggled to control his emotions. The room was cold yet beads of sweat lined his brow. He stood slowly in stunned awareness.

Michael had seen this before, not from Nichole, from himself. He had to have been eight, nine maybe, locked in a dark, damp closet for the better part of two days. Looking back he no longer remembered the offense, perhaps he had broken something. The beating that followed he would never forget. His back lined with bloody welts from a thick leather belt, thrown half-unconscious, as nothing more than discarded trash into the basement storage closet. He was certain his father tossed him in there hoping he would die. Screaming for help was pointless. It was the first, but not the last time his mind would betray him.

It was a type of madness, a darkness that engulfed him. He could still smell the stench of the sewer, feel the bugs crawling on his skin. His young mind thwarted into an atrocious, nightmarish abyss where there was no hope, no joy. Only the sound of his screams running through his head repeatedly. It was the same darkness that was now threatening to take hold of Nichole. He knew then and there he had to do something, anything to pull her out before it claimed her.

She trembled, her face buried between her forearms, still rocking in a catatonic like state, completely unaware of his presence. Grabbing a satin throw from the chase lounge at the foot of her bed he slid in beside her and gently wrapped her in a protective cocoon of emerald and white. To his surprise she stilled, but her breathing remained unsteady.

"My God, what did that bastard do to you," he mumbled barely above a whisper.

Taking each of her hands into his grasp, tenderly as if she were made of porcelain he drew them away from her face and into his chest.

"Nichole I need you to look at me."

Nothing, she sat unmoved, her head down.

"Listen to me, angel," Michael spoke, his voice calm, quiet, reassuring. "It's Michael. You're safe. You are here with me at La Cara."

Several moments passed in silence. The trembling stopped. Nichole shut her eyes tightly, her long thick lashes fluttering slightly.

Cautiously Michael began to caress her face delicately as he spoke.

"He's not here Nikki. That happened a long time ago. No one can hurt you here. I'd die before I let that happen."

A tormented sigh escaped her lips as she processed the words he spoke to her. She looked up and met his gaze a single tear rolling down her cheek.

"You know?"

Michael nodded, a heartbreaking sadness in his eyes.

More tears followed. Nichole had not allowed herself to cry in years. Crying meant feeling and she had withdrawn so far into herself that wretched night that now she rarely felt anything. Yet this night in the safety of Michael's arms her tears seemed endless. She sobbed uncontrollably. Weeping for the wrong that was done to her, weeping because of the fear she was forced to face every day of her life robbing her of all that she truly was, mourning the loss of the vibrant, carefree girl she used to be.

Michael held her close, his powerful arms encircling her, her head tucked safely against the warmth of his chest. Never before had he met a more amazing woman, strong, beautiful, a true survivor, yet fragile and vulnerable in his arms. She allowed him to share in her grief and to Michael that was sacred. Few things were to him he had seen much of the darkness of the world and suddenly thrust into his path was the brightest light of them all. They were alike the two of them, yet different, they complimented each other well. Lost in her he hadn't noticed exactly when the crying stopped or when she had drifted off to sleep. Tonight he was content to watch her breathe.

Steam filtered through the glass and marble bathroom like a thick layer of fog descending upon a mountaintop. The water would never be hot enough, the soap never powerful enough to make her feel truly clean. The logical part of her mind knew this. The emotional part propelled her to scrub viciously at invisible bloodstains that would never be erased until her skin was raw.

Nichole had awoken with her head nestled safely on Michael's muscular chest, their arms and legs entangled with one another. A more perfect place on this planet did not exist, of that she was certain. Yet, within moments a pounding in her head and the stinging of her swollen eyes had surfaced to remind her of all that had transpired a mere few hours before.

Dawn had not yet broken; La Cara was a tomb of darkness and silence as she stealthily slipped from Michael's grasp and into the shower. Shame, frustration, and fury coursed through her. She had lived this hell once. What loving God would allow such a cruel reminder at this point in her life? When she had finally allowed herself the right to live, the freedom to feel, she was being reminded that there is no greater hell than existing in a state of perpetual terror.

Michael had been a pillar of strength, gentle and kind and for that she was grateful, but she had never experienced that level of intimate vulnerability with any man and the newness confused her. She felt as if the very essence of her soul, the darkness, as well as the light had been ripped from her and displayed for all the world to view. His words replayed in her mind. He knew. Somehow, before tonight, he knew.

Nichole toyed with the idea of getting in her car and driving as far away from this place as her finances would allow, but deep down she knew running was never the answer. Neither was scrubbing her skin until it bled. She towel dried her hair and slipped into a white satin robe, opening the door slowly as not to wake him.

The room was aglow with candlelight and silhouetted shadows dancing throughout. Michael stood shirtless, dressed only in his black tuxedo pants stirring a cup of coffee. He was powerfully built, his skin dark and tanned with a hint of black stubble lending a dangerous quality to his perfectly chiseled features. Nichole stilled momentarily in silent awe, an unexpected heat pulsing through her. His ice blue eyes locked on hers, a slow sleepy smile formed on his face.

"Here, take this," he said placing the mug in one of her hands and taking her by the other led her to the sofa in the main room of the suite.

"Sit. I think we need to talk."

Nichole did as she was asked wearing nothing but white satin and wet hair and feeling surprisingly at ease. He sat next to her and said nothing as he brushed a loose tendril of wet hair away from her cheek and tucked in neatly behind her ear.

"My God you are beautiful."

She struggled for words. She clenched the warm mug between both hands and looked away.

"Are you okay, Nichole?"

She nodded focusing on the steam rising from her cup.

"I'm sorry, Michael."

"Sorry. What do you have to be . . . Nichole please look at me."

She had not been avoiding his gaze out of shame, she was however afraid that if she looked too long in his direction, lingered too close, she would melt away into a puddle at his feet or spontaneously combust by the heat that they shared in spite of what happened tonight or maybe because of it. She raised her head, her chin jutting proudly, her eyes glowing cat-like and exotic.

"Michael, how did you know what happened to me all those years ago?" she questioned.

He winced, his chest tightening. He feared she would hate him for his invasion into her private world. Perhaps unforgivingly push him away before he ever had a chance to make her his own yet, nothing short of the truth would do. She deserved an honest explanation.

"There is a lot you don't know about me, angel. The life I have chosen for myself has been complicated and competitive at times. I have friends in high places as well as enemies." His features softened as he spoke, as if relieved to finally be rid of the truth. "I make it a point to have anyone that I plan on working with closely investigated, perhaps I'm paranoid. A preliminary investigation showed you had a concealed weapons license and were well trained in martial arts. Normally I would stop there, but when I met you, talked with you, I had to know more."

He searched her face for signs of a potential eruption of fury and to his surprise he found none. He stood raking his fingers through his hair.

"Nichole, I swear to you I had no intention of violating your trust. I honestly did not expect to find what I did."

Nichole sensed his uneasiness. She was well aware of Michael's power, his position as well as the fact that had he not known in advance tonight could have been much worse than it was. She sat her coffee on the table and walked to him.

"Michael there is no way you could have known. I understand why you did what you did."

A look of genuine relief washed over him. "Then I'm forgiven?" he asked taking her by the hands.

"There is nothing to forgive."

They stood for several moments silent, lost in the mystery of each other. It was true there was a great deal of him she did not know. In her mind she vowed to take her time and enjoy discovering all there was to learn.

He pulled her to him, the heat of their bodies mixing in the coolness of the night. Glowing green eyes looked up to greet him. He had lived a hedonist lifestyle for over two decades. Money, women, power were in abundance for his amusement. He could have sex with a woman for hours and make her believe she was the only woman in the world and somehow this sable-haired beauty in his arms had done the unthinkable. She had become the only woman in the world to a man who had vowed never to love.

He placed a soft, tender kiss on her forehead, the tip of her nose, studying each detail of her face intricately as he trailed to the perfect pout of her mouth. Her eyes had burned through him since the first time he saw them, now they seemed to control him; the taste of her lips, the curve of her chin, sensual, delicate, perfect.

Nichole's head went back and a gasp escaped her lips as he bent to bury his face in the nape of her neck, breathing in deeply to take in the scent of her hair, her skin. She felt no fear, no hesitation. Somehow all the tears she had cried had served to free her. Emotions buried, left to fester were washed away. Her arms wrapped around him, willingly accepting all he had to offer.

Michael's heart pounded in his chest. This was not about sex for him, this was about making love to a woman who had taken control of his every thought since the moment he laid eyes on her, a woman who roused emotions in him that were all consuming and intense that they defied explanation. His mouth sought out her lips, kissing her lightly at first he nibbled on her upper lip, then her lower, sending a quiver through her body to her toes. A soft moan escaped her and fueled his passion, which he was already struggling to keep in check.

Michael knew that with Nichole he had to be especially slow and gentle. He wanted to take his time, to share himself with her in a way he had never done with any other woman before in his lifetime of vast experience. He deepened his kiss, his breath was heated, and he could feel the plump swell of her lips beneath his.

Nichole felt small in Michael's arms yet safe and protected. Her body reacted to his every touch, sensations long forgotten, renewed with every flicker of his tongue, each gentle caress of his capable hands through her damp hair, along the silken softness of her cheek, her neck.

Her body quivered and she fell into him, the heat of his chest easily felt through the thin satin of her robe. A slight groan escaped Michael's lips at the feel of her breasts pressing upon him. He struggled to maintain a slow and steady pace, fought his urge to drop to the floor and take her then and there. Nichole was special, Nichole was his undoing, every touch, every taste offered to him a precious gift.

With a subtle jerk, he lifted her as though she weighed not an ounce. He carried her to the bedroom, candles flickering in the breeze he created and tenderly laid her down on the bed. He handled her as if she were made of the finest porcelain. The desire that flowed through him was intense and fierce yet he forced an unhurried pace. He wanted Nichole to know the soft touch of a man, not only the hands that had brutalized her in the past.

For Nicole, time stood still, the world around her ceased to exist. Her breathing was rapid and shallow, her body ached to be touched, held, shared with the man who has saved her from herself, freed her in many ways. Michael lay beside her, quietly studying every feature. He touched her face again lost in her eyes, she flashed a sheepish knowing grin, giving him permission to explore further.

His hand fell to her shoulder and he carefully slid the soft satin from her skin, the robe falling in a cascading pool behind her. He sat in silent awe, a muted glance, which spoke a thousand words. Nothing existed beyond this moment and in the moment was heat and beauty, passion and a simple knowing that no two people that had ever lived had felt the same before.

It was then her body stiffened as she remembered . . . Nichole looked down, sadness in her eyes at the jagged scar the marred the side of her breast, another below her rib cage. Suddenly she felt ashamed and fought back the familiar sting of tears to her eye.

He knew they had to be there somewhere, hidden from the world. He read the article, *stabbed multiple times,* but the marks they left behind did nothing to take away from the beauty of her body, the beauty of her. Michael's jaw clenched. A flash of seething anger shot through him. The mere thought of any man touching her, daring to harm her sent his mind reeling for revenge, but now was not the time. He was overwhelmed by a need to reassure her. If she could only see herself the way he saw her.

He ran his fingertips lightly along the faded line, then followed the heat of his fingertips with soft, warm kisses. Her body shook in response, a soft cry escaping her lips. She ran her fingers through his hair as he used his tongue to make a slow wet circle around her nipple before greedily taking it into his mouth. Her back arched and she cried out as she watched this man that she was falling in love with take her body and arouse sensations in her that she had never known. The way he touched her, the unspoken language they shared was sacred, almost esoteric in nature.

Her head fell forward; she kissed his chest, his shoulders and whispered softly in his ear.

"Michael . . . I . . . I haven't been with anyone . . . not completely since it happened."

He stilled suddenly and rose his head to meet hers, she shook slightly, and tears filled her blazing cat-like eyes. Michel was shocked by her words and at the same time oddly pleased. He had never imagined a woman this beautiful was capable of living a chaste lifestyle, but her circumstances were extreme. What small part of his soul he had left to claim as his own was instantly in her possession.

"Do you want me to stop?" he asked his voice raspy, prepared to do whatever necessary to make this night perfect for her.

She shook her head, a tear escaping from her eye and cupped his face in her hands.

"No. I want you to make love to me." She paused and swallowed hard. “I didn’t want to disappoint you. It’s been a long time.”

His eyes widened in disbelief. He pulled her to him, holding her in a strong embrace, then tilted her forcing her to look at him.

“You listen to me. You could never disappoint any man. Not ever. Do you understand me?”

Again she nodded, a blush rising to her cheeks and slowly rested back on the bed, pulling him down with her. Nichole untied the robe from her waist, tossed it to the floor. She was breathless and dizzy from his touch.

Michael locked his eyes with hers as he ran his hands across her hip, down the softness of her thigh and met no resistance as he gently parted her legs and slowly rested between them. He did not dare to look away for fear the mere sight of her naked body beneath his would finish him off before he had begun.

The hunger, the need for each other was overwhelming, their bodies pressed together at they explored each other with fierce intensity. The fire that burned below Michael’s waist called out for release. He needed to be inside her, to be a part of her. He slid himself slowly into the wetness that welcomed him, never tearing his gaze from hers. He stilled. The fit was snug and he fought to maintain control.

“I don’t . . . want to hurt you, angel,” he spoke, his words catching in his throat.

Nichole struggled to form her words. Her body ached, she was melting into him, losing herself completely. Years had passed since she had been intimate with a man and never so completely as this.

“I’m fine,” she replied in a raspy voice her lips swollen and red.

Her hips rose to meet him, inviting him deeper inside her. Michael was certain he was on the brink of madness. Knowing she wanted him as urgently as he wanted her, feeling her body react to him brought him to the edge of sanity. He thrust himself into the warm softness of her gently over and over again. They clung to each other out of sheer desperation. Nichole felt as if she could never get close enough to him. It was extreme ecstasy in its purest form. There they made love. Two bodies moved in a single rhythm as dawn broke the horizon.

Michael held back until she screamed out in release. His mouth coming down on hers, swallowing the sound, and held her tightly to allow her to feel the full intensity of his climax, filling her, his body trembling. They collapsed in an entanglement of flesh and sweat, the flame from the candles slowly dying, both sources of heat now at rest.

Chapter 12

WAKING UP IN THE warmth of a man's embrace was almost a foreign to Nichole as it was fantastic. Since the night of her ill-fated attack she rarely dated. Four, five dates over the course of the past seven years, all completely low key and casual. Should the slightest hint of intimacy arise, Nichole was quick to squash it. It was a lonely existence, but it was safe. No chance of getting hurt, no hint of danger.

Yet now as her long lashes fluttered to life under the glare of the midmorning sun, her head lay softly on the chest of one of the most dangerously handsome men in America. A soft moan escaped her lips at the sudden realization that last nights' events were more than merely a dream. Nichole squirmed in a sleepy daze, Michael Collier had made love to her in such a painstakingly slow and sensuous way that her body ached for more at the mere hint of remembrance.

She stilled suddenly, Michael's hand now upon her cheek. His fingertips traced the line of her jaw, tilting her chin upward. The intense, raw emotion in the heat of his gaze was almost unnerving, but she managed a slow, sinuous smile.

"How long have you been awake," she spoke, her voice barely above a whisper.

Michael placed a gentle kiss on the top of her head, "one hour, maybe two." He winked with a gleam in his eye and a delicious smile upon his lips. The dark hint of whiskers on his normally clean-shaven face lent a menacing quality to his already intoxicating presence.

Shocked Nichole propped herself up on one arm to face him.

"Why didn't you wake me?"

"Because I was watching you sleep, you were dreaming," he said matter-of-factly, placing both hands behind his head as if it was something he did every day.

"Oh." She paused not certain if she should be flattered or embarrassed at the notion. "Oh, lovely."

What if she were snoring or drooled in her sleep. It had been many years since she shared a man's bed such things no longer occurred to her. Resigning herself to the idea she lay back down with her head on his chest, wishing she could disappear under the covers completely.

Michael could sense her innocent unease and found it quite captivating. Her beauty and her strength were what drew him to her. The fact that she was basically untouched by anyone, but him gave rise to a streak of possessive pride that surprised him. The way her body responded instantly to his touch, the way she had called out his name pulled at something deep inside him, resurrecting emotions he had buried long ago.

"Actually it was quite lovely, your eyes were fluttering, a few deep sighs, and the softest hint of a moan here and there. Very enticing."

Nichole reached for the sheets in an attempt to pull them over her head, but he quickly grabbed her under the arms and pulled her on top of him. His scent had mingled with her own and permeated the air around them, that mixed with the full-on heat of their bodies pressed together and Nichole melted in his arms. She could feel his instant arousal grow hard on the flat of her stomach.

Dropping her forehead to his, a coy grin splayed upon her lips. She taunted him. "Is there something I can do for you Mr. Collier?"

He let loose a low growl and crashed his mouth onto hers. One hand tangled in her long flowing hair he tugged gently at the nape of her neck, with the other hand he traced delicately the length of her spine, the smooth curve of her hips. His tongue probed greedily into her mouth, hungry for the taste of her lips, desperately clinging to her essence. Tilting her head to the side he placed a trail of soft heated kisses along the curve of her shoulder and then to her full, firm breasts. Burying his face between them, he alternated one then the other, inhaling her scent. Taking her nipples into his mouth he tugged at them gently with his teeth, fighting for restraint.

Nichole moaned softly in response, wetness building between her legs. Michael's touch consumed her, her skin flushed, her heartbeat pounding mercilessly in her chest. Her hips began to move in a slow circular movement against him, desperate to have the fullness of him buried deep inside her yet again. Michael's finger probed her opening and delighted in the soft silky wetness that greeted him. She was ready for him and wanted only him. He slid a finger into her and stopped cold when she visibly winced at his touch.

"What's wrong, angel? Did I hurt you?"

Nichole fought to steady her breath and speak.

"No, you didn't hurt me Michael . . ." she paused looking for the right words. "I'm a little tender . . . but in all of the right places. Last night was the first time in many years for me."

He gaped at her in amazement. She was passionate and brazen in their lovemaking, responded readily to him, it was easy for him to forget she had lived such a cloistered lifestyle for many years. The manly ego part of him swelled with pride and although he wanted to be buried deep inside her right now more than he wanted his next breath, he never wanted Nichole McCallister to associate him with pain of any kind. Michael quickly slid from the sheets and stood.

"Where are you going?" she asked, quickly grabbing a blanket to cover herself.

He leaned into her for a kiss. "To remedy the tender places."

He disappeared into the bathroom and Nichole heard the sound of running water, the scent of lavender bath salts permeating the air. He reappeared and took her by the hand, leading her into the room, candlelight throughout, warm and inviting, he stepped into the bathtub, and she eagerly followed his lead.

He pulled her to him, her back to his chest and buried his face in her neck, whispering softly in her ear.

"How's that?"

"Heaven," she replied, "Pure heaven."

They sat in silence for a while, holding each other, thinking thoughts neither of them dared to say out loud. Not now, not yet. When Michael's hand absentmindedly traced the outline of her scar Nichole flinched.

"I'm sorry," he said, quickly pulling his hand away. Nichole turned to face him.

"No, you have nothing to be sorry for. It's part of me and I've accepted it. I'm not used to anyone else accepting it."

Michael grabbed her by the hands and kissed them softly. It was as if a storm was brewing in his eyes, the ice blue now almost a dark gray and in them strong, indefinable emotion. When he spoke his voice was soft, yet severe.

"You are incredibly beautiful, Nichole, never ever feel like you have to hide any part of yourself from me."

She smiled a bittersweet smile and he cupped her face in his hands, stroking her cheek softly with the tip of his thumb.

"Angel, I know last night was not what you had planned. It's not what I had planned either, believe it or not. I had wanted to be with you for a long while now. I never intended to act on it and with everything unfolding the way it did I need to know you don't regret what happened between us."

Surprising both herself and Michael she began to laugh.

"Regret it . . . no, I don't regret it, Michael." She looked around as if struggling for the right words. "Have you ever lived through a situation so painful, so inconceivably horrific, that something inside of you breaks? You don't know what part of you it is or where it is, all you know is that you no longer feel anything. There's no pain, no pleasure, only numbness . . . and the worst part is you don't know how to fix it or even if you want to fix it because feeling absolutely nothing is much better than feeling the pain, even if it means never smiling a true smile ever again."

"Yes. Yes I have," he replied with sadness in his eyes all his own, "I know exactly what you mean. You learn to function among normal, feeling people, but in reality you're an empty shell going through the motions."

"Exactly," she whispered, turning to face him, stunned by his admission. "Until one day," she continued, "until one day when you least expect it someone walks into your life and changes everything. Then suddenly all of those feelings that had lain dormant for many years come bubbling to the surface and suddenly you're no longer hollow inside, you're alive for the first time. The sun shines brighter, the sky seems bluer, and suddenly you have a soul again."

He smiled and kissed the tip of her nose. "Exactly," he whispered, brushing back a lock of wet hair from her face.

She gazed at him in awe. This man was still a mystery to her yet in his eyes she felt as if she could see through to his heart, to all of the unspoken secrets it held, a shrouded pain, not unlike her own.

"How do you know?"

"Excuse me?"

"How do you know what I mean?" she asked. "Since the day we met you seemed to understand me in a way no one else ever has. You've expertly handled my neurotic idiosyncrasies with a delicate touch before you had read the article. You had to have survived your own personal hell for that to be possible . . . what happened to you Michael?"

He held her hands tightly and let loose a deep sigh. He had spoken the words out loud only once in his lifetime and was met with a rejection he had yet to forget. Those that knew what he had endured as a child had been there to witness it, like Tom. For decades he lived in the shadow of his personal truth, burying the pain, locking away the bitterness and anger out of fear that once unleashed they may consume him completely.

He hesitated for what seemed like an eternity. The woman before him was unlike any other soul he had encountered in his time on Earth. Nichole was beautiful yes, she was also genuine and trusting despite the depravity life had forced upon her.

"When I was born," he finally spoke, pulling her closer to him, "my mother died giving birth to me . . ."

"Oh God," she interrupted, "I had no idea, I'm sorry."

Michael rhythmically stroked the palms of her hands with his thumbs, his expression trancelike as if he were a million miles away locked in the pain of the past.

"My father, was a cruel man," he continued. "He never wanted a child and when my mother died and he was left to raise me on his own he started drinking. I don't have a single memory of him without a drink in his hand. I became his personal punching bag. The older I got, the more creative he became with his punishments."

Nichole felt sick to her stomach. She had never imagined a man as successful and powerful as Michael Collier could have come from such wretched beginnings. She had mistakenly assumed he has been born with a silver spoon in his mouth, nothing like this, never this. She climbed into his lap and wrapped her arms around his shoulders.

"Michael please, I'm sorry, I had no idea. You don't have to talk about this if this makes you uncomfortable. Living through something like that is heinous enough, I didn't mean for you to relive it."

He cupped her face in his hands and placed a gentle kiss upon her lips.

"Oh, angel, I know the cause of your nightmares it's only fair that you know the cause of mine. My father is a sadistic bastard, but it was because of what he did to me that I am able to understand you. I shut my emotions off like you said. I made myself a success to spite him and I've used money, power, and women to fill the void inside myself for as long as I can remember."

Nichole hesitated, his words stung and for a moment she began to doubt herself, to question Michael's motives. Perhaps last night was a result of one drink too many coupled with the extreme emotions of an intense situation. Perhaps she was reading far more into their current circumstance than was warranted.

"You've been through hell Michael and that I understand, but please I don't want to be another body to fill the empty place inside you. I don't deserve that."

He grabbed her by the arms and pulled her back to him, locking his legs around hers to hold her in place.

"Not you, angel, don't ever think that. I'm not a fool. I know my reputation, but you are not like the other women who have been in my life, don't entertain that thought for a second. Knowing you the way I do, knowing all that I know about you, I may be a son of a bitch, but I never would have taken you to my bed if my feelings for you weren't real."

He could feel her relax within his arms and held her there tightly, breathing her in, relishing in the connection between them that had completely rendered him a defenseless fool. He kissed the back of her hand, the sensitive spot on her wrist and left a wave of heated kisses up the length of her arm.

"You, Nichole McCallister, are a gift that I do not now, nor will I ever deserve."

Chapter 13

TOM STOOD STARING HELPLESSLY at the mound of papers and carelessly tossed books before him. He knew there was a desk under there somewhere, a hell of a way to start a Monday morning. With Michael constantly on the road, all local business fell into his hands.

He dropped his briefcase into a large leather chair, left word with Tina his secretary to hold all calls and began sifting through the clutter. He had to close on a shopping mall and small office building, attend a teleconference with the Atlanta office and review half a dozen leases all before lunch.

Barely an hour had passed when the door to his office cracked open slowly and Tina poked her head in. She was a quiet, even-tempered, petite woman in her early forties.

"Excuse me, Mr. Hogan. I hate to interrupt, but Caroline Collier is on line two."

Tom dropped the lease he held and jerked his head in her direction.

"Caroline? Are you sure?"

Tina rolled her eyes in disgust.

"Pretty sure. I told her you were busy and asked to take a message. She said she has already talked to your wife and knows you are here. She said if you won't take her call she'll come down here and camp out in front of your office until you agree to speak with her."

Tom's jaws clenched, he leaned back in his chair massaging his temples.

"That sounds like Caroline. Thanks, Tina, I'll deal with her."

Tina paused before making her exit.

"Mr. Hogan, is she as horrible as she seems?"

Tom began laughing hysterically.

"Honey you don't know the half of it. Caroline Collier is an evil, self-absorbed, soul-sucking harpy."

Tina's eyes widened.

"I see. Well, good luck to you then sir."

Tom looked at the phone with dread, bile rising up in his throat as he picked up the receiver.

"Caroline. What a pleasant surprise," he spoke sarcasm dripping from every word.

"Where is he, Tom?" Her shrill voice screeched through the receiver.

"Where's who?"

"You know damn well who. That bastard you call a best friend. And don't play stupid with me and pretend you don't know where he is because I know firsthand that Michael doesn't as much as scratch his ass without letting you know about it first."

Tom grimaced as his hands balled into fists. He had never known hatred of a woman until Caroline Collier. She was beautiful; blonde hair, blue eyes, long legs and big tits, well cultured and powerful in her own right, but she had no heart and no semblance of concern for anyone other than herself.

Tom spoke through gritted teeth.

"He's out of town and will be for several months. Actually now that I think about it, he'll be out of the country entirely for the next year," he lied.

"Well then," she demanded, "I highly suggest that you earn that grossly overpaid position of yours and find him. That decaying piece of flesh that fathered him had a massive stroke last night. They say he's brain dead and they need Michael's permission to pull the plug.

He needs to get his ass back here and deal with this and see to it that they can stop bothering me." She screamed her final words, slamming the phone in Tom's ear.

Tom yanked the phone away and stared at it in momentary disbelief.

"Bitch."

"Purple?"

"It's not purple. It's mauve."

Michael looked from the array of wallpaper samples spread out before him and then up at Nichole.

"Angel, it's purple," he spoke matter-of-factly, suppressing a smile. "I don't care what names Crayola comes up with, purple is still purple and I can't work in a purple office."

Frustrated Nichole slammed her hands down on the desk in front of him.

"You're impossible. It won't be your office for long and then it will be my office and I like mauve," she exclaimed.

"Purple," he corrected, unable to hold back a devilish grin.

Nichole took a step back, hands on her hips and glared at him. She wore a pastel green, form fitting, silk summer dress that plunged at the neckline and accentuated her luscious curves, the green of her dress appearing to make the green of her eyes glow with intensity.

"Michael, let's be realistic. A few months from now when the center is running smoothly you'll be gone, off God knows where embarking on your newest conquest."

She regretted the words before they finished spilling off her tongue, a clever double entendre, or Freudian slip perhaps.

Michael looked at her sharply, his expression grave.

"Is that what you think?"

Nichole looked away.

"I didn't mean that the way it sounded."

Michael ignored his phone as it chirped in his jacket pocket, his black shirt, and black hair mixing to add a dangerous look to the seriousness in his eyes.

He had made love to her in a way most women only dreamed of, freed her from the desolate cage of a world in which she lived, yet he had made her no promises. She was not going to fool herself into thinking she could tame a man determined to live free of being bound by anyone.

Reliving the night repeatedly in her memories Nichole wondered how many other women had known the magic of being made love to by Michael Collier, then quickly banished the thought from her mind. It was too painful, too horridly obscene to think of him with anyone else.

His arms wrapped around her from behind. Startling her he held her to him tightly, his chin resting on her shoulder, his mouth pressed against her ear.

"Is that what you think?" he asked, his voice low and sensual. "Do you truly believe you were nothing more than a conquest to me?"

Nichole bit at her lower lip inhaling deeply. She could barely think with him this close to her, nevertheless form coherent words. She freed herself from his grasp and faced him in silence, searching his face for the answer he sought from her.

Michael held her close, tracing the line of her jaw with the soft caress of a fingertip and left in its wake a coursing heat that Nichole felt down to her toes. If it were a sin to enjoy his touch, Nichole would gladly give up her place in heaven among the saints for a single kiss. Dear God, she hoped she was wrong. The world disappeared when he looked at her, touched her and when they made love she was certain time had stood still.

An impatient pounding vibrating the glass of the front door interrupted them. Michael swore under his breath. The building inspector had shown up early. Nichole moved quickly to open the door when Michael stopped her, a smoldering look in his eyes. He held her wrists lightly in his hands.

"This conversation is far from over."

She nodded, feeling as if her heart had skipped a beat.

"I know."

Within minutes, the building inspector was followed by the carpet installers, tile layers, and painters. Nichole was again up to her ears and nose in the whirl of electric saws and paint fumes. She was thrilled to see the boyish good looks of Max Porter as he unexpectedly walked through the front door.

Michael watched from the makeshift office window as Nichole beamed up at him, throwing herself eagerly in his embrace. He recognized him instantly as the man he had seen with Nichole outside the parking garage at the oceanfront. He left the phone to ring a second and third time unanswered as he watched how freely she spoke with a man Michael was growing to envy despite knowing not a thing about him. The muscles in his jaw tightened with each breath of laughter that escaped her lips. He was being overprotective; Michael tried to reason with himself, the sting of jealousy being a foreign emotion to him. Raking his fingers through his hair he turned away. When his cell began to buzz yet again he snatched it from his jacket pocket nearly tearing the silk lining.

"What," he bellowed.

"You know after dealing with Caroline all morning on your behalf I expected a warmer reception."

"Caroline? What the hell did she want?"

Tom filled Michael in on the details and he laughed at the irony of it all. They wanted his permission to pull the plug on the bastard. No. Not today. No stranger dressed in hospital scrubs would be bestowed the honor of putting an end to the life of the most miserable, sadistic, son of a bitch that ever breathed. Tomorrow Michael would personally make the trip to Texas and pull the plug himself. He'd waited for this moment for most of his adult life. He alone had earned the right, for it was he alone who still bore the scars of his darkened past.

"Have Tina call the airlines and then email me the flight information. I'll fly out in the morning and handle it."

Michael's emotions were all over the place, his mind spinning in all directions at once, Nichole returning unnoticed.

"Where are you going?" she asked startling him.

"Texas," he said coldly as he sat to review a spec sheet.

It had not escaped her that his mood had undergone a rapid transformation in the few moments she was out of the room. Curious as to what may have prompted such a sudden turnabout she probed further.

"Michael, is something wrong?"

He folded his hands atop the desk and looked at her with angry gray-blue eyes.

"My father has had a stroke. It doesn't look like he's going to make it I'll be gone for a few days."

"Oh, Michael, I'm sorry."

"Don't be," he said plainly. "The only reason I'm going is to make sure the bastard dies."

She stood silent uncertain of what to say. Nichole's attacker had been a complete stranger, but Michael's was family. The complexity of the situation was too much to process. There were no words to right the wrongs he faced as a child or wise declarations for the task he now faced.

Michael took advantage of her silence to ask a few questions of his own.

"Who was the man you disappeared with earlier?"

She was bewildered for a moment and then it occurred to her. He had been watching her with Maxie. Could there be more to his foul mood than his issues with his family? Could he possibly be jealous? Michael Collier, jealous? Was he capable of petty human emotions?

"His name is Max Porter. He was the person who found me after I was attacked." She stilled as she spoke, her voice sullen. "I was tossed in a thicket of bushes and vines. If he hadn't found me, I would have died."

Michael tensed, the mental picture her words created in his mind was more that he could bare. More than once he had wished he were there that fateful night, had been there to see her safely home, untouched by brutal hands, unfettered by the cruel harshness of life. Despite his chagrin at the thought of sharing her with another man in the slightest way, he was grateful for the Max Porters of the world. He could not wrap his mind around the concept of a world without Nichole in it. For a man who had sworn to never live his life bound to another under any circumstance Michael Collier was failing miserably.

"He stayed with me," she continued "until the ambulance arrived, rode with me to the hospital and came back every day until the doctors assured him I was out of danger."

She reached out and touched his face.

"Michael he's my best friend. That's all he is, honestly. And he's a good man."

He pulled her into his lap, cradling her, stroking her hair. She had a narcotic effect on him. Nichole McCallister had the ability to turn a completely phlegmatic, levelheaded, powerhouse of a man into an overly sensitive, bumbling fool. He knew he should thank God for Max Porter and he did, but at the same time he found himself envying the closeness of the bond they shared.

Dear God, what was happening to him? Where once there were rules now there were none. His business, the most important aspect of his life was becoming and invasive distraction and all he could think about was this charmingly mischievous vixen that had stolen what was left of his common sense as she was quickly working her way into his heart.

He ran his fingers through the silken softness of her hair and turned to bury a feather light kiss at the nape of her neck. The mere scent of her, the slightest brush of her skin brought back the scorching memory of the magical passion they had shared the two nights before. Pride be damned he needed this woman, wanted this woman for his own.

His lips brushed her cheek and then found their way to the perfect pout of her mouth. He kissed her softly at first, a patient lover leading a forbidden carnal dance. He felt Nichole turn and press against him, her body eagerly responding to his touch. When a soft moan escaped her lips something inside him shifted. His mouth became demanding with a possessive need to touch, to taste, to feel every inch of the miraculous body within his arms. His heart pounded in his chest as he resisted the urge to take her then and there, on the floor, atop the desk, he needed to be inside her, to feel the snug fitting warmth of her closing around him.

It was then her words played back to him. A conquest, she thought herself a mere conquest in his eyes. Grudgingly he pulled away breaking the kiss and cupped her flushed face in his hands.

"Oh my angel," he said, his voice raspy as he struggled to maintain his composure, "I want you more than I have ever wanted any woman . . . but not here, not like this. You are far too precious a gem deserving of only the finest life has to offer and when I return I fully intend on spoiling you rotten."

Nichole fought to catch her breath. His kiss had left her light-headed and dizzy. Her lips felt as if they were swollen and on fire. Her body ached for more and yet her heart swelled at the tender, gallant display of Michael's restraint. Never had she known a man to put aside his physical needs for a semblance of virtue and propriety. He truly was an enigma, one that required infinitely more investigation. An investigation she was looking forward to almost as much as she was the spoiling.

Chapter 14

MICHAEL WAS GRATEFUL HE had decided to have the corporate limousine meet him at the airport opposed to his vehicle. With fortune came a certain degree of fame no matter how desperately he had tried to avoid it. The last thing he needed right now was to see in print that he had been caught with a brandy before breakfast in the first class section of the airplane. But here inside his cocoon of darkened steel and tinted glass he was free to numb his senses undetected.

He hadn't expected to feel apprehensive about seeing his father after all of these years. The fact that he was in a vegetative state didn't seem to make a difference. A man as vile as Stephen Collier must have retained the ability to reach out from beyond the grave and still inflict pain.

The weather seemed to reflect Michael's mood. Morning looked like night. A black and slate gray cloud filled sky whose only brightness were fleeting flashes of lightning strikes followed by explosive blasts of thunder. Thick heavy sheets of rain pelted the earth flooding the streets, slowing traffic to a near halt.

The hour's drive from the airport to the Shady Oaks Nursing Home turned into three. Michael was grateful to have a skilled driver as they passed car after car abandoned at the roadside. He wanted it all to be over and done—pull the plug, sign the papers and have the miserable prick incinerated.

Tomorrow he would fly back to Virginia, spirit Nichole away from her duties and spend what was rest of the day and all night making love to the one woman who had replaced all others in his mind and in his heart. A slow smile spread appeared as he thought back to the night of the auction. Remembering how she responded to his touch stirred a fire inside him. Her soft moans and subtle cries, the most powerful aphrodisiac he had ever known. Her body fit his as if the heavens had formed her especially for him. She was the missing part of him he had searched for all his life.

The sleek stretch limo snaked its way up the tree-lined winding drive. Michael downed what was left of his third brandy, squared his shoulders, and prepared himself for the task ahead. Dressed in a dark navy blue Oscar de la Renta suit, his expression grim, he was an imposing figure as he strode through the tempest and into the sterile fluorescent light of the reception hall.

Two women shared the duties of the information desk, one young, one old and both equally willing to assist him.

"How can I help you, sir?" the elder of the two spoke first.

"I need to speak with someone in charge of a patient of yours. Stephen Collier," he said oblivious to the suggestive looks and abundant cleavage of the younger receptionist.

"Are you family?"

"My name is Michael Collier," he said plainly.

She entered Stephen's name into the computer and his personal information flashed on the screen before her.

"Oh, you're his son."

A quiet moment passed. Michael stared at her unable to publicly acknowledge that the man they spoke of was indeed his father. Clearing her throat she spoke to break the uncomfortable silence.

"His room number is 309. I'll have the attending physician meet you there. He'll be able to better explain your father's condition to you.

Michael nodded and made his way to the third floor.

It had been twenty-two years since Michael had come face to face with his tormentor. Seeing him now, frail and thin and hooked up to machines seemed somewhat surreal. The vision Michael had imprinted in his psyche was that of a huge, bellowing, house of a man whose only range in temperament varied from miserable to uncontrolled fury. Yet now, Stephen looked small, much older than his years, and peaceful. Never once in eighteen years did Michael ever recall his father looking peaceful.

Ten years previous Michael had received a call from the hospital informing him of his father's first stroke. It had left him unable to walk and with considerable memory loss. Despite his hatred of the man, Michael had his attorneys deal with the details and had him moved into the best nursing home in the area. He paid for his therapy and medication, saw to it that Stephen would never want for anything, but he did it all from the safe distance of a boardroom.

Having grown from a boy to a man did nothing to quell the horror that had been ingrained in his psyche all those years ago. Post-traumatic stress they had called it. A psychologist had diagnosed him when he was only twenty-four. He had no desire to seek out psychological help, but it was part of the deal he had made with the courts after nearly beating a man to death one night outside a club in New Orleans.

Michael and Tom had traveled to Louisiana to celebrate the successful closing of their first piece of real estate. Tom Hogan's then fiancé, now wife had been attending college in the area and she had agreed to put them up for the weekend. On their first night out a drunken sailor in town on leave had made Jocelyn his target for the evening. When Tom interceded he received a left hook to the jaw and Michael, who had been watching from a distance snapped. He had spent the rest of the weekend in jail, was put on probation, and had to submit for a psychiatric evaluation. He went grudgingly. He didn't need a Ph.D to tell him that all those years with his father had royally fucked up his head, that he was already brutally aware of.

Now he had come full circle, Stephen was the helpless one and Michael had been granted the power to determine the moment of his last breath. Michael sought out the sole machine responsible for keeping his father alive, his gaze trailing the length of the power cord to its place in the wall. Inhaling deeply his hands began to shake and he stepped closer to the bed. He had spent his childhood doing anything and everything to make his father love him. His animosity spurred from years of fear, pain, and rejection. Michael knew it had to end. He would put his pain to rest, leave his past behind and walk away.

His heart pounded in his chest. He had lived this moment a thousand times over in his mind and yet as his fingers traced the cord to the socket in the wall something inside failed him. He clenched the plug in his hand, the muscles in his arm tensing, his body shaking. Despite the pain, despite the nightmares that still plagued him, he had somehow grown beyond the hate. His short time spent with Nichole had changed him in ways he never dreamed possible. For the first time in his forty years, life had true meaning, meaning beyond the materialistic, beyond massive displays of wealth and power. He had something to live for that was precious. This life was not his to take.

Blinking back tears he accepted defeat. Michael reached out his hand, resting it on the lifeless, skeletal shoulder of a man who had never once shown him a hint of kindness.

"Goodbye dad," he said, wanting to feel strong yet his mind bending to the dark turmoil simmering below the surface.

So many memories, and unanswered prayers, pent up raw anger and hurt brought to the surface, even in a coma the man had the ability to bend him, but he would never break him, of that Michael was certain. For now he was content to go home and lick his wounds until his dour mood had passed. Tomorrow he would hop a plane and rush back to Nichole because she alone was all he needed to be reminded that despite the horrors in this world there did exist spectacular moments of pure joy.

As he left the building, he was greeted with the unexpected warmth of sunlight beating down on him. The storm had passed, the skies quieted. The Furies themselves, perhaps appeased by the sacrifice left at their hands, for Michael a bittersweet ending to such a brutal history.

Later that night the nursing home's attending physician, in the presence of two witnesses, removed all forms of life support from Stephen Collier and marked the time of death.

Michael chose to abandon his small glass and drink straight from the bottle. He hurled it across the room, the Waterford crystal shattering into thin shards, disappearing into the flames. The temperature outside neared one hundred degrees and yet he sat bare-chested in front of a roaring fire, a trademark sign that he had succumbed to another dark mood. He would sit in a near catatonic state and watch for hours as the flames reduced the wood of a once powerful and mighty tree to cinders and ash.

He sat unmoved at the sound of the front door opening. He heard keys jingling and the click of high heels on the hardwood floor approaching from behind.

"I need to remember to fire that grounds keeper for not changing the locks," he said, not bothering to turn around.

"Nice to see you too." The woman spoke in a tone matching the bitterness that greeted her.

"Caroline, unless you are here to tell me that you put your pitchfork down long enough to sign the papers we have nothing to say to each other."

"Come now pet," she said standing next to him, "your visit with daddy dearest not all you had hoped it would be?"

Caroline reached out to drag her nails through his thick black hair, stopping at his neck, knitting her fingers through his thick locks and forcing his head in her direction.

"Take your hands off of me you miserable bitch."

Michael's voice was harsh, his face expressionless. He stared past her, through her, the flames reflecting in his eyes. Her touch repulsed him. God how young and stupid he must have been. No piece of ass or real estate was worth selling your soul to a she-devil.

"Why are you here?" he asked. "What could you possibly want from me?"

Cold and conceited she donned an iniquitous grin, bloodlust in her eyes.

"I thought perhaps you may want to renegotiate the terms of our arrangement."

Michael's stomach turned sour. Beyond the fact that he had consumed more liquor in the hours that he had left his father than he normally had during a full weekend of celebration, he was becoming brutally aware of the all the poisons that had contaminated his life throughout the years. He yearned to wash himself free of all it, wipe clean the slate in one monumental cleansing motion.

"Well," he stood, his eyes glared, as a man possessed, you were wrong. What I want is for you to go away." His voice became increasingly louder. "What I want is for you to never darken my doorstep or sully my life with your wretched presence again. You will not get as much as a penny more out of me. You wanted my money Caroline and you got it, you've sucked every ounce of life out of me that I had to give. Sign the fucking papers or don't, at this point I could care less, but I want you out of my house *now.*"

Caroline set her jaw, a mocking smirk upon her face.

"You mean our house don't you dear? We picked this house out together remember?"

She began to stroll the room, tapping a finely manicured nail on pictures that hung the walls, then grasped from the mantle a vase that had belonged to Michael's mother. It was the only thing he had left of the woman who had died giving birth to him, the only possession among his millions that he truly valued.

"Now Mikey," she continued, "you haven't forgotten the good old days have you? We paid cash for this house and then celebrated by making love right here on . . ."

Michael cut her off, his stomach lurching at the mention of their ever having made love.

"The only thing good about my days spent with you is that they're over. God help the next poor bastard you spread your legs for."

As he turned to leave the room, the sound of his mother's vase crashing against the marble floor assaulted his ears and a battle ensued. The insults flew through the air like daggers, Caroline smashing everything glass that was not attached to a wall. The last thing Michael remembered was his bottle of brandy crashing dangerously close to his ear, shards splintering across his face, narrowly missing his eyes.

He woke confused in his bed. His throat was on fire, his head threatening to split in two. When Caroline stepped nude from the master bathroom, towel drying her hair he was certain he was trapped in the grip of a lucid nightmare.

"It's about time you woke up."

"What the hell do you think you're doing," Michael said with pure disgust.

"Why, lover, you wound me." Her voice was laden with faux sweetness.

Michael sat up quickly horrified at the realization that he was lying naked under the sheets.

"No . . . there is no way," he protested. "You manipulating banshee, God himself could not produce enough liquor to make me sleep with you again.

Caroline Collier stood tall, unwavering, her nose in the air, her chin jutting out proudly and smiled.

"Oh Michael, I can assure you, God had nothing to do with it."

Chapter 15

THE SUN WAS SETTING by the time Michael pulled into Nichole's drive. His flight home delayed for over an hour because of storms in the area, his patience wearing thin after the first ten minutes. A fresh wave of regret washed over him as he tried desperately to remember the details of the previous night. How could he have had sex with that woman? It wasn't possible was it? By the time he reached the peninsula, he decided it was better left forgotten. He was anxious to get to Nichole and prayed to whatever god that would still listen to a man like him that she would not be able to sense his guilt or ask too many questions. She could never know.

He spied her immediately from inside his car. She stood barefoot at the far corner of her house admiring a freshly cut bouquet of calla lilies and Canterbury bells, the breeze dancing through her hair. The slamming of the car door drew her attention away from the flowers. Michael made his way toward her with a strong, determined stride. She looked at him questioningly, but he said nothing. He cupped her face in his hands and looked down at her, his eyes burning with a fierce urgency.

Nichole began to speak, his mouth crushed down on hers swallowing her words. Tiny bolts of electricity shot through her, her knees felt weak and she lost her grip on the blossoms she held—yellow, pink and purple falling softly around her painted toes.

"Go pack," he said, releasing her.

""Pack?" she asked, struggling to maintain her footing, the heat from his kiss leaving her shaky and weak? "Where are we going?"

"It's a surprise."

"If it's a surprise how do I know what to pack?" she asked mockingly.

Michael arched a brow and studied her momentarily.

"Comfortable, casual, enough for three days," he said, patting her behind. "Now go we have a long drive ahead of us."

They made the trek in under seven hours. Nichole dozed in the passenger's seat, waking now and again to adjust to a more comfortable position, smiling all the while as she slept. Spontaneity in Michael was something she had never expected. He was always disciplined and in control, his every moved planned out weeks in advance.

Michael snuck stolen glances at her as she slept. So beautiful he thought to himself, so precious. Not even in a drunken stupor would he have been able to do something as senseless as to jeopardize what he had with her. It was impossible. Nichole was the only pure and decent thing to ever come into his life. The magnitude of it all weighed heavily on him.

The purr of the motor died as Nichole opened sleepy eyes toward a night sky overflowing with twinkling lights that seemed close enough to touch. She stepped from the car and stretched her arms skyward as if trying to steal away one of the shimmering celestial lights for her own. Before she knew it, Michael was upon her, his arms locked around her waist pulling her hard against him.

"Where are we?" she asked. Her sleepy voice had a sensual languid quality to it.

"My refuge."

Michael pointed a few meters ahead in the direction of a faint light that glowed between the trees.

"I had this cabin of mine built about five years ago. I come here from time to time to escape."

Nichole rested her head on his chest and listened to the tranquil night sounds that surrounded her. Crickets chirped in all directions, the rustle of leaves in the night breeze and in the distance the faint trickle of water flowing over rocks.

"We're in the mountains," he continued, looking down at her. Her eyes closed, a soft smile on her lips. "Come on, angel, let's get you inside."

The cabin was in reality a six thousand square foot log home with vaulted ceilings, an internal balcony that overlooked a massive great room, and a double-sided fireplace that could be viewed simultaneously from the master bedroom and master bath. Her eyes widened as Michael walked through the structure turning on dimmed lights. The look of childlike wonder on her face stopped him in his tracks. The wonderment of her and her ability to retain such an irreproachable innocence after what life had done to her amazed him. In many ways, her light chased away the darkness that Michael had carried around inside himself for so long. She represented hope and joy and all the things that were actually good in this world that he had long since forgotten.

Michael had seen to it that the cabin was prepared for their arrival. Fresh linens, a stocked pantry, a bottle of wine was chilled and waiting in the master suite. He carried their bags to their room and Nichole poured them each a glass of wine.

"Michael," she spoke hesitantly," how did things go in Texas?"

He searched her face momentarily for any signs that she may know of his duplicity. No he decided, there was no way she could have known and vowed that she never would know. He turned from her and spoke staring blankly out the window into the darkness of the night.

"Not quite what I had expected. My father . . . he . . . he was a brutal man Nikki. I only went so that I could personally be the one to end his miserable life. When I got there . . . I couldn't do it." He let out a sigh and raked his hand across the stiffness in his neck. "Maybe I'm a coward."

His words tugged at her heart. There truly was so much more to this man than he allowed the world to see. She walked to him and took him by the hands, looking up at him with the most mesmerizing eyes he had ever seen.

"You're a lot of things, Michael Collier, but a coward isn't one of them. Bitterness can serve a purpose, but that purpose is short lived and then you have to let it go before it destroys you. Life has a way of turning us into people we never knew we wanted to be."

He looked at her, shaking his head slightly and totally at a loss for words. Young, beautiful, and wise, the combination was staggering. But tonight no words were needed. Tonight Nichole was strong where he was weak. She felt brazen bold and sensual. All the years spent cloistered like a nun cried out for sinuous release. She wanted nothing less than to make love with this man for hours on end until her body surrendered in spent weakness.

Her hands slid up the expanse of his chest, looking longingly into his eyes as she deftly unbuttoned his shirt to reveal rippling muscles and a soft patch of dark hair covering them. The wetness of her mouth glided expertly across his skin in the form of light, silken kisses.

He lowered his eyes watching her, wanting her more by each passing second as he ran his fingers through her hair, down her back and resting them on her firm derriere. He pulled her to him, lifting her silk camisole over her head. Two firm breasts rose to greet him, the taught pinkness of her nipples brushing against his chest. Nichole drew her nails lightly across his stomach and Michael groaned softly, shivers rushing through his body.

"Dear God, woman," he said his voice raspy, his words breaking as he spoke. "What have you done to me?"

The kiss that followed was filled with heated passion and urgency and all-consuming need. They continued undressing each other in a slow ritualistic fashion, the golden light of the fire filling the room, a trail of clothes littering the ground in their wake. Michael scooped her up and lay her gently on a bed covered in rose petals, shades of crimson and white whirling in the air and landing on her, mixing with the strands of her hair, resting on the velvety softness of her naked flesh. Rembrandt, Matisse, Botticelli, hell Michelangelo himself had never created a work of art more beautiful than the one lying in his bed at this moment he thought to himself.

Nichole propped herself on her elbows, petals falling from her hair, Michael slowly lowering himself atop her, straddling her, pressing his forehead to hers. He distracted her with a kiss as he reached for his wine glass on the table beside him, tilting the rim so that drops of the cooled liquid ran down her neck and across her already erect nipples. She let out a scream of playful laughter as his mouth followed the trail sucking lightly as the droplets pooled near her navel.

Nichole's body squirmed beneath him. The coolness of the wine followed by the warm wetness of Michael's mouth had a dizzying effect on her senses. She fought the urge to surrender to his slow, attentive touch. To resist would be madness yet tonight she wanted control, it had been too many years since she had played the role of seductress and never once with a man like Michael Collier. It was his turn to squirm.

With one sinuous movement, she wrapped her legs firmly around his waist, pulled him atop her. and rolled over, pinning his hands to the bed with hers. Michael laughed aloud, but was quickly rendered speechless by the sight he beheld. Nichole hovered above him a virtual goddess, a sensual, passionate look filling her eyes, her head tilted to the side with waves of sable hair cascading across her breasts and delicate rose petals clinging to her skin.

His breath caught in his throat, his mind being assaulted by a barrage of emotion, desire running rampant through his body, every inch of him reacting to her touch. She fascinated him. Nichole McCallister was more than he had ever dared to dream a woman could be. He knew himself to be completely undeserving, as he reviewed in his mind the time wasted on twisted, tawdry affairs spent enmeshed in carnal lust in search of an elusive level of heaven that could only be found in this one woman. Worth be damned, his need for her was too great to deny.

Nichole used her locks as a weapon of torment, skimming the softness across his chest and moving in a slow fluid movement down his torso and over his stomach. On all fours she stalked catlike down the length of his body, her tresses taunting the skin of his hips and thighs and then taking her time to circle repeatedly the length of his hardened shaft.

Michael's body writhed as if he were suffering. How easily pleasure and pain melded into one. She had bewitched him, he couldn't take his eyes away from her, but her taunting seduction was becoming more than he could bear.

"Nichole," he spoke, his voice low and raspy, "I need to be inside of you. *Now.*"

A coy smile appeared upon her lips as she spread her legs and slowly straddled his hips. She bit hard on her bottom lip, easing him gently into the warm wetness of her body, welcoming him. He filled her completely and she embraced the pressure within her. Placing both hands firmly on his chest she steadied herself and began to rock back and forth in slow rhythmic waves.

Michael groaned low in his throat. This was sheer insanity. He struggled to remain still, to allow her to control their lovemaking, but his senses were overwhelmed. She was warm and wet, such a perfect fit. How could a woman virtually untouched display such flagrant eroticism and bring him easily to his knees? He had been with a multitude of women, had turned love making into an art form, yet this exquisite creature riding him expertly had brought him to the brink within minutes. He was falling quickly into a magical madness from which he hoped to never return.

Nichole began to hurry her pace as a soft muffled cry escaped her lips, Michael's hips rising to meet her. She locked her eyes, moist with tears, on the steamy depths of his haunting gaze, her back arching sharply as tiny convulsions rushed through her, gripping him tightly, pulling him deeper and deeper inside her body. At this moment, he belonged entirely to her. Mind, body and soul, a possession wrought by emotions and sensations that defied explanation.

Michael quickly gathered her into him and with one final thrust, let loose his seed, filling her, spilling into a pool of milky dampness between them. Nichole collapsed on top of him, her body shaking, her heart pounding. Kissing the top of her head he held her close, so close it was if he were afraid to let her go. She was everything he never dared dream existed in this world, but she was real and in his arms and he knew he would never be the same man again.

The light of the moon had faded with the dawn and Nichole was entranced with her surroundings. It was if the rest of the world truly had melted away, its pressures and stresses lost among undulating mountain ridges, hardwood forests, and vast meadows overflowing with wild flowers.

For three days there was no talk of childhood traumas, tragedy, or past heartaches, the past stayed where it belonged, the future left a mystery. They existed only in the now, making love in the afternoon sun amid a field of endless color before God and all his creation, dinners at dusk, fireside by a tranquil lake nestled inconspicuously among the trees. This was her heaven, a magical, mythical utopia that dreamers dream of, that poets speak of and that every woman aches to find.

On their last morning in their mountainous sanctuary, Nichole woke early, her body wrapped in the warmth of Michael's. When he slept it was easy to imagine him as a young boy, his hair tussled about his forehead, his features sharp and guarded when awake, softened when he slept. His words replayed in her mind. The torture, the torment he had endured at such a young age, years before she had been born. They molded him; shaped him in ways that allowed him to connect with her, understand her own brokenness.

Nichole blinked back tears and shook the thoughts from her mind. She wouldn't taint this sacred place brooding in darkness. She looked at Michael, an ebony lock curled at his temple, reaching softly as not to wake him she twirled it between her fingers. They had laughed and played like teenagers in love and shared passion intense and overpowering. That is what she would take with her; the beauty, the love. It was pure and unblemished and it was theirs to treasure.

Chapter 16

CAROLINE COLLIER, CHRISTENED CAROLINE Colette Villejoin knew only the beautiful side of life; the beauty and, of course, the misery she sadistically inflicted upon other people. Over indulged since birth as the only child of Senator Villejoin she was catered to and pampered, her every wish granted. Private school, ballet lessons, tours of Europe, she grew to expect and became increasingly ungrateful with each passing year. Her grace and beauty she considered her birthright. Women were intimidated by her, men adored her.

Empathy and basic human compassion seemed to be missing from her DNA, a true narcissist in every sense. Power, wealth, and beauty, she chose her lovers accordingly. By the age of twenty-four, her sirens song had broken many hearts. Having no true capacity to feel love for anyone other than herself she moved quickly from one victim to the next, retracting her talons only long enough to sharpen them.

When she met Michael Collier at a campaign function for her father, she knew without question they would be a perfect match. He was devastatingly handsome, already powerful in his own right and was often referred to as Texas' next "billion dollar man." The fact that he seemed ambivalent toward her at best made the challenge that much more enticing. So she hired a private investigator to find out all there was to know about the newest member of the Billionaire's Boys Club

She had learned that Michael Collier was a self-proclaimed bachelor. He had never willing sought the love of another and consistently rejected any and all attempts to entrap him into the world of monogamy or domestic bliss. He was married to his career, his fortune the only mistress to hold his devotion and yet he appeared to lack and actively sought out an increasing measure of political influence. That was where she came in.

When presented with the prospect of a union as a political move, another rung on the ladder leading to his success, the concept of marriage for convenience held an appeal he found difficult to resist. Caroline was undeniably beautiful with a body more than capable of filling his sexual needs, not to mention taking on a wife such as a woman in her position would lend with it an air of respectability he lacked and in the end the statuesque, platinum blonde with menacing gray eyes won the prize.

Caroline was remarkably convincing in her role of the supportive, loyal, and adoring wife. She was a passionate lover, championed all his business ventures and always willing and eager to be the perfect hostess at a moment's notice to any high dollar client who happened into town for a night.

Over time, Michael himself began to soften to the illusion she had created. On a night late in December after two bottles of wine and a heated session of passion Caroline had inquired about a scar on Michael's back. Letting his ever-present guard down, he confided in his young bride of the sordid details surrounding his childhood. Instead of compassion and understanding she responded with disgust, disgust not at the savage treatment that he had endured, but at the prospect of it ever being discovered and the effect it could have upon their position in society.

Emotionally Michael withdrew into himself completely that night. It had been a hellish feat at best to speak the words aloud, yet to have them met with revulsion and a total lack of understanding was a humiliation too great to bear.

His vision now clear, his heart cold but safe, Caroline became increasingly transparent. More than once Michael caught himself absentmindedly shaking his head in wonder as she used her beauty and charm to manipulate politicians and CEOs with the grace of a southern belle. To those she viewed as a threat, she carefully hid jagged barbs of insults wrapped within a package of sweet flowing words and compliments, falling deaf on unsuspecting ears, but never missing their target. Michael witnessed several of her carefully orchestrated displays with a new awareness.

With the business growing by leaps and bounds and Caroline's social status increasing daily they spent less and less time together. What connection they shared, if there ever was one, quickly dissipated. Michael sought her out only for sex. The one thing they undisputedly did well together was fuck. No pretenses, no illusions of love, raw and animalistic, satisfying carnal trysts.

It was purely accidental that Michael would one day discover her most heinous and unforgivable deception, duplicity so great that it would result in him revering her with nothing but pure hate and abject revulsion each time he looked at her. He immediately sought a divorce, a divorce she passionately contested. No man had ever left Caroline Villejoin and she would be damned if Michael Collier were the first. It was unthinkable and she would never stand for the public humiliation.

Using the political connections that Michael had once actively sought out Caroline had managed to drag out the divorce proceedings for years now, continuously changing her demands, switching attorneys, and repeatedly being unable to appear in court in a bitter attempt to prolong the suffering she could cause Michael.

Her most recent esquire, Jonathan Cole had a reputation for being tenacious, money hungry and virtually unbeatable. Keeping an accurate list of current Collier holdings and properties was no easy task, after reading the morning paper he called Caroline with baited breath.

"Caroline darling, tell me you've seen this morning's Regional Highlights section of the newspaper."

"No. Why?" she demanded, patting dry her translucent skin having finished her morning swim.

She covered the phone with her palm and ordered her maid to bring the Herald poolside immediately. Tossing the front page, sports and commentary to the ground she froze when she came to the article

Jonathan was referring to. On the front was a picture that comprised half of the page, an image of Michael standing with a strikingly beautiful, dark-haired woman dwarfed by a massive building in its last stages of construction. The headline read, *Local Midas Turns Steel Into Gold In Virginia.*

Caroline's face contorted, her eyes filled with bitterness and loathing.

"That no good prick. That's where he's been hiding."

Seething with rage she hurled curses through the air, her heart pounding in her chest.

"I'll contact Hogan and Mike's attorney. We need to find out everything we can about this new property and add it to our list of his assets."

Caroline was quiet, deep in thought. She lived in a five million dollar estate that sat on twenty acres of elegantly manicured gardens, a tennis court, and an Olympic-sized swimming pool. She employed a full twenty-four-hour staff and had a bank account that would take several lifetimes at least, to burn through. No, she had to take more than money from Michael. Each time she had asked for an increasingly outrages sum he readily agreed just to be rid of her. This time she would go for the jugular, the press be damned.

"No, Jonathan, wait. Don't call Tom, don't call anyone," she paused. A smile spread across her face at the deviousness of her idea. "Actually yes I want you to call my travel agent."

Michael Collier was a man caught in the grip of his folly. He had finally fallen from grace, broken hardened rules he used to define his life and staggered willingly past the point of no return. More than once he shook his head in wonder at the stark reality, yet what mere mortal in his position could help but do the same.

The woman he shared every night with for weeks now was not only smart and capable and infinitely enticing, but had faced a darkness he alone could comprehend and had managed to defy her demons their victory. She was hope, a light in the darkness and a passionate lover whose touch he could not resist.

The few nights he had spent apart from her he found it impossible to sleep, already accustom to the feel and warmth of her body molded to his. His appetite for her was insatiable and showed no sign of waning anytime soon. He was proud when she stood beside him and possessive. His touch was the first she had known for most of her adult life and he longed to keep it that way, despite his inability to say the words she longed to hear.

Michael was quickly becoming a part of her world, the people in it kind and decent, a stark contrast to those who had once filled his life. He cringed at such a brutal reminder. He would have to find a way to rid his life of that heartless bitch who undeservingly shared his name if it meant calling God himself down from the Heavens. One way or another he needed to free himself completely and be able to offer Nichole more than merely his bed.

For now the crunch was on. Construction was all but complete and Michael was faced with forty stories of stark white walls and bare floors. Paint samples, carpet swatches, and furniture brochures were strewn throughout the main corridor. Nichole and Michael could agree on nothing. She argued his tastes were too dark and brooding. He countered he was running an office building and not a day spa and despite their best attempts at compromise they stood at a standstill. The sound of voices drew his attention from the mounds of catalogs on his desk.

"What's this?" he questioned turning to face the two women approaching him.

Nichole nodded toward Estelle. "I've brought the voice of reason," she said smiling.

A smirk rested on Michael's lips, as he raised a suspecting brow.

"Uh-huh. For some reason, I doubt that." He took the older woman by the hand and lightly placed a kiss on the soft wrinkled skin. "I know an ambush when I see one."

From the moment Nichole had introduced him to Estelle Peterman he had been unable to deny her a thing. She won him over instantly with her feisty, willful ways and her tender, unwavering concern for Nichole.

The old woman jutted her nose in the air in feigned offense. “I’ll have you know young man that I am perfectly capable of making my own decisions without being influenced by either of you.”

Michael laughed aloud. He hadn’t thought of himself as a young man in a long time but he still wasn’t convinced. He cast a wary glance in Nichole’s direction, her eyes widening at his silent accusation.

“What?” she questioned defensively. “You heard the lady, she makes up her own mind.”

Extending and arm to each of them he gallantly surrendered. No man stood a chance against these two, but Estelle quickly wiggled free of the light hold upon her arm. She burst through the heavy wooden door of the main office, a woman determined to fulfill her mission. Fully covering the desktop and spread across the entirety of the floor stretching to the far corners of the room were splotches of color, small squares of tile and patches of carpet fabric of various fibers.

She threw Michael a scolding look and then turned to shake her head disapprovingly in Nichole’s direction.

“Well,” she said, “I can see I have my work cut out for me now don’t I. Nikki honey, you should have called me sooner.”

Michael crossed his arms in front of him and rolled his eyes toward the ceiling.

“Please Estelle, tell me you don’t have an affinity for the color purple.”

“It’s mauve,” Nichole retorted in her the most frustrating tone she could muster.

Estelle dropped the handbag she carried and flumped down into Michael large leather chair, the size of which appeared to dwarf her thin frame, her demeanor, however, was larger than life. She had been given a job to do and she took that seriously.

“That’s enough out of both of you,” Estelle demanded. “This is a mess and I have work to do. Michael take Nichole out and buy her lunch and make it someplace expensive,” she continued, sneaking a wink in Nichole’s direction.

Michael relented immediately without argument. Quickly he took Nichole by the arm and fled the room and the accusatory glare of the determined old woman who had usurped him of his power and momentarily taken control of a multi-million dollar piece of real estate.

When they returned nearly two hours later, they entered the room warily, Michael cracking the door open barely an inch, peeking silently into his workspace and hoping to avoid another scolding. He never knew his mother, but in his mind he envisioned her to be a lot like Estelle Peterman. What he saw both surprised and delighted him. Order had been restored to the room and Estelle had laid out in interior designer precision the perfect compromise of colors and patterns to appease both he and his dazzling protégé.

“Well, what do you think?” Estelle asked proudly.

Michael smiled and bended to place a gentle kiss upon her cheek. For the first time in forty long years, he was totally content with his life and grateful for the amazing women that filled it, both of them.

Chapter 17

"MICHAEL WOULD YOU STOP it," Nichole shrieked batting away his wandering hands as he tried to cup her soapy breasts.

"No," he replied flatly.

"I thought you said we should shower together to save time. We have to meet the mayor in an hour."

A soft sensual laugh escaped him, "I lied."

He turned her from the force of the water to face him. Trails of suds streaming down the length of her near perfect body, slippery and wet she easily slid into his grasp.

"Oh now you're lying to me are you," she replied with mock offense.

Her face brushed his chest and she was unable to ignore the swollen part of him that had risen to greet her.

"It was an innocent white lie. Besides I've never made love to you in the shower before."

Beads of water trickled down her face. Michael stood hypnotized studying the delicate angles of her jaw, the rise of her cheek and the subtle slope of her nose.

"The Michael Collier I met four months ago would never stop to consider putting anything before his precious business. Yet here you are resorting to trickery for sex and at the expense of missing your own ribbon cutting ceremony," she said, trying to goad him. "Dare I say you are a changed man, Mr. Collier."

Michael winced, his expression growing grim. Nichole was right he was a changed man, changed so drastically and completely that she could not possibly begin to comprehend the magnitude of the transformation that she alone had caused. Once hardened and cold, driven by dark torment and now a man in love with life, filled with hope and helplessly falling in love with this amazingly beautiful creature in his arms. She was light, she was beauty and grace, and yet the words remained muted on his tongue. It came as a sad realization that in forty years of living he had not once told another human being that he loved them. Those few words had the ability to make a man completely vulnerable and vulnerability was the one thing he feared.

His arm wrapped around her waist and held her securely to him, his free hand gently skimmed the water from her face.

"You're right," he said, "I have changed. I've changed in ways you'll never understand, angel. I never saw it coming, but there you were and I couldn't stop it if I tried."

His gaze held such heat that Nichole forced herself to look away before she was lost entirely in his eyes. There would be hordes of people left waiting for them, the mayor, the media, and half of corporate southeastern Virginia.

He turned her chin lightly forcing her attention back to him and held her there, his mouth hovering dangerously close to her own.

"And I have never simply had sex with you. From the first time I ever dared to put my hands on you, I made love to you . . . with you. No other woman on the face of this earth can claim as much."

She whimpered softly as his mouth came down on hers, her body reacting to his words, his gentle touch. She could no sooner deny him her body than she could deny the sun the right to shine, both unexplainable forces beyond her control.

How they made it to the building on time before the start of the opening ceremony Nichole had no idea. The number of fires left to be put out far exceeded the number of days that preceded the opening of Collier Tower. To make matters worse, Michael had been contacted by the heads of the City Council and the City Planning Commission who eagerly proposed to turn the opening into a formal affair with local media coverage and a reception to follow. They had hoped to combine a ribbon cutting ceremony at the Creative Arts Center with a groundbreaking ceremony for the future Museum of Contemporary Art in an effort to portray to the public a renaissance taking place in the Virginia Beach area. Michael reluctantly agreed.

With countless hours of grueling work and many sleepless nights behind them the impressive structure had been made ready with no time to spare. Michael and Nichole now stood alongside Mayor Edwards on a stage erected early that morning and looked out at the massive gathering of spectators that had crammed in the newly paved lot, the acrid smell of asphalt stinging the air. The reception to follow was by invitation only and would be held at Calypso's, a four-star restaurant that had taken residence on the penthouse floor.

Michael smiled affectionately when he caught sight of George and Estelle Peterman among the crowd. He had grown increasingly fond of the spirited old couple over the past month. When Nichole had enlisted Estelle's help for the final decorating details of the main corridors and the various conference rooms, George faithfully trudged behind. Michael and the old man formed an easy friendship over hot wings and pre-season football in the video teleconferencing room leaving the ladies to their designs.

Max Porter had arrived in time to grab a spot next to Nichole's parents. They had come from their home along the southern tip of North Carolina's outer banks and stopped to make a brief appearance before heading to Norfolk Airport to catch a plane to Aruba. They were celebrating thirty years of marriage with a three-week excursion to paradise compliments of Michael.

Tom Hogan flew in from Houston and sat in the front row with Clayton Muller, the head developer of the Creative Arts Center. Channel ten had cameramen strategically positioned throughout as well as reporters from several surrounding newspapers. Had Michael known that the completion of his latest project would turn into such a publicity stunt he may have chosen to abandon the project before it began, but having Nichole come into his life made it all worthwhile.

Speeches were given at length both my Mayor Edwards and Clayton Muller. Michael kept his monolog brief but took the time to introduce and thank both Nichole and Tom for their endless contributions to the project and stopped to point out and publicly thank Estelle for her decorative flare.

Dusk had set in and the sweltering heat of late August in the South was becoming too much to bear. Nichole prayed silently for some form of breeze and yet the air remained thick and still. Discretely she slipped from Michael's side into the background, her hand grasping her midsection, a wave of nausea coursing through her.

As he concluded speaking Michael snuck a concerned glance over his shoulder. Nichole had regained her composure and quickly waved him off. Feeling queasy and damp with perspiration she was still a breathtaking sight to behold. In a snug fitting beaded halter silver gown, her hair piled atop her head, her sun-kissed skin made the glow of her cat-like orbs even more dramatic.

Tom joined Michael and with Nichole they approached the red velvet barrier that spanned the entrance of the building as Clayton took his place in the barren adjacent lot. The crowd quieted, faint rumblings of traffic were heard in the distance. As Michael positioned himself to cut the ribbon a woman's voice called out from among the sea of faces.

"Wait."

A ripple of movement began in the center of the audience as a lone sleek figure clad in a red silk gown slipped into the middle isle and stalked forward. A look of horror spread across Michael's face, Tom's jaw dropped and Nichole's eyes widened in confusion. A stunned silence enveloped them as the woman neared with strong determined strides, her head held proudly, her glare locked on Nichole.

Once upon them she focused her attention on the mayor.

"In a moment such as this a woman's place is beside her husband, don't you agree, Mayor?"

Instinctively Nichole looked questioningly at Tom. He blanched, swallowing hard and it was then that the realization struck her. She felt as if she had been thwarted by some indomitable force, suffocating, her eyes narrowing on Michael, time had been suspended and everything moved in slow motion. Her jaw dropped slightly, the sound of her heartbeat thundering in her ears, the look in her eyes piercing Michael to the core.

Caroline, determined to draw out their suffering turned to Michael. Wearing high heels she nearly equaled him in height. She was unarguably a striking and formidable presence. There was nothing delicate about Caroline Collier.

"I'm sorry I'm late, Michael," she said with a satisfied simper. "I did so want to surprise you."

Nichole searched Michael's face frantically for some form of explanation, but his focus had turned to Caroline, his jaw tightly set, murderous rage filling his ice-cold blue eyes. Tom quickly recovered and spied Michael holding the scissors that were to be used to cut the ribbon. He clutched them defensively as if he intended to use them as a weapon.

"Mike," he whispered through clenched teeth.

No response.

"Mike," he repeated raising his tone this time drawing his attention.

Tom's eyes darted to the right and then back again.

"The cameras, Mike. Cut the damn ribbon."

A hum of murmurs began among the audience confused by the delay and then quickly erupted in applause as the material was severed, two separate waves of velvet wafting to the ground while simultaneously a reverberating clamor of sorts was heard in the distance signaling the birth of the Collier Creative Arts Center.

Immediately the crowd began to disperse, people milling about eager to escape the heat and the pungent stench of tar beneath them. Max urgently pushed his way forward. He knew he had to get to Nichole, get her out of the camera's eye and away from the probing questions of the reporters now upon them.

If anyone knew the unlimited depths of Nichole's strength, it was Max Porter. He was the one who had held her hand and literally watched helplessly as she stared death in the face. He was the one to support and comfort her on her ever winding path as she railed against her fears and struggled to build a new life for herself, but he'd be damned if he'd stand by and watch some manipulative shrew deliberately humiliate Nichole before the all-seeing world.

He stopped suddenly when Estelle appeared before him blocking his path. Estelle was a woman not easily shaken yet today her expression was frantic and her voice laced with trepidation.

"Maxie, did you know Michael was married?"

"No," he replied gravely, "and I'm pretty sure Nikki didn't either."

George stepped forward with genuine concern.

"Son, you get her the hell out of there."

"I intend to, sir," he said, making a beeline for Nichole.

Chapter 18

Michael conceded, had he actually strangled Caroline it would be caught forever on videotape and broadcast on the eleven o'clock news leaving him with no chance of escaping a prison sentence. He was an animal caught in a trap and would have sooner chewed off his leg to free Nichole the humiliation she was about to endure than to have to stand and watch her suffer.

The reporter concluded his interview with a few questions for Caroline. She replied with her usual tone, oozing with sweetness and southern charm.

"Well, to be honest," she said, "Michael was rather secretive about this project. I understand he received unlimited help from his little assistant Ms. McCallister."

The first barb was thrown. Tom turned his head away from the camera and winced. He couldn't bring himself to look at either Michael or Nichole.

"Of course," she continued, "I am thrilled the project is finally completed and I'll be able to have my husband home again. I mean honestly, we've only shared the same bed once in the past six weeks."

This barb she hurled with precision, its serrated edges aiming directly for Nichole's heart and meeting its target head on.

Max reached Nichole as the news correspondent signaled the conclusion of his coverage of the Collier Creative Arts Center and signed off, but the damage had already been done.

"Gentlemen," Max said taking Nichole by the hands, barely glancing at them as he spoke and ignoring Caroline completely, "I'm afraid I'm going to have to steal this magnificent woman away from you for a bit. Nikki, if you please? I need your help with something."

Without hesitation, he quickly spirited her into the building and down the hallway to the main office. Nichole fell into her chair, slammed her elbows on the desk, and rested her head in her hands. Tightly she squeezed her eyes shut and grimaced in a futile attempt to block out the world around her.

Max walked to her and kneeled at her side. His heart ached for her. He was the first to notice the subtle changes in her since Michael had come into her life. It was there in her smile, in her laugh. It was in her willingness to try new things, venture out into the world without her protective shell with the innocent eagerness of a child. All the rape had taken from her, Michael had given back.

"Nikki," he said, "talk to me. I need to know what to do to help you."

Nichole slowly turned to him and stunned him with a sheepishly, beautiful smile.

"How is it that during every major crisis of my life you are the one to come to my rescue?"

She reached out and affectionately caressed the side of his face. He had expected tears, yet found strength, anticipated a resurgence of ancient fears and he was met with determined eyes. The transformation of Nichole McCallister may have been brought about by Michael, but it quickly became clear that it wasn't dependent upon him.

A sense of relief washed over Max and he stood looking down at her.

"You have definitely made my life a bit of a challenge at times, but I wouldn't have it any other way," he said, smiling and exposing a dimple in his right cheek that Nichole loved so much.

"You're okay then?"

Nichole rose from her seat elegant and proud.

"I'm furious and I'm confused and I'm hurt, but I need answers.

For tonight, I'm going to hold on to furious and save the rest for tomorrow." She let loose a sigh and continued. "There will be tears. Of that I'm certain, but I'll be damned if I let that bitch out there see them."

Max couldn't help but smile. He liked this Nichole.

"Don't think you're off the hook," she said walking to him making a gesture as if dusting off one of his shoulders. "I fully intend on putting that to good use in the near future."

Nichole wrapped her arms around him, her head falling softly against his chest.

"I do love you, you know that?" she asked, looking up into his soft brown eyes.

Max kissed the tip of her nose.

"And I you," he replied.

"Maxie, why can't we run away together? It's that whole gay thing isn't it?"

He laughed and held her tighter to him.

"I'm afraid so, beautiful."

"Damn, I never could compete with that," she said, smiling up at him

Max cocked his head to the side and looked at her questioningly.

"Did you ever tell Michael?" he asked.

"Tell him what? That you're gay?"

Max nodded.

"No . . . why . . . should I have?"

Still holding, her Max arched an eyebrow and looked at her as a big brother would, had he caught his little sister with her hand in the cookie jar.

"Nikki," he spoke almost as if to scold, "you know damn well Michael gets irritated every time I come around you. If I dare say so myself, I think he's jealous."

Nichole's expression brightened.

"Exactly . . . You should go, Maxie, I need a few moments alone. No doubt Michael will not be far behind you and I need to be prepared for whatever confrontation that is about to take place."

Max was hesitant at first. He wanted to be the one to confront the bastard with his fist to Michael's jaw, but he knew Nichole needed to deal with this her way.

"Are you certain? I can wait outside and take you home. I don't want you to be alone tonight, Nikki."

Nichole hugged him one last time. "I'm certain. I'll be okay I promise. I'll call you as soon as I get home."

Michael immediately began to stalk off in the direction in which Nichole and Max had disappeared when Tom caught him by the arm.

"Let her go, Mike, give her some time to cool down."

"Let her go," he said in horror. "If I don't find her and try to explain this fiasco before she leaves I'll never see her again."

"What about Caroline?" Tom asked. "She's up there right now rubbing elbows with the mayor and all your investors. Are you going to let her get away with this?"

Michael began to grow impatient.

"I don't give a damn about her right now," Michael said, jerking his arm free from Tom's grasp. "That miserable bitch can slither back to whatever rock she crawled out from under. She's taken everything from me Tom. Ruined everything good and decent that has every come into my life since the day I met her."

His eyes grew wild thinking back to the day he had discovered that the only thing totally pure and innocent to ever come his way had been destroyed before he knew it existed.

"Or have you forgotten Tom," he continued his voice exploding through the now abandoned lot, "that, that totally self-absorbed, maniacal, sorry excuse for a human being aborted our . . . my child because children were never a part of her plans."

Tom groaned. As much as he would like to, he'd never be able to forget that day. He and Michael had decided to cut short their workday for a day of fishing on Michael's boat. Michael had misplaced his key for the small yacht and knowing that his meticulous and well-organized wife held extra keys to all their properties and vehicles he headed to her armoire in search of a spare. It was there he found the discharge papers from a women's clinic a two hours' drive away and with it instructions for post-operative outpatient care following an abortion that had taken place three days before while she was supposedly on an out-of-town shopping excursion. Before the night was out Michael had had all Caroline's things packed, the locks on their main estate changed and was on the phone with his attorneys to begin the divorce proceedings, thus beginning a long, out of control war between the two that would drag on for years.

Tom remembered, he remembered all too well and stepped aside, yielding to the pain in Michael's eyes.

By the time Michael had reached her Nichole sat alone, staring out a window into the darkness with a vacant look in her eyes, feeling hollow inside. A waning moon had made an appearance in the night sky and cast a silver glow upon encroaching clouds that threatened to conceal its beauty.

Nichole sat unflinching at the sound of the heavy wooden door as it swung open, then closed behind her, keeping her back to the intruder who dared to disturb her solitude. Without looking, she knew it was Michael who had come. She felt his presence, felt the change in the air around her and to her dismay her body responded to the knowing.

Nichole knew Michael would seek her out, knew he would find her wherever she went and surrendering to the inevitable she waited patiently in the office they were to share. Half relieved, half dreading the confrontation about to take place her pulse fluttered at his nearness. Still she sat motionless in the shadows of the moonlight that broke the darkness around her, hoping against all hope that by some small miracle Michael would find the words to right this wrong. It was a violent tug of war between heart and mind that she shrouded with her face set in stone. As he approached her heart fought against what she already knew. This would be good-bye.

The sound of her heartbeat echoed in her ears as he stood before her cocooned by the silver rays of moonlight, blocking her view of the night. Her gaze moved slowly up the length of his body, knots forming in her stomach when her eyes met his. Those ice-blue orbs, now the color of a stormy sea held caged within them an undeniable pain, a pain that matched her own. Quickly she turned away to stare into the blackness, into nothing.

Michael reached out to touch her. Deftly she stood and backed away to put distance between them. She needed strength, needed control and yet every breath she took was filled with Michael's scent, every movement she made encapsulated with a dizzying warmth that radiated off his body. His body, a body she knew intimately, strong yet tender. When he was near it was almost as if some invisible force had the ability to reach inside her and hold in its transparent hands her fragile soul.

"Angel," Michael spoke with desperation in his voice, "please, please let me explain."

Nichole clenched her hands into fists to steady their shaking and inhaled deeply. She spoke coldly making a vain attempt at indifference.

"That was quite a performance out there tonight, Mr. Collier. My kudos to your wife."

"Nichole please don't . . ."

She cut him off and stepped further away. Saying the words out loud, *your wife,* Michael's wife, those words, and the meaning behind them cut her to the core.

"When you told me that there was much I did not know about you I had no idea how monumental an understatement you dared to make." Her words came quickly now, cutting and clear, the bitterness of betrayal on her tongue to mask the hurt inside. "I knew you had your demons Michael, your secrets, ones that allowed you to easily sense my own—but dear God a wife. You're married Michael? How could you? How could you have sex with me, make love to me the way you did, make it seem real . . ."

"Damn it, Nichole, it was real," he demanded. "It is real."

Nichole continued as if she had not heard him speak . . ."When all the while my private affairs, the whole clouded history of my life had been laid open to you by your henchmen. Did I make such and easy target, Michael?"

He could barely make out her silhouette across the room as the clouds wafted carelessly about overhead snuffing out what little light there had been. She was moving further and further away from him, not only physically, but emotionally as well and it filled him with trepidation. Michael reached out and tugged at the beaded cord of a stained glass lamp, a dimmed honey colored light filling the room. Quickly he made his way to where Nichole stood, blocking her path to the door. Lightly, cautiously he placed his hands on either side of her face and slowly persuaded her emerald gaze to meet his. He spoke with passion and anguish.

"Angel, listen to me, please. That woman out there tonight is my wife on paper alone. She has been stonewalling my attempts at a divorce for years now. She is wicked and manipulative and does everything she can to make my life a living hell, but I do not now nor have I ever loved her."

Michael drew her closer. Never had he known such desperation. This raven-haired beauty, brazen and strong had been his undoing in many ways and yet awaken within him the need, the desire to love and be loved. His closeness, his touch, the look in his eyes all proved too potent a mixture, Nichole was losing her resolve.

"Then why, Michael, why did you marry the woman?"

"Because," he said, winding a tendril of her hair loosely around his trembling fingers, "I was young and stupid and power hungry and she was willing and well connected. I was wrong not to tell you the truth from the beginning and for that I'm sorry, but honestly Caroline is a part of my life I wanted to forget. I was hoping to be done with the whole sordid mess and save you from ever having to deal with her." He raked an unsteady hand through his hair. "She's poison to everything she touches. I truly never meant for her to ever have the opportunity to hurt you."

His voice and the intensity it contained, his passion-filled presence intoxicated Nichole's senses and confused her mind. Michael felt her relax within his grasp. Tenderly he placed a light kiss on her forehead, the tip of her nose and each beautifully painted eyelid. His lips soft and gentle as the beating of angel wings and for a few precious moments she allowed her mind to forget.

When Michael spoke again his words were barely above a whisper.

"You were never a target, my angel. Please believe that."

And it was then the silence was broken in her mind. Caroline's words replayed, echoing in her ears. They had shared a bed, Michael and his wife. Her body stiffened and she pulled away.

"No . . . no, no, no," he pleaded, "don't do that. Don't turn away from me, Nichole."

Again her body started to shake, her eyes held and accusatory glare.

"Did you sleep with her, Michael?" Her voice trembled as she spoke.

Michael closed his eyes and drew in a deep sigh, yet said nothing.

"Michael, when was the last time you made love to your wife?" Nichole demanded, rage renewing within her veins.

"Made love to my wife." He spewed the words as if they were tainted with poison, repulsed by the mere notion. "I have never made love, as you put it, to that woman."

"Semantics, you know damn well what I mean." Her eyes narrowed on him with a scathing look. "When you went to Texas, after the charity auction, did you leave my bed to crawl into hers?"

He said nothing. It seemed as if he had lapsed into a catatonic state as the realization struck him. Caroline had won yet again. Michael knew he could try and deny what he was still unsure of, but he had changed in many ways and it wasn't in him to look Nichole in the eyes and lie. His hopes, his dreams of a future with her plummeted and he stood shell-shocked before her.

"Answer me," Nichole commanded.

Michael was suddenly a man defeated. With a stricken look, he faced her.

"I don't know."

"You don't know?" Nichole was momentarily stupefied, her hands made flailing gestures as she spoke. "How the hell can you not know if you slept with the woman or not?"

Michael leaned against his desk, his hands supporting his weight. A distant loneliness wrought his face, surprising Nichole that in the midst of her rage she had to fight the urge to reach out to him.

"If it did happen it happened the night my father died. I went home, lit a fire, and proceeded to get exceedingly drunk. Caroline showed up and we had a huge fight. It was pretty ugly. All I remember is thinking she had left and going to the liquor cabinet for another bottle. When I woke up, I was in my bed naked and she was coming out of the bathroom. She says we had sex, but my hand to God, Nichole, I don't remember any of it."

It was all too much to process, so many untold truths, lies, unwelcome realities assaulting her simultaneously, her new world of passion and bliss crumbling before her and the man she thought she knew better than any other was now a stranger. She felt suddenly dizzy, warm, and cold at the same time and fought to suppress the urge to wretch. Seeking refuge she made her way to the door, but Michael stopped her, folding his arms around her from behind. His lips brushed her ear as he spoke, his words soft as velvet.

"Nichole please, don't walk out on us. We can work this out. Please give me a chance."

At this stage in her life after knowing so many, Nichole hated tears. She had cried and hurt for too long. She desperately wanted to be strong, to show him he hadn't and couldn't hurt her, but it was seemingly inescapable. She felt the familiar sting well up in her eyes.

"I can't, Michael." She cried softly as she spoke. "I can't. I don't know what's real with you and what isn't and after everything I shared with you. I'm not that strong."

She paused and swallowed hard, bringing her hands to her face.

"I'll never know what's true and what isn't. You know trust is everything to me and right now I don't understand why? Was it lust? Was it the challenge of it for you . . . what?"

Michael held her tighter, pulling her body into his as if trying to make her a literal part of him so that she could never leave. This was unfamiliar ground to him. He had never lost a woman he had truly cared about before because he had never let himself ever truly care. He could feel the shudder of the stifled sobs wracking Nichole's body as he held her and he hated himself for being the cause of them.

"I'm well acquainted with lust, angel and there are many women I have wanted in my bed for that reason alone, but you . . . not you." He could barely recognize the sound of his voice, his words trembling as he spoke. "Those women came to my bed willingly and I always made it clear to them that I had nothing more to offer. Hell, I honestly never believed I was capable of love. I assumed I was born broken, until you. Dear God what you did to me. I love you Nichole. With all my heart and soul, tainted as they may be I do love you."

A sob escaped her lips and for a moment she went limp. She was suffocating in a sea of emotions and uncertainties. She wanted to run, as fast and as far as was humanly possible anything to make the hurt stop.

Breaking free of Michael's grasp she clutched the handle to the door and flung herself through the opening. She never looked back and Michael watched as she slipped farther and farther from sight.

Chapter 19

NICHOLE DROVE HER SUV down a long and winding country road that was void of human life. Tall pines towered overhead and lined the shoulder as squirrels and rabbits darted haphazardly in front of her. Max Porter sat next to her, patient and silent not quite knowing where he was going or why. The only thing he was certain of was of the beaming smile on her face, one he hadn't seen in well over a month now. Since the all too public fiasco at the grand opening of Collier Creative Arts Center Nichole had been withdrawn and sullen. Rarely were her eyes free from the sting of tears. To Max, it was far too reminiscent of nightmarish days long ago, of pain he had hoped to never see on her face again. There were no physical injuries this time around, only emotional. It was plain to anyone who knew her well that the scars left behind ran deep.

Nichole made a sharp left turn, stopped the car with a jolt and climbing out motioned for him to follow.

"Come on, Maxie, hurry. I want to know what you think?"

He followed her for over twenty yards through grass and brush, stopping in dead silence at the structure before him. For several tense moments he stood perplexed and motionless, arms crossed in front of him as if he were contemplating the machinations of the universe.

"Okay Nik, I'll bite," Max said with a look of trepidation upon his face, "what is it?"

Nichole rolled her eyes and waved a hand in the direction of the worn and ramshackle yet substantially sized building before them.

"This, my dear friend, is the future site of McCallister's. I'm going to open my own restaurant," she said with self-assurance and a slight childlike bounce in her step.

Max bit down hard on one of his fingertips. He didn't want to tell her what he truly thought. She was too happy, too enthusiastic and after all she had been through recently how could he dash yet one more of her dreams. Be supportive he thought to himself, yet still caution her.

"Honey, are you sure about this? I mean, where did all of this come from? I didn't know you wanted to open up a restaurant. And not to sound too pessimistic but is there actually a building under all the plant life?"

In front of them stood an old Colonial Georgian style building, covered with and endless maze of ivy and moss, growing across the stairs and up the side of the building to the roof. Trees and overgrown bushes crowded it from all sides. A bird flew into a broken window on the top floor. Four immense pillars lined the entrance.

Reluctantly, Max stepped closer. He pushed through the weeds and saw that this house was built on a crawl space and literally shuddered at the thought of what might be living beneath it. Nichole rushed to his side and grabbed his hands in hers.

"I know what you're thinking, but hear me out, please." Her mouth formed the perfect pout as she spoke. "You know I can never go back to working for Michael. I have to do something and I want something of my own Max. Something I can be proud of."

She looked at him and her eyes pleaded for mercy.

"Okay, that I can understand, but why this, why now? Why not wait a longer until your brain has had a chance to rest from the hell you went through?"

Nichole stilled, within an instant her demeanor shifted from that of a carefree child to a woman with the weight of the world on her shoulders.

"I'm pregnant, Maxie."

It took a few moments for her words to register and when they did he forced a bittersweet smile and hugged her tightly to him, his chin resting atop her head.

"Oh, honey."

Max held her for a few moments in silence. He wanted her to be happy for her, but the situation was so damned complex. Tilting her chin, he looked into eyes. The uncertainty in them tore at his heart.

"I thought after the attack, I thought the doctors said you would never be able to have children?" he questioned, more confused than ever.

"That's what they have been telling me for years. I resigned myself to it, made peace with it but apparently they were wrong," she said placing her hands on her stomach, "very wrong. Trust me I was dumbfounded when I found out. I never dreamed it possible, but I want this baby Max."

Max smiled equally dumbfounded. This baby was a tiny miracle no one could ever deny that. The horror inflicted on Nichole's body that night was unspeakable, her losses were great. Perhaps this was the Heaven's gift for such great suffering.

"Honey, I'm thrilled for you, but I have to ask have you told Michael?" he questioned.

Hormonal and choked up by his reaction, Nichole was afraid to speak for fear she would burst into tears if she opened her mouth. She merely shook her head.

"Are you going to tell him?"

Nichole began to pace, leaves and twigs crunching under her feet as she spoke.

"How can I? He has a wife, a miserable bitch of a wife that enjoyed humiliating me in front of hundreds of people, but a wife all the same. How pathetic would I look going down there to inform him I'm carrying his illegitimate child?"

"You could never look pathetic Nichole."

"You know what I mean. Maybe I'm being selfish, yes it's totally unfair to the baby. I don't have it in me to deal with him right now. Maybe someday, but not now."

Max put his arm around her shoulder and directed her toward the stairs.

"Nikki you don't need to explain it to me. I understand. You do what you need to do when you need to do it."

The midmorning sun poked its way through the canopy of leaves overhead and formed beams of light all around them as they walked. Once inside, Max was pleasantly surprised. Aside from all the dust, cobwebs, and stray mouse running to and fro, it was quite charming. Pieces of antique furniture left behind to fade into time were scattered throughout the many rooms. There was a small service elevator in the enormous kitchen that led to a hallway on the upper floor. Many rooms had hardwood floors, the others with carpet in desperate need of replacing. One room contained a huge fireplace large enough for Nichole to stand in. There were chipped statues of cherubs and old faded paintings that hung on the walls. The overall scene was hauntingly enchanting. In his mind's eye, Max began to see the possibilities. There was still much more to consider.

As he walked, he pondered and the questions began to flow.

"How much land came with it?"

"Seven acres. Originally it was much more, but it's been sold off in bits and pieces over the years?"

"And plumbing? What about central air? How old is the furnace?"

One of the reasons Nichole always trusted Max's opinion and often turned to him for help was that he was a thorough businessman. He thought things through realistically, with a cool head and she had prepared well for the inquisition.

"The plumbing," she replied, smiling, "is in excellent shape, the central air wasn't installed until about twenty years ago and a new AC unit and furnace were part of the deal."

He sat cross-legged in the middle of the floor in what appeared to be a grand dining room. Grabbing Nichole by the hand he pulled her down next to him and sat quietly looking around.

Nichole knew he was starting to weaken. His expression was still skeptical, but she could see it in his eyes that the wheels in his mind were already churning out ideas. Max looked at her out of the corner of his eye.

"And who my dear, may I ask, do you plan on having help you run this place one you get it fixed up? You know real estate. You don't know anything about running a restaurant."

Nichole tilted her head to the side with a coy smile perched upon her lips and batted her lovely eyelashes for all she was worth. They both began laughing. Max grabbed her hand and kissed her fingers.

"Why is it I cannot refuse you?" he asked.

"Because you love me," she said confidently, "and because you know damn well this can work. We can do this Maxie I know we can."

If anyone could pull this stunt off Max knew that Nichole McCallister would be the one to do it. She had come prepared for the battle, the surrender, and the clean up after. In the back of her Escalade, hidden under a ton of old towels were mops, buckets, cleaners of all kinds and an industrial strength box of garbage bags. Immediately she opened all the windows to rid the place of the musty smell and worked herself near exhaustion by knocking down cobwebs, dusting, and sweeping while Maxie stayed outside clearing away brush and debris and pulling down the myriad of vines that clung to the manor.

After many hours had passed, the two of them alone, had managed to erase the outward signs of abandonment that time and nature had ravished on the long forgotten stately home. Nichole had worked through a bout of morning sickness, pausing only momentarily to try to force down some water and a piece of fruit. She was only six weeks along, but the child that was forming inside her had clearly begun to make its presence known in the form of nausea and fatigue.

Just before dusk she emerged through the massive front doors and spied Max knee deep in garbage bags filled with trash and weeds, fighting off the first barrage of the evening's mosquitoes and looking equally exhausted. Nichole took a seat on the stairs and he wearily climbed them and sat down beside her.

"You know," he said, wiping sweat from his brow, "this is going to cost some money. We can't do all of the work that needs done around here by ourselves, especially with you in your condition."

"Not as much as you might think," Nichole said sounding optimistic. "Ever since my dad retired he uses any excuse he can to get away from my mother for a while. She's making him nuts; he's going to start coming up on weekends to help out. The Peterman's are going to pitch in also. Estelle is amazing when it comes to interior decorating, plants and landscaping and her husband George is going to redo the hardwood floors."

Max smiled and shook his head. Nichole had ambushed him and he knew it. He laughed aloud in spite of himself.

"Okay Nikki, here's the deal. If I'm going to get involved in your crazy scheme, I'll put some money up toward the cause. I'll cover supplies, dishes, furniture, whatever you need," he said. His expression was pained, filled with concern. "I know you Nik, you're going to push yourself too hard. If you want me in this, you have to promise to take it easy for you and for the baby."

The sun began to fade quickly in the distance, crickets and other creatures of the night welcoming the darkness, each with their individual song, a much welcomed cool breeze blowing Nichole's hair from her face.

"I promise, Max," she said, resting her head against his shoulder. "I need you to be sure about this. I don't want you to give up so much until you've had time to actually think about it. I don't want you to end up resenting me if this doesn't work for whatever reason."

Max wrapped a dirty arm around her shoulders. He drew in a breath and smiled. Whenever life appeared to settle down a bit or threatened boredom, he could always count on Nichole to liven things up for him.

"You've known me for how many years?" he asked.

Nichole laughed. "Too many."

"Then you know I wouldn't do it if I didn't believe it could work. Besides you've done all the legwork. That's the hard part."

Max held out his hand.

"Partners?"

Nichole beamed through tired eyes. "Partners."

Chapter 20

SHE ONLY CRIED WHEN no one was watching, usually in the shower at the end of a long day, where the sounds of the water beating on the glass door muted the echoes of her sobs. Nichole hated the crying, despised having to face yet again, a pain so deep, and intense it felt as if it resonated from within her bones. She longed in vain to live in a world that was safe, a certain world into which she could bring her unborn child and be assured protection. But that was a world that would never exist and she grudgingly accepted the fact.

She wore a brave face for her family and friends, stuffing her fears and heartache from view while immersing herself in her restaurant to busy her troubled mind. Yet when night would fall and silence surrounded her, thoughts of the man she still loved in spite of the lies told and thoughts of their child that grew inside her descended upon her mind overwhelming her emotions. Michael Collier was a man she knew more intimately than any other on Earth and yet all she had known was built on deception.

She struggled with the grief of her loss, grieving a man who still lived. A man who walked and talked, laughed and breathed under the same blanket of darkness that each night hid her tears. As her breasts swelled and her belly grew, she repeatedly ignored the temptation to reach out to him. In her mind's eye, she could see him, moved beyond words to learn of the baby they had created together. In her daydreams, he was there holding her, reassuring her, hand on her stomach amazed at the movements beneath. Those dreams she knew, were flights of fancy created by the hormones and the silly idle wishes of a new mother-to-be.

Nichole now coveted a deception all her own. Unable to face further rejection or humiliation she resigned herself to raise the child alone. Michael could never know. Having been knocked down one too many times by the harshness of life, she needed this baby as much as the baby needed her. It was her reason to get out of bed every morning, her reason to succeed, the only reason she had for wanting to live at times. If Michael knew, he might try to take the child from her and that would be a final blow from which she knew she would never recover.

Over the next few months, she threw every ounce of energy she had into giving 718 Settlers Cove a facelift. Everyone around her appeared to join in her enthusiasm and was willing to lend a hand. Max Porter worked tirelessly throughout the evenings and through the weekends to locate suppliers and furnishings. He cut down trees and mapped out areas along the walkway and throughout the front lawn to be landscaped by the capable and long too idle hands of Estelle Peterman.

Estelle had picked out a handsome array of Holly bushes and various shrubs that would hold their heartiness throughout the winter months, along with a stunning variety of perennials that would bloom each year adding accent to the old manor perfectly. The area surrounding what would one day be McCallister's Restaurant began to take on the appearance of a beautifully tamed prairie.

Estelle's husband, George, was enjoying his share of the work far more than he had expected. He hadn't performed his craft in years and took delight in restoring the old hardwood floors. Together he and Nichole had chosen a perfect burgundy wine colored carpet for the main entrance. But it was her father Frank who showed up every Friday around noon and stayed until late every Sunday evening without fail that pulled at her heartstrings the most.

Frank McCallister was a relatively quiet man, but when he had something to say that he deemed important people usually listened.

He had worked hard for over two decades with the local ship building company, had endured two tours in Vietnam, a rough and tumble sort of man from a large family of boys that was easily tamed when his daughter was born. He had salt and pepper hair with a receding hairline, stood six feet tall, and weighed in at close to two hundred pounds. All in all, he was a big teddy bear that tended to grumble a lot. At the time of Nichole's attack, the only thing that kept him from hunting down the bastard that had hurt his daughter and killing him was knowing how desperately she needed him home with her and not in jail himself. It left him frustrated and helpless and that was how he felt now, helpless. He tried to be around as much as he could to not only help, but to watch Nichole closely to see to it she didn't over exert herself and he truly enjoyed the time they spent together reconstructing the ancient beauty.

It was early evening on a Saturday. Frank had finished adding a beautiful gypsum plaster molding to what would soon be the Grand Dining Room. He had stepped down from the ladder, with his hands on his hips and a beaming smile admiring the work he had done when Nichole poked her head around the corner. She was dressed in an oversized t-shirt and loose cotton running pants, beads of sweat on her brow, she appeared these days more fragile, yet still beautiful. Entering her fifth month of pregnancy she had a glow about her and could still light up a room with her smile. Pregnant and hard at work, growing a new life inside her, and giving life to her surroundings she had found purpose.

"You've done good daddy," she teased.

Frank turned with a slight jolt, half embarrassed to be caught in such self-admiration. He walked over to his daughter and wrapped an arm around her shoulder.

"You know honey," he said, "when you first told me about this idea of yours . . . I have to admit I was a bit skeptical. Yet in a few short months, she's risen like a phoenix from the ashes."

Nichole looked from the ceilings to the floors and smiled.

"Yes, she has. Now if we can get her up and running before this baby is born."

His smile quickly faded and was replaced with a look of concern and stern reprisal.

"Nichole McCallister, I don't want you pushing yourself. Your health and the health of that grandbaby of mine are far more important than any of this." He waved his arm in an outspread gesture. "You have plenty of people willing to do the hard stuff, let us do it. This place is up to code and will be ready in a month or two. I want you resting young lady. Worry about hiring the staff and that you can do from your office."

Nichole smiled tenderly, her face upturned to watch with humor as her father continued to grumble.

He caught a glimpse of the coy expression on her face and made one final attempt at being stern. "I'm serious Nichole. If anything happened to you or that baby . . . well . . . your mother would make my life a living hell."

Nichole rose on tiptoes to kiss him on the cheek.

"Yes sir," she said obediently as she decided to let him win this round or at the very least let him think he had won. It was a trick she had learned from her mother when she was a little girl. Whenever her father felt it necessary to be protective and raise his hackles a few bats of the eyes, a coy smile and yes sir or two would quickly appease his foul mood.

It was the beginning of December, gray skies dominated the days, and darkness came early. Fall had finally conceded to the chilled air of winter and for that Nichole was grateful. Growing her baby, Michael's baby, inside her sent her body on a rollercoaster of hormonal fury. She was always too hot, continuously exhausted and now that her morning sickness had faded her appetite reigned supreme.

The flash of headlights dancing briefly across the still bare windows surprised her this late in the evening. She opened the door to a welcome gust of frosty December wind laced with the aroma of roasted chicken and Dutch apple pie. From the two cars that had arrived and parked in the lot, exited Estelle and George Peterman and their daughter Jenna whom Nichole hadn't seen in well over five years and from the other her mother and Max Porter, all carrying food, drinks, and a hearty appetite.

The sight of their cheer filled and loving faces brought tears to her eyes. It was then that Nichole realized that despite her circumstances feeling sorry for herself would accomplish nothing and that she had much to be grateful for. Few people in this world had as many truly loving people to make-up their lives and the knowledge that both she and her baby would always be blessed with them by her side moved her.

Half way through the apple pie Jenna spirited Nichole away from the group. She was almost ten years older than Nichole was and when they were children Jenna had informally adopted her as the baby sister the stork never delivered. During Nichole's days in the hospital she sat in turn keeping a vigil at her bedside. Obligations with her job in Seattle kept her way from home most holidays, but upon hearing of her friend's latest quandary and with Christmas near she felt an urgent need for a long overdue visit.

"Nikki, I don't mean to pry," she said, her voice barely above a whisper, "and don't be angry with my mother, but she told me all about your situation and everything about this Michael Collier fellow."

Nichole gave her an understanding smile.

"Of course she did," she laughed. "I would have never expected anything less from your mom."

"She only told me because she's worried about you, about the baby."

Nichole took a sip of her water and motioned for Jenna to take a seat next to her. All this mollycoddling and having those dearest to her walking on pins and needles around her was beginning to become tiresome. She knew what they feared, that she would once again snap under the weight of the pressure upon her and revert back to the fragile, frightened girl she once was.

"Jen, I appreciate what you are trying to do, I appreciate what all of you are trying to do, but this isn't like before." She paused for a moment breathing deeply, trying to collect her thoughts. "What happened with Michael stung like hell. It still does I won't try to deny that. I'm stronger than I was back then because of him. He hurt me yes, he also brought magic into my life. He gave me back to me and I'll be grateful to him for that alone for the rest of my life."

Jenna saw the look in Nichole's eyes. There was sadness, that was to be expected, but there was also strength and it was a strength she would rely on greatly in the months ahead. Jenna knew firsthand that being a single mother was not for the faint of heart and that Nichole would have her work cut out for her. She also knew she would not only brave but master the unknown ahead as she did every other task set before her.

"Okay," she conceded, "if you ever need anything Nikki, please call me."

They stood to rejoin the others. "I will, I promise," Nichole replied.

Jenna wrapped her arm around Nichole's shoulder and leaned in to whisper in her ear.

"When you get to the hospital, tell them you want the epidural, all the pain killers they'll offer," she said with a wink and a grin.

Nicole erupted in laughter. "You're as bad as your mother."

They sat that evening on the floor in a circle of laughter, food, and merriment. Max and Frank had built a fire that crackled and warmed the room with a golden-colored hue. The women took turns placing their hands on Nichole's stomach, feeling the light squirms underneath as the men made wagers on the baby being born a boy or a girl. It was a circle of love. Nichole was almost undone by the attempt that the people closest to her had made to make her feel special for one evening.

For the first time since the passing of summer, Nichole allowed herself to exist in the moment. Her heart was light and she smiled a true smile, not a forced illusion for the benefit of others. And although she paused for a brief moment of sadness, a pang of longing for the one man who would have made the night complete, she was learning her way without him. Under this night's darkness, she would not cry.

Chapter 21

NINE O'CLOCK ON A Friday night and the last thing Tom Hogan wanted to be doing was driving back to his office in downtown Houston. He had forgotten his wife's anniversary present in his top desk drawer and if he didn't have it to give to her tomorrow morning there'd be hell to pay. As he rode the elevator to the thirty-second floor he decided that seeing the smile on Jocelyn's face would be well worth the trip. Married twelve years, three kids and she was still as beautiful as the day they had met. Tom considered himself one of the lucky ones. Most of his friends were having affairs or divorced at least once. Michael's divorce being the messiest he had seen outside of the tabloids.

It was Michael's office light that solely lit the darkened hallway greeting Tom when the elevator doors opened. He glanced at his watch to see if he was right about the time. The hands pointed to 9:25.

Tom hadn't missed the metamorphosis Michael had undergone. During his stay in Hampton Roads, it was apparent even through the phone that Michael had mellowed, his laughter would come in hearty, frequent bursts, he joked and made light of disruptions at the office that would have, under normal circumstances, sent him into a tirade. In general he seemed to be enjoying each moment of his life, his rough, calloused edges softened by the touch of one amazing woman.

With Nichole now out of the picture all that had changed. He showed no emotion, not joy, not anger, not once did he shed a tear. He was empty inside as if there were nothing left but a hollow, desolate space. Despite the efforts of those around him to break the catatonic like spell that held him, he remained silent and withdrawn.

Ah, Tom thought to himself looking down at the sealed document laying atop his desk. If this doesn't bring a smile to_his face nothing will. It must have been delivered after he had left for home, but he was not going to miss the opportunity of hand delivering this one himself.

When he opened the door to Michael's office, he found him at his desk, all of Houston a light against the night through the window behind him. Contracts and leases were strewn before him, still wearing the same clothes he had worn into work at six in the morning, except now his sleeves were rolled up exposing his muscular arms and his tie lay in his in-box. Michael looked up at the sound of the door swinging open.

"Mike, what the hell are you still doing here?" Tom asked.

Michael put down the papers he had been reviewing.

"Working," he said flatly. "What's your excuse?"

"I forgot Jocelyn's anniversary present in my desk."

"I can see where that would be a problem," Michael acknowledged, taking a sip of his coffee that was now lukewarm at best.

Tom shifted on his feet.

"Actually I have a present for you too," he said, laying the sealed manila envelope in front of him.

Michael said nothing. He broke the envelope's seal and removed the contents. Glancing the front page he remained stone-faced. Inside his stomach turned sour. Too little, too late he thought to himself.

Dumbfounded Tom flopped down in the chair across from him.

"Michael, what the hell is wrong with you? Your divorce is final. You're rid of the bitch for good this time. You should be celebrating, singing from the rooftops."

Michael raised an eyebrow and leaned back in his chair. He appreciated his friends concern, but was in no mood for this conversation.

"Listen, man," Tom continued, "this isn't you. Jocelyn's worried about you, hell I'm worried about you. You have no life. All you do is work. Jesus Christ, when was the last time you got laid?"

A muffled groan escaped Michael's lips. He raised his hands to his head and squeezed at the temples. Getting laid was not going to fix this. How many times had he scoffed at the foolishness of men who allowed their hearts to become victims of a woman's indifference only to now stand dazed and confused by the same crippling emotion that pulled at his chest. Experience was a cruel teacher and time had done nothing to ease the pain.

Tom had rescued Michael from his demons before, pulled him from the pit of hopelessness more than once, but those times were different. At least then he still had an ounce of fight left in him, now there was nothing. He had become a shell of the man he knew well. In a last ditch attempt to get him to open up he questioned further.

"Mike, man, I know the divorce was rough on you and you lost the old man this year . . ."

Tom's words were stopped short by a burst of near hysterical laughter.

Michael stood to pace the room, shoving his hands in his pockets.

"That's what you think this is about," he said stunned, "Caroline and the old man? Tom, don't be gullible."

"Then what the hell is it, I know the thing with Nichole was fucked up to say the least, but you have to let it go."

Michael stared unblinkingly and waved Tom off with a stiff shake of his head. This was his pain to handle alone. He held no desire to talk it through, share his feelings, or bare his soul. He simply wanted to forget. After several moments of passed silence, Tom conceded surrender.

"Fine, I'll let it go. Only if you agree to get the hell out of here and join the land of the living," he said. "One beer, that's all I'm asking and I'm off your case."

Michael closed his eyes and drew in a sharp breath, best to go along and get it over he thought to himself.

They rode around for close to half an hour when Michael finally agreed to a small sports bar few people frequented. Several widescreen TVs, a different sports channel on every one, never too crowded and the beer was cold.

After a few drinks and some idle chatter, Michael seemed to be enjoying himself. He had loosened up considerably and the dour expressing the hung on his face had softened. Agreeing to one game of pool before heading home for the night, Michael racked the balls while Tom headed to the bar for another round. In Tom's absence, two women had taken it upon themselves to approach Michael from either side. Women always approached Michael and he had usually welcomed their advances, but that was what seemed like a lifetime ago. Oh how the mighty had fallen.

Both women were young, mid to late twenties, both attractive, both looking very disappointed as they walked away. Tom had taken notice and strained to hear the conversation taking place. How many years now had it been that he had lived vicariously through the carnal exploits of Michael Collier, benefited through the innocent flirting of the sister and or friend that was passed over breaking the monotony of his otherwise faithful persona.

"What's up with that?" Tom questioned, nodding in the direction of the women now seated at a table across the room.

Michael glanced over his shoulder and turned back to the table. It was his turn to break, the pool balls made a harsh crashing sound, the four ball dropping into the right corner pocket.

"They invited me back to their hot tub," Michael said, sounding bored.

Tom looked again at both young ladies and then at Michael. "Both of them?"

Michael simply nodded.

"Two, corner pocket," he said, mapping out his shot with his pool cue.

"And you said no," Tom said, astounded.

"I did," he replied without emotion.

That's when it hit him. He had known the man most of his life, thought of him as more a brother than friend and yet there was much he had never come to understand of Michael Collier. Tom knew opening this door was like opening Pandora's Box, but he had to be certain.

Jocelyn should be doing this he thought to himself. This was her area of expertise not his and yet curiosity had the best of him. Tom took his shot at the table and missed.

"Mike, can I ask you a question that is none of my business?"

Michael smirked.

"Since when did you ask permission for that?"

"Have you heard from Nichole since you returned from Virginia?" Tom asked, watching him closely.

The brief smile on Michael's face faded quickly. A stern "no" was his reply. He pointed out his next shot hoping the conversation would end there.

"Left side pocket."

"I'll be a son of a bitch," Tom said half to himself, half to Michael. "You honestly fell in love with her. You're still in love with her."

Tom knew Michael had truly cared for Nichole, but he thought it an obvious case of lust mixed with some loyalty born of shared tragedy. The same kind of loyalty Mike had shown to him, his disdain for abuse, his need to rescue a helpless victim based on his empathy he kept well hidden. But never did Tom think him capable of being completely in love with any women. Michael himself had said he was too broken inside for that to ever be possible.

Tom's words hung in the air as the balls danced around on green felt. The eight ball dropped. Michael took a last drink of his beer, laid his pool stick down on the table and left the bar not saying a word.

Returning home, he fought the urge to sleep. Sleep brought with it little in the form of escape. The nightmare always began the same way.

A blackness all encompassing, thick and ominous. There was no breeze and yet a putrid smell hangs in the air. He fumbles around in the darkness for what seems like forever until a gray fog appears in the distance. He walks slowly at first, toward the eerie haze, the echo of his footsteps ringing in his ears. He walks for hours and yet the only light present continues to move farther and farther away.

It is then that the muffled cries of a familiar voice pierce the silence. As if propelled by a mystical force he is suddenly cast into the center of the gray mist. The only color, red, blood red, so much blood.

The cry belongs to Nichole. It is the night of her savage attack. He reaches out and is unable to touch her. Distance has no meaning here. He slips again and again in the crimson liquid puddle at his feet. He can see her hair matted and tussled, an outstretched arm, but never her face. He sees only one face, the face of the man who brutalizes her. He stands to confront Michael and in his face, the face of Nichole's assailant, Michael sees his own face.

At first the dream was fleeting, once or twice a month, and only the darkness. Recently, however, it came more frequently, almost every night and horrifying in detail. Many months had passed since he had held Nichole in his arms, made love to her, had become lost in her eyes and yet not one moment went by when she did not weigh heavily on his mind. Awake or lost in the hard-won respite of sleep she was there, tormenting his thoughts, tearing at his soul.

Chapter 22

"PLEASE COME OUT," NICHOLE pleaded, looking down at her swollen stomach. "Please baby. Mommy is ready to hold you in her arms now."

Nine months pregnant and four days past her due date, Nichole was growing increasingly weary. Her body ached, her hands and feet were swollen and twice in the past month her back gave way to muscle spasms, muscles not used to supporting the load of the rapidly growing bump she carried, still, not the slightest contraction, nary a sign of impending labor.

She sat uncomfortably on the sofa, her feet propped up on the ottoman her mother had given her. Her long sable mane draped across her shoulders as if a blanket and a fire burned in the hearth before her. Spring had broken the dreary spell of winter, yet at night the winds grew cold still.

McCallister's had opened on schedule two months before. It was a night she would always remember. Unlike the grand opening of Collier Tower, there was no drama, no unwelcome intrusions. Nichole had spent the first hours on pins and needles expecting a crisis. After the fiasco with Caroline Collier, she tried to be prepared for anything. If the skies opened up and the four horsemen of the Apocalypse arrived for dinner, Nichole planned to have a table ready for them. But on that night the skies held their thunder, the locals arrived in droves and word spread quickly of the finest dining experience to be had in the Tidewater area.

McCallister's ran like a well-oiled machine in her absence. Max had taken the lead four weeks into operations when Nichole's obstetrician ordered her on bed rest. Her blood pressure was dangerously high and the ultrasound technician may have detected a slight murmur in the baby's heart. She was assured that neither was an uncommon occurrence and was told that she needed to rest until her child was born.

Nichole grudgingly agreed. Remaining idle for weeks at a time served as its own form of torture, but for the baby that she and Michael had created, there was nothing she would not do.

And she sat, a cup of tea in hand, Estelle Peterman checking in on her every few hours and her mother on the phone every few minutes.

The waiting was becoming unbearable, she had too much time in which to do nothing but think. Her emotions swung like a pendulum inside her, from excitement to frustration, giddiness to apprehension, but most of all fear. She was afraid of labor, afraid of raising a child on her own and afraid of what the future held. She wanted more than anything to have Michael there at her side reassuring her. He weighed heavily on her mind this night and sleep eluded her. She stared at the phone fighting the urge to reach out to him yet again. The passage of time has a strange effect on a person. The hurts inflicted are eased, the lies told soon forgotten and all the memory truly holds on to is the love that was shared. A whirl of sadness surged through her.

She needed an outlet, a porthole through which she could channel the sorrow welling up inside her. Holding in such fierce emotions could not be healthy for her or the baby, that she knew, turning from the phone, she headed for her desk, tore a notebook from the top drawer and began to write.

Michael,

I have wanted to talk with you desperately over the past few months. I've called your name out in the darkness, prayed to the powers that be, I've tried willing you back into my life through memories of you and I but the result is always the same. You're never there. I've resorted to taking pen to paper and writing a letter you'll never receive, words you'll never read but need to be spoken if for no other reason than to free my mind of you and possibly allow me to live my life without your memory forever present to haunt me.

In my life I have learned grief and sadness, heartache and pain. I've somehow survived terror and madness, obsession. I've been brought to my knees from sorrow and fear and I have known love. Love and passion, joy, sheer bliss, all too fleetingly but they have been mine. And like you, I held them tenderly at first only to cling too tightly when their time with me was through. I have learned that life is a cycle, all things pass only to come again. I no longer cling tightly these days. I have learned that when it's time you must let go willingly or have what you hold most dear literally ripped from you.

My God I miss you. I often wonder how life or any truly loving God could bring you into my life only to take you away after such a short time or did I actually chart this insanity into my world, a poorly written Shakespearian tragedy in which I play the ill-fated lead. To say that I loved you seems far too simplistic. The word love is grossly understated and overused and yet in this life it is the only word available to describe the all-consuming whirl of emotions, the hunger, the need that I've come to know since you. For want of a more perfect word, yes I have loved you without pause since the day we met.

With patience and a gentle touch you broke through the horror I used to define myself and rescued the tormented soul inside and for that I will be forever grateful. Never did I imagine that a time would come in my life when I would be the one to walk away from you, from us, inconceivable. However I know now that life can conjure up circumstances that are often times unimaginable to the people who are forced to live through them.

I wish I could count the number of times I've tried to logically explain you away, attempted in vain to hate you for the hurts you caused me, the lies you told, only to covet a deception far greater in the end. I've tried to dismiss you as an infatuation, a dream of an overactive imagination. Dear God I'd love to know that you were real, that we were real. As real as this child that we created, a little girl yet to be born. My only hope now is that she will someday forgive me for not letting you into her life but to lose her as well as you would destroy me. I hope that one day you will both be able to forgive me. All my love, my heart and my soul.

Nichole

Nichole sat in silence; a tear stained face and read aloud the words she had written. The better part of a year had passed and still the pain was raw. She folded the letter carefully, crossed the room, and tossed it into the smoldering embers of the fire. The paper's edges quickly took to flame and her most sacred emotions were reduced to ash within seconds. It was then the emotional was to be put on hold as the physical pains began.

"I've . . . changed . . . my mind." Nichole struggled with each word, but those words echoed throughout the delivery room. "I want . . . the epidural."

Her hands clenched tightly around the collar of Max Porter's shirt making it difficult for him to breathe.

Max smiled and wiped her brow with a cold cloth. "You can do this Nikki, you're the strongest person I've ever known."

"Maxie, I'm tired," she said, "how many hours can this possibly take?"

Max looked almost as exhausted as Nichole. They had both been up for close to twenty-four hours. The physical strain was taking its toll on Nichole, whereas Max's strain was primarily mental.

"This little one is stubborn, like her mama," he said keeping a wary eye on the blood pressure monitor.

The labor had begun slowly at first. The contractions were irregular coming once or twice an hour. Nichole remained calm and waited, filled with anticipation each time her abdomen tightened. At around three in the morning, they grew in intensity and were spaced twenty minutes apart.

She woke Max, who had been sleeping in her guest room since the end of her eighth month. Each night at the close of business, when the last of the guests trickled grudgingly though the exit door of McCallister's, Max would oversee the staff's closing duties, prepare the following day's bank deposit, lock the doors behind him and return to his temporary domicile. Without fail, Nichole would be waiting up for him and insist upon an intricately detailed play-by-play of the night's events. Being unable to play the slightest role in her business venture irritated Nichole to no end. Max would talk for hours ignoring his need for sleep to placate his expectant friend.

He had been lost in sleep for only an hour when she roused him, the grimace on her face telling him all he needed to know. He threw on his Old Dominion sweatshirt and cap and called Frank and Aggie to tell them the time had come. Nichole was admitted and while being adorn with the required attire of paper gown, fetal monitor and blood pressure cuff, Max waited outside for her parents and filled out the necessary forms.

"Almost there," the nurse announced snapping off her latex gloves. "Your parents have arrived, I'll send them in now."

Her father was the first through the door, he kissed Nichole lightly on the forehead and handed her a giant stuffed teddy bear. It was her mother that caught Nichole's attention.

"Mother," Nichole said, a wary expression on her face.

"What is it, honey?"

"What do you think you're going to do with that?" she demanded pointing a swollen finger at the video camera she carried under her arm.

Aggie's eyes rolled in her head. "Your father said you'd make a fuss about this. I'm going to film the baby being born."

Nichole's mouth dropped open in horror.

"Um, *no,* you're *not.*"

She was becoming irritated. Her husband and daughter were always on the same side, the opposite side of the one which she was standing.

"Nichole Marie McCallister, listen to me. This is a perfectly natural experience . . ."

Nichole protested, cutting her off midsentence.

"Mother there are many perfectly natural experiences that occur every day in my life and I don't want those on film either," she said sarcastically.

Max couldn't help but to laugh out loud in the midst of all the chaos. Never in his wildest dreams could he have imagined the ways in which Nichole McCallister would alter his life. And yet here he stood, thirty-something, gay male, business entrepreneur, birthing partner, in what was about to become a virtual reality sitcom. Still shaking his head, he took his seat beside her bed, clasped her hand in his, and held on for the ride.

Three centimeters quickly turned to four and four into five. Five centimeters stalled flat. For over three hours, there was no change and her contractions actually appeared to ease up. The nurse assured her that with a first delivery these things tended to happen, which did nothing for Nichole's demeanor. She patted Nichole on the hand and said she would inform her obstetrician. He may consider breaking her water to move things along a bit.

At the time, that sounded like a good idea. Faced with a giant plastic knitting needle probing her uterus, not good. Nichole had attended every Lamaze class on time, read all the books for first-time mothers, and diligently sifted through every website with a stork on it. She somehow imagined having a baby would be exactly like you see on television, the mother has a pain, the water breaks, the baby is born. She never envisioned herself inching her way up her hospital bed trying to escape the mean doctor with the pointy stick.

Not long after, the contractions returned full force and yet her progress lagged. As the sun set, marking the end of yet another day Nichole grew impatient. She wanted the pains to stop, wanted to hold her baby in her arms and dear God, she wanted to sleep. She tried to lend gravity a hand by walking the halls and entertained briefly the idea of high impact aerobics, anything to feel comfortable in her own skin again. What she hadn't counted on was how physically taxing the actual pushing could be.

For over an hour, she grunted and groaned her way through mind numbing counts of ten. When the delivery nurse informed her that the first baby is always the most difficult delivery, but that her next would come more quickly, Nichole successfully resisted the urge to scratch out the woman's eyes. Finally, after what seemed like endless hours of labor the time had come.

"Okay Nichole," her OB spoke, "she's crowning. Make this next one count."

Nichole bore down one last time, drawing every last ounce of waning strength. Hanna Grace McCallister was born. The cord was cut and a cry to rival that of her mother's erupted from her tiny newborn lungs. Nichole collapsed into the pillows behind her and melted into a flurry of laughter and tears. Her father clung to the delivery nurse like a second skin as she carried his granddaughter squirming and squealing to be cleaned and weighed. Aggie was snapping enough photos to rival the British paparazzi and Max breathed a huge sigh of relief.

Within the hour, Nichole was settled into her room on the maternity ward with her daughter sleeping, at last, in her arms.

"She's amazing Nikki," said Max, who felt as if he were floating somewhere between extreme exhaustion and euphoria.

Nichole was tracing each tiny feature of her daughter's perfect face with her fingertip.

"She looks like Michael," she said, her words tinged with sadness.

"She does," he admitted. "Are you okay? You haven't mentioned him all night, I left it alone, but I know you would have much rather have had him holding your hand tonight than me."

Nichole's face softened when she looked up at him.

"Not so. This was my decision Maxie and I've made my peace with it. Yes I miss him and yes I do still love him, but I'm going to be fine and I couldn't have done all of this without you and still remained sane." She leaned in to place a kiss on his cheek, "Thank you."

"Thank you," he said before leaving, "for letting me be a part of this night."

Nichole laughed. "Like you had a choice."

Finally alone with her daughter, Nichole counted each tiny finger, each little toe, marveled at how completely perfect she was, and gave a silent prayer of thanks to God for the amazing sleeping angel in her arms. It would be a daunting task, raising a daughter alone in an uncertain, dangerous world, but oddly she was unafraid. Hanna was returned to the nursery so that her mother could rest. Nichole struggled at first, to find a comfortable position, the adrenaline had worn off, and her body was now reacting to what it had been forced to endure. Eventually the sheer exhaustion pulled her into a welcomed slumber and over a thousand miles away, under a moonlit Texas sky, Michael Collier slept a dreamless sleep.

Chapter 23

NICHOLE HAD SPENT COUNTLESS hours during her pregnancy painstakingly designing and decorating the most elegant and enchanting nursery her mind could conjure up. She spared no expense, as what was once a sparsely furnished spare bedroom gradually transformed into a chamber of luxuriousbeauty. It was a suite to rival that of royalty, befitting any true princess or at least, an heiress to a real estate dynasty.

Soft flowing satin of the palest shades of pink and white, handsewn, lace adorned the room from end to end. Hints of pastel green ribbons and golden-flecked cherubs were positioned subtly throughout the space, surrounding a circular crib of white wrought iron. The crib itself was topped with a domed canopy dressed with lace-trimmed tulle and satin bows. From the ceiling hung a handcrafted miniature chandelier of clear crystal, gilded in gold. During the daylight hours, the beams of sunlight that broke through the windows would shine upon the prisms casting star-like reflections throughout the room. During the hours of darkness a mere flick of a switch would encase the room with a soft, delicate light specifically designed as to not offend new eyes.

In a word, it was perfection and by all appearances Hanna McCallister was equally as perfect; a squirming, squealing, seemingly flawless gift from the gods. Atop her tiny head, she donned a thick smattering of ebony hair, dark as night and soft as newly spun silk. Her eyes were clear and bright with hints of green already shining through the newborn blue. With flawless skin, a button of a nose and the perfect pout of a mouth, her beauty was to be outdone only by the power of her lungs.

Appearances are oftentimes deceiving. The surface of the water seemingly smooth as glass, calm and inviting, all the while beneath the waters' edge there lies in wait an invisible threat as dangerous as it is illusive.

Staring out the window babe in arms, Nichole welcomed yet another sunrise with waning enthusiasm. The inherent joy of all new mothers, the euphoric bliss marking the end of forty weeks of morning sickness, backaches and swollen ankles that was Nichole's by right was repeatedly squashed by the guilt she carried inside her each time she gazed the innocent face of her daughter.

The child she had carried for nine months, the magical creature that nursed at her breast had a father she would never know. Adding to her torment was the unshakeable suspicion that Nichole felt to her core, something was desperately wrong with her daughter.

"Nikki," Estelle spoke as she entered the room, "give Hanna to me. Go back to bed and get some rest."

Nichole stood unmoved for several somber moments as the sky began its transformation from gray to golden.

"You think I'm right, don't you Estelle?" she asked, still staring, almost as if she were unable to move.

Estelle's slipper clad feet scraped the carpet as she walked. Originally Nichole had insisted that having someone stay with her after returning from the hospital was unnecessary, but after a few short days she had realized how greatly she had underestimated the effects that childbirth and sleep deprivation have on the body. Everything below her neck was sore, aching, or swollen. Her hormones seemed to fluctuate minute-by-minute, peaceful and relaxed one moment, dangling on the verge of tears the next.

When Hanna was first brought home from the hospital, she slept as any breastfed newborn, two sometimes three-hour stretches, but with her first three months of life her pattern of rest became increasingly erratic and unpredictable. Out of desperation and in a state of sheer exhaustion Nichole finally asked for help. Estelle and Maxie took turns staying one or two nights a week and her parents alternated shifts during the weekends.

Estelle took a seat on the sofa patting the cushion next to her.

"Come. Sit. Bring the baby to me."

With tired eyes and a heavy heart, Nichole did as she was told. Estelle studied the babe asleep in her arms.

"Did she nurse?"

"Barely," Nichole replied sounding frustrated. "A few minutes here, a few minutes there. I broke down and tried the formula they sent home from the hospital. She wanted nothing to do with it."

Estelle looked long and hard at the size of the child's arms and tiny legs. She was no doctor but over the years she had had a hand in rearing scores of children and it was clear to her aging eyes that Hanna was not gaining the weight most infants should.

"When she's crying, have you felt her stomach? Does it ever feel unusually hard? Does she pull her legs up?"

Nichole massaged her temples and thought for a moment.

"Colic you mean? I don't think that's it. Sometimes when I'm holding her against me I could swear it feels like her heart is about to pound out of her chest."

Estelle paused and thought on that for a moment. It was possible that if the child had worked herself into a state that her heart rate would go up, yet she had held many a child in the midst of a full out tantrum and it was unlikely to notice the heartbeat that strong unless one made a point to look for it.

"What did her pediatrician say when you took her in for her check-up?"

The pediatrician spent a total of five minutes in the room with her. His nurse took all her measurements, asked the important questions, and administered her shots. All the doctor did was look in her eyes and ears, squeeze a few things and gave a quick listen to her chest. He claimed all babies, especially ones that are breastfed sleep less and tend to not gain weight as quickly.

"What about her heart racing? Did her have an explanation for that?" she asked her voice dripping with sarcasm.

"I hadn't noticed it at that point," Nichole replied, shaking her head. "This is something more recent, over the past week I'd say. The other day she was crying so hard I swear her lips looked almost blue."

The old woman wore a pained expression. For the past month, she had tried to hide from her own suspicions that there was indeed something amiss with Nichole's most valued treasure. She had suffered so much already. Not this, not now. Standing, Estelle placed a sleeping Hanna in the spare basinet kept by the sofa and turned to Nichole. Slowly she nodded.

"I agree with you. I wish with all my heart that I didn't, but I think something may be wrong."

Before the last word had rolled off Estelle's tongue, Nichole had felt as if she had been kicked in the stomach. Her motherly instinct had been sending out alarms for days now, yet hearing her silent fears confirmed by a woman as wise and experienced as Estelle Peterman made it all somehow seem real and extremely urgent.

Nichole's head fell into her hands suddenly feeling the need to wretch, her heart raced, her mind filling instantly with the all too familiar darkness of despair. The rape she had survived, losing Michael she had survived, carrying a child alone and starting her business she had survived, but this, to lose the one thing she loved more than life, how could she survive this?

"Nikki, listen to me." Her voice was stern and commanded attention. "Just because something may be wrong with Hanna does not mean it is something that can't be fixed. Don't panic, don't imagine the worst. That helps no one, fixes nothing."

Nichole struggled to pull herself together. Estelle's words rang true. She knew if she let her thoughts drift to a dark place she would be of no use to anyone. Her daughter needed a mother that could think straight and take the appropriate action, not some blithering mass of useless tears afraid of what the future might hold. She stood and paced the room silently for several moments, her mind struggling for answers. Taking Hanna back to the pediatrician the hospital had recommended was pointless, the man suffered from an excess of ego and an extreme shortage of compassion and his competency in her opinion was still in question.

"Take a shower, get the baby ready. There is an old friend of George's on the staff at the Children's Hospital in Norfolk. He owes us a favor. I'll make the call and ride down with you. Let me make all the fuss. Ole Doc Wellington will do anything to shut me up."

Estelle, true to her word, was indeed the one to make a fuss. Bounding into the office of Virginia's most renowned and respected pediatrician, she laid out her demands with clarity and excess volume, leaving the medical receptionist and Nichole, wide-eyed, mouths gaping.

The dark-haired, gray-eyed woman, outfitted in brightly colored scrubs barely had a chance to speak before she was informed that Hanna McCallister was about to be the good doctor's newest, most favored patient and although they had no scheduled appointment they would not be leaving until the child was thoroughly examined and all questions were answered to their satisfaction.

As Nichole filled out the necessary forms, her thoughts wandered. She longed to be anywhere but here, facing yet again, another potential life-altering crisis, searching desperately for answers, yet dreading those same answers with equal intensity. She was sick of the struggle, tired of the fight and her soul ached for better days.

Somewhere they existed. Days where life flowed with you, instead of the persistent rail against you, defeating all your hard won efforts. Moments of bliss and love and laughter, those moments were fleeting, but they were indeed real. She had known them in her past and she longed desperately to have them come again. For now, the sadness, the fear, the feeling of sheer desperation had laid claim to her and called her their own, unwelcome companions in her search for something more.

A nurse had come to usher them into an examination room in twenty minutes time. Hanna was again weighed and measured, the results recorded in her file. She fussed considerable as most babies do when stripped of their warm clothing and exposed to harsh lights. To Nichole's welcomed surprise Dr. Wellington immediately followed, an older, distinguished looking gentleman, with thinning hair and a kind face.

"Ladies," he said, extending his hand. "I hear you have some concerns you'd like to discuss."

This time Estelle held her tongue. She had made their way through the front door and landed the first appointment of the day. They were being taken seriously. Her job was done.

Nichole stood, holding her daughter close to her, wrapped in a blanket of soft organic cotton to shield her from the draft. She spoke her worries with as much confidence and strength she could muster.

"May I hold her?" he asked calmly. "When her heart races, is she usually crying and upset?"

Nichole thought for a moment and shook her head.

"Not always," she said. "It has happened several times when she is as quiet and still as she in now. After it happens she usually begins to cry, oftentimes uncontrollably and then she seems completely exhausted, but she won't sleep."

The pediatrician shook his head, his face wore and expression of deep contemplation.

"There are some test I would like to run on Hanna today if that would be all right with you Ms. McCallister. From what you have told me of the behaviors Hanna has been exhibiting and from what I've heard, I have my suspicions as to what may be the cause of her distress, but I cannot say for certain without some blood work and a few tests, all noninvasive."

"What are your suspicions telling you, doctor, and please do not bullshit me?" Nichole demanded.

Dr. Wellington smiled, Nichole McCallister was proving to be as feisty and demanding as his dear longtime friend Estelle. Her influence on the girl was clearly evident. "Nichole I don't want to say anything until I'm certain. There is no reason to make yourself sick by getting upset about what-ifs. Let's first identify the problem, if there is one and if there is, then we determine the best way to fix it. Is that okay with you?"

Nichole seemed to calm down a bit. She searched his eyes for sincerity and merely nodded her response. She liked this man, he was rational yet understanding and his credentials were beyond reproach, yet she grudgingly handed over her beautifully fragile, ebony-haired baby girl and hoped against all hope that they were horribly wrong.

Chapter 24

ON THE FIRST THURSDAY of every month Nichole religiously dressed her daughter, gathered their things, and made the drive from Williamsburg to Norfolk prepared to spend the better part of the day behind the pastel colored walls of Mercy Children's Hospital. Each visit identical to the one before, Hanna was weighed, her blood drawn and then whisked off to be hooked up to a series of machines that would gauge her cardiac function and assess the size of the hole in her heart.

The process was physically as well as mentally draining on mother and daughter alike. After spending almost three weeks in the hospital fighting for her life after being raped and brutalized, Nichole despised every sight and sound within the sterile walls yet she fought to put up a good front for her daughter's sake. She played and laughed with Hanna, held and rocked her in the attempt to distract her from the whirring of the machines and the needles that probed her otherwise perfect skin, month after agonizing month the same routine, the same disappointing result.

The child's mental development was ideal, leaning toward advanced, but at eleven months old she was still not gaining weight as she should, still tired easily and the hole in her heart showed no signs of closing. Dr. Wellington conceded defeat. He had hoped that his tiny patient's body would progressively heal itself and that his intervention would not be needed. Disappointed yet highly optimistic as to the outcome he took Nichole by the hand and tenderly delivered the news. The operation was finally set for the week after Hanna's first birthday.

At eight AM on Monday morning, a week to the day that Hanna turned one Nichole watched stone-faced as the most precious thing in her life was wheeled away from her, disappearing behind two imposing cold metal doors. She walked her way down the hall in a daze, her hair pulled back in a long thick ponytail, dark circles under her eyes. She made no attempt at sleep the night before preferring instead to sit and watch her daughter breath in the darkness.

The waiting room was already filled with familiar faces, each holding silent vigils of their own. Estelle Peterman sat knitting a blanket of lavender and white for Hanna no doubt, her husband George at her side. Their daughter Jenna had flown in from Florida and was involved in an intense conversation with Max Porter at the back of the room, her father paced the floor mumbling softly to himself and Aggie her mother sat in the corner, rosary in hand praying for divine intervention. Nichole was no longer certain she believed in God, but if there was some omnipotent being that lived in the sky and granted wishes as he saw fit Aggie McCallister would be sure to find his direct line and badger him into submission.

When Nichole walked through the doors to take her place among them they quieted, all eyes turned in her direction. She spoke not a word, shed not a tear, she took a seat at the far end of the room and simply stared into nothingness.

"Uh oh . . . this is bad," Jenna said, leaning into Max.

Leaning forward, hands clasped in front of him Max nodded in agreement, his ever- present easygoing smile turning into a frown of concern.

"She's resigned herself to the worst and she's starting to shut down."

Jenna began to panic and grabbed Max by the hand.

"We have to do something. I can't sit here and watch her disappear into that dark hole again. Don't you remember how carefree and in love with life she used to be before . . . that night."

Max raised his brow in confusion. “No, no Jenna I don’t.”

“Shit, Max, I’m sorry. It seems like you’ve always been a part of this ragtag extended family of ours. Sometimes I forget how you and Nichole met.”

His expression turned grave. “I never will.”

Jenna groaned. She could never begin to imagine the horror he had experienced that night, stumbling upon a complete stranger, beaten and bloodied, clinging to life. He had held her hand through each painstaking moment until the ambulance arrived.

For the better part of an hour, they allowed Nichole her space, giving her time to hopefully sort through things on her own. Nichole statue like and unmoving almost as if she were frozen in time, no one dared to say a word. Finally, unable to bear another moment of the solemn quiet, Max stood and nodded in Nichole’s direction. “Come on let’s go get our girl.”

Frank McCallister had stopped his pacing and turned to join them when the cool hand of Estelle Peterman reached out to stop him.

“Frank, let the kids do it. If we all pounce on her at once, she’ll feel more overwhelmed than she already is. Maxie has a way with her that no one else does and Jenna makes a good buffer. Let them try.”

He nodded and stepped back resuming his sentinel duties. Jenna took a seat on Nichole’s left, Max on her right, each taking one of her hands in theirs.

“Nikki, please don’t do this,” Jenna spoke. There was no response, Nichole continued to stare straight ahead, unmoving.

“Nichole, listen to me,” Max said, twisting so that he was within her line of view. “You cannot climb back inside your shell of self-imposed solitude and hide. Hanna needs her mother.”

Nichole tightened her grip on the hands that held her and flashed Max her best how fucking dare you glare.

Max had done his research on trauma victims. He knew that when a survivor was exposed to a trigger they would often disassociate, the mind begins to shut down unable to cope with the approaching threat. They could become lost inside themselves for days, weeks, months at a time. The key to preventing it was to interrupt the cycle as soon as possible. Determined to prevent Nichole's further descent into madness he pushed harder. Having her furious with him would be a small price to pay.

"If you're disappearing again, hiding from reality," he said reaching into his back pocket and pulling out his cell phone, "at least call Michael and tell him he has a daughter so that Hanna will at least have one parent able to take care of her when she comes out of this."

Nichole yanked her hands free from their grasp, ragging furry emanating from her stormy eyes, in one smooth motion she snatched the cell phone from Max's hand and ran out of the waiting room and into the hallway.

"I cannot believe you said that to her. What the hell were you thinking, Maxie?"

"It worked didn't it, he said drily, "every day after I found Nichole I went to visit her . . . at the hospital, at home with her parents when she was released. Three months, Jenna, that's how long it took for her find her way out of the catatonic state she was in and speak for the first time since she had been raped. She can hate me all she wants right now, but I'm not going through that again and I'm not letting her put herself through that again."

Jenna nodded in agreement, raking her hand through her short blonde hair. She looked tired; worry could exhaust a person quicker than any amount of physical exertion.

"You go after her and do damage control," she replied, "I'm going to go and try to find out if there is any news on Hanna. It's been over two hours there has to be some word."

Nichole fought back the tears that surfaced in her tired eyes, tears of rage, frustration and an overwhelming feeling of defeat. Clenching the cell phone in her hand she pounded out each number of Michael's mobile from memory. There was no fear, no trepidation, only fury coursing through her. Life had been cruel one time too many and she was being forced to face the unforgiving onslaught of it yet again on the second worst day of her life or was it the third?

Her body stiff, her jaw clenched, she held her breath as the phone began to ring, one, two, three, no answer. She was about to disconnect when she heard a woman's voice.

"Hello." Nichole froze, no it wasn't Caroline's voice. She could never forget the sound of that shrew's screeching. This was someone new.

"Hello," the voice repeated.

Nichole swallowed the lump in her throat along with her pride.

"Michael Collier, please," she replied, managing to conceal her true emotions from the words as she spoke.

"Mike is busy at the moment. He's in the shower, but I'll be joining him momentarily if you'd like to leave a message." The woman's tone was oozing with exaggerated sweetness as if marking her territory with each syllable.

Nichole grimaced and balled her hands into fists. She felt sick and silently admonished herself for being such an unsuspecting fool.

"No . . . there's no message." She disconnected and hurled the phone with every ounce of energy she had left. It crashed into the wall before her, echoing through the otherwise abandoned corridor and shattered at her feet into a burst of tiny bits of flying plastic.

Max reached her in time to witness his cell being reduced to nothing but projectile pieces of shrapnel. Grabbing her by the arms he attempted to steady her trembling limbs. She was seething with a fire in her eyes that penetrated the pale blue walls surrounding them.

"Dear God, Nik, what the hell happened? Did you actually call Michael?"

Nichole wrenched free of his grasped and pushed him away.

"Did I call him," she fumed, "did I really call him? That's what you fucking told me to do isn't it? Yes . . . I called Michael and his new piece of arm candy answered and was more than happy to let me know that he was in the shower and that she would be joining him soon if I wanted her to give him a message."

Max's eyes widened in horror, a wave of regret settling over him

"Nikki, I'm so sorry." He struggled for the words to make this wrong right. "I never considered . . . you were starting to disappear on us again. I had to stop it." He leaned against the wall for support, slunk to the ground, and buried his head in his hands.

She looked over at him seated on the floor, looking as defeated as she felt. Nichole had been infuriated with many people in her life, her attacker, Caroline Collier, Michael, but never Maxie. Truth be told she wasn't angry with him at all. She was angry, at the world and its cruel realities, exacerbated by life itself and its never-ending barrage of tragedy and trial.

She made her way to him, plastic and metal crunching beneath her feet as she walked. Taking a seat on the floor next to him, she lay her head on his shoulder and sighed.

"I truly am sorry, Nichole, I'd never deliberately do anything to hurt you," he said grabbing her hand and squeezing it tightly.

"I know and I appreciate what you did. I'm not exactly thrilled with the way you went about it."

"I hate to ask," he spoke sounding almost as mentally and physically drained as Nichole felt, "but did you leave a message?"

Her face jerked up to meet his.

"Hell no." She smiled, "I smashed your phone instead."

Max scanned the floor in front of him, "Yes . . . I noticed that."

Nichole laughed for the first time in weeks, all the tension, all the anxiety leaving her body with each heartfelt giggle. She had lost all track of time, gave no notice to her surroundings until the sound of approaching footsteps drew her attention down the hallway.

Jenna was running toward them, Dr. Wellington trailing behind. Nichole stood quickly suddenly feeling as though she may be sick. The entire day has been surreal, like walking around in a nightmarish trance that would not end. As they drew near she felt paralyzed, unable to move, knowing full well that they proceeded as either emissary's of hope and life or agents fate sent to rip her heart out.

Within moments Jenna's face came into view, the bright, beaming smile upon it was unmistakable. She wrapped her arm around Nichole's and motioned impatiently for Dr. Wellington to hurry his stride. Wearing his operating room scrubs, his padded feet shuffled to great them.

"Nichole my dear," he said reaching out to her, "you're beautiful baby girl did wonderfully. She is in recovery right now. When she wakes up she'll be moved to NICU and you can see her then. It's shouldn't be too long."

Nichole felt a million butterflies swarming in her stomach. It was over, it was finally over.

"Then she's okay?" she questioned, her voice trembling seeking further reassurance. "The operation is over and my baby is going to be okay?"

"The operation was flawless, no complications, she was a real trooper" he reassured her. "Now she'll still need to spend about a week here in the hospital, she'll be on antibiotics to stave off the threat of infection and we will give you a list of nutritional guidelines to follow when you leave here, but there is no reason Hanna should not have a long, perfectly normal life."

She threw her arms around him and held on tightly.

"Thank you, thank you, a million times thank you," she cried.

"You are more than welcome." He smiled and released her. "Now why don't we go to the waiting room and let everyone else know the good news. According to my staff, your mother has lit every candle in the chapel and they are afraid she might set off a fire alarm soon."

They all laughed in unison, the sound music to Nichole's ears. Nothing else mattered now, not Michael or the tart that was undoubtedly naked with him at the movement. Whoever she was she could have her stolen moments with him because Nichole knew that she had and always would have the best part of Michael Collier, the living breathing daughter that they had created together. Nothing could take that away from her now.

Chapter 25

JOCELYN HOGAN DID NOT particularly care for so-called charity fund raising events. It was not that she had a problem donating money to a worthy cause, but rather found it tedious to spend endless hours with a group of wealthy pious politicians who spoke time and again of helping the less fortunate all the while patting themselves on the back for the one decent thing they did each year.

Being privy to the world of Michael Collier brought with it frequent exposure to men of great wealth and influence. Heads of state, congressmen, and CEOs from major corporations around the world had all rubbed elbows with her husband at one time or another, oftentimes leaving her with a growing distaste for bureaucracy and corporate greed. Having moved among them for many years she knew she would never truly belong and over time began to excuse herself more and more often from the frequent invitations to garden parties and campaign fundraisers delivered to her doorstep on a weekly basis.

Tonight's affair was different, however. This particular event was sponsored by Michael Collier and was to benefit abused and battered women. For a cause as worthy as this one she would don her favorite frock, smile her best smile, and laugh at every mundane, antiquated joke that came her way, anything to get a senator or judge to cough up an extra thousand.

Jocelyn was a no-nonsense woman of class. She was well educated; having paid her way through college, a highly respected pediatrician and a cornerstone of the community. When Michael enlisted her help, she enthusiastically accepted. Michael willingly opened his home for the gala and Jocelyn had handled the rest.

There was a sizable turnout; almost everyone invited had shown as well as several who had taken it upon themselves to appear unasked. It was an election year and the ballroom overflowed with elect hopefuls and their wives all preening like peacocks as sounds of the Viennese Waltz drifted through the estate.

"Tom." Jocelyn attempted a whisper.

"Tom," she said, again a hint of urgency in her voice this time as she tugged on the sleeve of his jacket.

"What is it honey," he said, leaning in to hear her more clearly.

"Who's the tart draping herself on Michael's arm?"

Tom followed Jocelyn's gaze. Across the expanse of the billiard room seated at the end of the bar sat Michael Collier and what appeared to be his date for the evening, a tall, rather statuesque woman in a scarlet tight fitting gown.

"Oh, her," Tom replied, sounding a bit disgusted. "Christine something or other. I can't remember her last name."

Jocelyn remained focused; you could almost see the wheels turning in her mind. She tended to be a bit protective of Michael. She loved him for all he had done for Tom before she had come into his life and after. She loved him because Tom loved him and because she truly believed in her heart that behind Michael's icy façade, which he displayed to the world, lay a tender, kindhearted man much in need of acceptance, desperate to experience an unwavering, unconditional love.

"Jocelyn." Tom sounded wary.

"I'll be right back honey," she said, releasing his arm.

Tom grabbed her by the wrist before she could escape. There was suspicion in his voice.

"Jocelyn, let it go, just for tonight."

"I want to talk to Michael for a minute. He's drinking heavily again, I worry. I'll be right back," she said, patting him on the hand in a mute attempt of reassurance.

Some may have called Jocelyn Hogan meddling, but Tom knew she did what she did only because she truly cared. She was a true romantic at heart and was among a select few on the planet who still believed in happy endings.

With her casual flare for persuasion, she successfully freed Michael, from what she deemed to be nothing more than a gold digging harlot obsessed with her own vanity. She corralled him into his library under the guise of an unforeseen complication with a donation made during the evening.

The room was dark and brooding, not unlike Michael himself. Its walls lined with rare and vintage books, many first editions dating back centuries. Goblet pleated draperies, the color of burgundy wine blocked out the sun, casting shadows throughout. Before Michael had a chance to speak, Jocelyn had led him to the sofa that sat alone before a flameless hearth.

She swallowed hard. “Michael, I lied. There is not a problem with the donations.”

Michael arched a brow suddenly quite curious. It was completely uncharacteristic of Jocelyn Hogan to lie about anything. He wasn’t altogether certain she knew how.

“Okay, Jocelyn,” he said becoming intrigued. “What is this about?”

“Michael, I know you are going to say this is none of my business and please don’t be angry with Tom. He only told me because he does care about you.”

Michael raised the glass he carried to his lips, draining the final few drops. The spark in his eyes long since lost, a dour foreboding every present in his expression, he questioned her.

“What’s on your mind, Jocelyn?”

She paused for a moment in an attempt to arrange the words in her mind.

“I know about Nichole McCallister. I know that you loved her, I know what that lunatic did to her . . .”

Michael tensed visibly, the muscles in his jaw clenching taut. He cut her off before she could speak. His words were sharp, his voice tinged with bitterness.

"Oh really, and do you know what my lunatic ex-wife did to her? Did Tom fill you in on those lovely details as well?"

"Yes, he did. But that is what Caroline did to her Michael not you," she said, attempting to place the blame where it truly belonged.

At that, he laughed a nearly sinister laugh. His countenance was encompassed in a darkness so deep it was if he were a mere shell, the light from his soul entombed in some far off distant place, leaving him hollow and empty inside.

"And do you suppose that because it was Caroline standing there, humiliating her in front of hundreds of people, instead of me that it hurt her any less?"

He moved to a table across the room, lifted a brandy decanter, and filled his glass.

"Michael, please hear me out," Jocelyn pleaded.

He tore off his tie as though it threatened to suffocate him and tossed it to the floor at his feet. Continuing before Jocelyn had a chance to speak again his voice rang through the darkened room.

"Nichole literally survived hell, Jocelyn. She was raped, beaten, brutalized, and left to die. What was left of her she locked away from the rest of the world for years and by some damned miracle of God she opened up for an undeserving bastard like me. What she gave me was the most sacred, precious thing she had to offer and by lying to her the way I did I may have very well spit in her face."

Jocelyn was awestruck. She sat in stunned silence. What had happened to Michael Collier and who the hell was this man in front of her. She had known Michael for as long as she had known her husband, he was godfather to their eldest son, they had worked and vacationed together. Their lives had been intertwined from end to end for almost two decades and she had never witnessed him entirely passionate about another human being. For that matter, she had never known any man to hold such fervency for any woman. At that moment, she almost envied Nichole, a woman she had yet to meet.

"Michael," she spoke, her voice softer, more sympathetic. "After going through the horror that she did, for Nichole to open up to you, she had to be completely in love with you. That kind of love doesn't go away."

"It's been years Jocelyn," he said, cynicism dripping from every word, "I'm sure she's moved on to someone who deserves her far more than I."

Jocelyn stood to put them on even footing.

"Oh, like you've moved on?" she challenged. "You said it yourself, it's been years and you're still completely in love with her. You drown yourself in your work and your brandy; you cut yourself off from the decent people who truly care about you and parade around shallow, empty women like the one you're with tonight. What the hell is wrong with you?"

Michael stiffened. Her words had wounded him. Sitting down the brandy he carried he walked to the door, his expression was severe, a furrow knit in his brow. Contacting Nichole now, after so much time had passed was not an option. How was he to put the matter to rest when the world around him served as a constant reminder?

"You know, Jocelyn," he said his voice a low grumble, "even a drunken, workaholic, womanizing, prick like myself, likes to forget, for just a while, all he's lost."

His words hung in the air and rendered Jocelyn mute. She had never meant to insult him, only to jar him into action, nudge him into the direction where his heart belonged. Holding hands and coddling would never do with Michael Collier. She made an attempt at the tough love approach, but she had never expected this reaction. The room suddenly felt cold and lonely, as if reflecting the true inner feelings of its owner. Michael made his exit with no further words, the sound of the door clicking lightly behind him.

Jocelyn searched in vain the rest of the evening to locate Michael and make amends. She searched the gardens, the wine cellar, walked every inch of his lavish estate. Enlisting the help of her husband proved to be futile as well. It was as if Michael had literally vanished. They returned home well after midnight. With Michael nowhere to be found Jocelyn felt it her duty to see off every last guest and secure the estate.

Returning home sleep eluded her despite her best effort

"I have to fix this," Jocelyn declared aloud to a darkened room as she sat up in bed with a jolt, frustrated at her thwarted attempts at sleep.

Tom lying next to her drearily opened one eye. The clock read three in the morning, his head still pounded from the night's festivities. He knew this was coming but had hoped it would at least wait until the sun had made its appearance, but Jocelyn's constant tossing and turning had secured a restless night for them both

"Jocelyn, there is nothing you can do at this hour. Please go to sleep and we'll sort it out in the morning."

"No Tom," she said, sounding almost desperate, "you didn't see his face. There was so much sadness in his eyes, he looked completely lost. I have to do something to fix this."

Tom grudgingly sat up in bed, his eyes bloodshot and burning.

"You can't fix Michael Collier, Jocelyn. Believe me I've spent the better part of my life trying to pull him out of the wreckage of his childhood this . . . this is different." Tom raked his fingers through his tousled hair, let loose a frustrated sigh and continued. "Honey, ever since he met Nichole no rules apply to him. She struck a chord with him, reached a part of him no other human being has ever been able to reach, and since that night when Caroline put herself on public display in Virginia, Mike's been bound and determined to punish himself."

Jocelyn reached for a glass of water on her bedside table. Sipping it slowly she listened halfheartedly as her husband spoke. Why did men always have to be so damned stubborn she thought to herself? Eager to make love, slow to love and when they finally do they lose all good sense.

She knew she needed to take matters into her own hands. Tom would never approve. She resolved to keep the matter to herself. If Michael was too stubborn to contact Nichole and content to wallow in his own self-pity then she would have to take the step that he was not willing to take for himself. She would find a way to reach Nichole McCallister herself, it would take some time and proper planning but was Jocelyn was determined to pull this off.

Michael may have known many women in his life, however, he had yet to truly understand them. But Jocelyn Hogan knew what countless other women who had loved and then lost had known. We may walk tall with a brilliant diamond gleaming on our hand and a captivating smile, but a woman never forgets that special one that got away, the one that stole her breath simply by being in the room with him, the one that held the power to suspend time with a touch. In the heart of every woman lies a secret she treasures, its value immeasurable.

Chapter 26

IT HAD TAKEN JOCELYN Hogan several months' time to clear her schedule at the hospital, research the whereabouts of Nichole McCallister and concocted a somewhat believable story about visiting her old college roommate in New York for the coming weekend. Locating Nicole had been the easy part. A quick search on the internet and McCallister's website appeared equipped with address, phone number, and hours of operation. Jocelyn maneuvered the site in hopes of finding a picture of the woman whose life she was about to intrude upon to no avail, but at least her name was there listed as the restaurant's owner.

Coming up with a story to cover her whereabouts, took some creativity. She contacted her old roommate and sorority sister and enlisted her help. Together they agreed that a quick trip to the Big Apple was her most viable option. In truth, they had been discussing a reunion for quite some time. Tom would be less apt for suspicion. And in her mind Jocelyn justified her lying to her husband with the knowledge that she was doing something good for two people who deserved to be happy. He may not have agreed with her methods had he known, yet she hoped that the ends would justify the means.

The week passed by slowly and her apprehension grew. With the logistics of her plan easily secured, Jocelyn now fretted under the weight of the realization of the true impact her actions may have. Tom discovering the truth was one thing, but should Michael ever know . . . she shuddered at the thought. Michael could never know plain and simple. He would never forgive her for interfering, even if it was for his own good and worse yet it could damage the relationship he had with Tom.

There was also the matter of approaching Nichole. Jocelyn knew she could not simply walk into McCallister's, request Nichole's audience and over a cup of coffee happen to mention that she was a long-time friend of Michael Collier and "oh by the way he is still desperately in love with you and miserable without you." The woman would think she was mad. Not to mention the possibility that Michael may have been right when he said Nichole had likely moved on with her life. What then? It was all too much to consider.

Jocelyn threw herself into her work, taking on extra patients to busy her mind, yet between each case of the flu, mysterious rashes, and the odd item stuck in a tiny nostril she rehearsed repeatedly in her mind the words she would say once face to face with Nichole McCallister. The woman had already been through so much in her lifetime the last thing Jocelyn wanted to do was to open old wounds. In the same respect she could no longer stand by and watch Michael destroy himself.

During the evening hours, she avoided her husband as much as possible. Tom always knew when she was hiding something and this was the biggest secret she had kept from him over the entire course of their marriage. She had resolved to tell him the truth once she had returned, but not a moment sooner. Theirs was a good marriage, solid. It was built on trust and mutual respect for each other and love and although they rarely argued, when they did it was often over her tendency to "interject herself" into matters that were not her concern. Or at least that was how Tom had put it; his polite way of saying she stuck her nose in where it didn't belong. This escapade was sure to inspire their biggest argument yet.

When Friday had finally arrived, she sent Tom off to work with a kiss and the reassurance that she would call once she was safely on the ground. Once inside the airport she swallowed hard, steeled her shoulders, and boarded the plane bound for Williamsburg Virginia. It wasn't until they were actually in the air that she breathed a sigh of relief. It was too late to turn back now.

Following up on the reputation of the establishment Jocelyn had secured herself a reservation for one under the name of Jocelyn Edenton. Although she had never met with Nichole, never spoken to the woman, Tom had and she wanted to eliminate the slightest chance of suspicion of a connection between the two. Edenton was her maiden name, the name christened upon her by the Holy Mother Church and the name she had recognized for the first twenty-two years of her life, it was the safest alternative.

The reservation had been made for six thirty on Saturday evening. Jocelyn had spent Friday pent up in her hotel room fighting her doubts and the undeniable urge to abandon her intricately concocted scheme altogether. It would have been much easier to hold up at the bed and breakfast she had chosen for the remainder of the weekend and fly home on Sunday sure to preserve the status quo. Yet each time she had resolved to do so, Michael's words from the night of the charity event echoed in her mind. The look in his eyes that night, desolate and defeated, and Jocelyn felt responsible for bringing it all to the surface.

Michael Collier truly was an enigma, darkness and light, made of flesh and blood with a touch of the immortal. He was as unbeatable as he was broken. And the only woman that lived and breathed capable of reaching him was now within reach, behind the walls of this enchanted eatery, tucked away in the woods.

With a sinking feeling in her stomach, Jocelyn spied her watch. The time had come. Having spent the past thirty minutes observing McCallister's from the safety of her rental car, it quickly became apparent that the a reservation was not only a necessity, but must be met on time. Despite the chill in the air, a line had formed between the imposing columns that marked the entryway and down the staircase into the lot. Nichole McCallister had done well for herself indeed.

Having maneuvered her way to the hostess station Jocelyn was immediately seated at a quaint table with a full view of the overflowing dining room. She had ordered a glass of wine and half-heartedly scanned the menu, finding herself surprisingly relaxed, soothed by her surroundings. The soft candlelight blending with the crackle from the fireplace and tranquil music set the tone, having a sedative effect on her nerves as she spied the crowd hoping to distinguish Nichole from among them.

Her server approached to take her order, a young attractive girl with her hair pulled back at the nape of her neck, her uniform pressed and spotless. "Have you decided what you would like to have for dinner this evening?" she asked.

Scanning the menu one final time Jocelyn had chosen a ginger teriyaki glazed salmon and fresh grilled asparagus. Putting forth the best innocent smile she could muster, she handed her menu over to her server and spoke. "Does the owner happen to be in this evening?"

"Ms. McCallister or Mr. Porter?

"Nichole McCallister, is she in?"

"In an unofficial capacity yes, Mr. Porter is working the floor tonight" the girl replied. "Ms. McCallister is in the office trying to catch up on some paperwork, but she could be here for a while since she has her daughter here helping her out."

The remark was innocent enough yet the words caused an instant reaction in Jocelyn who struggled to keep her composure.

"She has a daughter I had no idea. How old is she?"

"Hanna . . . almost two I think, she's quite a handful," she answered politely. "Do you need to speak with Ms. McCallister? Is there something wrong?"

Jocelyn quickly put her hands up in protest. "No, no nothing's wrong. A friend of mine had recommended this restaurant, she said I would adore everything about it and you know she was right. I traveled a long way and I was hoping to pass along my compliments to the owner."

"Of course, I'll put in your order and I'll let her know."

She quickly downed her glass of wine and fidgeted in her seat. A daughter, nearly two years old. Jocelyn did the calculation in her mind. The numbers added up, could it be possible? Jocelyn was quickly becoming an expert liar, a thought that would normally trouble her, but the true weight of the situation was weighed upon her and her thoughts tripped over each other, unable to form a coherent thought despite her best efforts.

In an attempt to steady both her racing mind and trembling hands, Jocelyn closed her eyes and focused on taking slow, deep breaths, holding each for several seconds, and exhaling slowly. She was about to put on the single, solitary, most important performance of her life and it had to be believable.

Time seemed to drag on, each moment tormenting her with apprehension. Her dinner arrived and though it looked absolutely delectable, her appetite failed her. She picked at the vegetables and managed a mere two bites of fish. Her thoughts were miles away on the forlorn expression of Michael Collier and the crushing effect this new reality could have upon him if it were a reality. When Nichole approached the table, Jocelyn was caught completely off guard and jumped slightly in her seat.

"I'm sorry I didn't mean to startle you," Nichole spoke, extending her hand in welcome. "I was told you wished to speak with me."

Jocelyn stared, momentarily speechless at the figure before her. Long dark flowing hair, a beautiful winning smile, and the greenest eyes she had ever seen looking back at her. It was easy to see why Michael had fallen for this woman. She put down her napkin and stood.

"Please, Ms. McCallister, have a seat."

"Call me Nichole."

Both women took as seat at the table opposite each other. Nichole offered a welcoming smile, Jocelyn swallowed hard in her throat and somehow managed to regain the power of speech.

"Thank you for joining me. As I told your server a dear friend of mine had been in town on business and she recommended your restaurant. I decided to take her advice and I must say I'm glad I did. It's quite elegant and soothing. I wanted to extend my compliments."

"Thank you," Nichole replied. "It does mean a lot to me when our patrons go out of their way to reach out to us. But you've barely touched your meal, is there something wrong. I could send it back for something else if you don't like."

"Oh no, that's not it at all . . ."

Jocelyn's next words were cut short by the sound of a childlike giggle headed in their direction. Closely followed by a tall light-haired gentleman and several of the staff.

Nichole laughed and stood. "Come here Hanna," she said, extending her arms to the most beautiful child Jocelyn had ever laid eyes on.

"Sorry Nik, she escaped again. Said she had to go to the potty and when Janey attempted take her there she took off in the other direction."

Nichole scooped up her daughter in her arms and kissed her on the cheek. "I'm sorry Ms., I don't know your name."

"You can call me Jocelyn."

"I'm sorry, Jocelyn, this is my daughter Hanna. As you can see she is very determined and a bit of a handful."

Jocelyn could hear the sound of her heartbeat ringing in her ears. Her legs felt as if they might collapse from beneath her. The child held in front of her was the spitting image of Michael Collier. She had the same black hair, same mouth, same smile. The only difference was that her eyes held within them the identical captivating emerald color as her mothers. There was no doubt this was Michael Collier's daughter and that changed everything.

Chapter 27

Still struggling to steady her herself, Jocelyn called the airline. She had to be on the first flight home in the morning. She had to talk to Tom. No matter how furious he was going to be with her, she knew she had to not only tell him the truth about her whereabouts, but all that she had learned.

Michael Collier had a child, a child whose existence had successfully been concealed from him for several years now. She didn't blame Nichole. Jocelyn was a mother. She couldn't begin to imagine being totally in love with a man only to discover a wife cleverly hidden in the shadows, being publically humiliated and then to discover you're carrying his child. No, she knew that had she been in the same position she would have likely done the same.

Jocelyn squinted back tears. My God, she thought to herself, the woman must have been devastated. After meeting Nichole, Jocelyn knew without a doubt that it was not malice that prompted her to keep Michael's child from him but fear. The sadness in her eyes had been unmistakable. Never had two people needed each other more than Nichole McCallister and Michael Collier and the child they shared needed them both.

The sound of the front door opening startled Tom Hogan, who drowsed lazily beneath the covers. Jocelyn wasn't expected home until later that evening yet to his surprise it was she who stood waiting for him in the foyer as he trudged down the stairs.

Jocelyn bit down hard on her bottom lip, inside she was trembling. He had to know the truth and there would be no way around the argument sure to ensue. Eventually she hoped he would come to see the necessity behind all she had done.

She stared at her husband, not yet out of the clothes he had slept in, stubble on his face and never had she been more grateful for the simplicity that was her life. Having Michael Collier in their lives had proved to add all the drama she could handle.

"Tom," she said, "come into the kitchen. We need to talk."

Tom said nothing, but followed as instructed. He was clearly confused, hesitant, yet curious.

He lowered himself into a chair at the kitchen table, his gaze following his wife as she helped herself to a cup of coffee in silence. He had never witnessed her so perplexing, or secretive. Briefly he entertained the thought that she had been having an affair. Whatever was bothering her something was desperately wrong. Unable to bear the silence any longer he spoke.

"Jocelyn, what's this about?"

Hesitantly she turned from the window, a pained expression on her face.

"Tom, I lied to you. I didn't go to New York this weekend. I was in Virginia."

He completely missed the significance of all she had said. All that registered was the lie. Oh God she was having an affair.

"Why did you lie? Why didn't you tell me where you were going?"

Jocelyn gritted her teeth. He wasn't going to make this easy.

"Tom, I went to Virginia," she said again hoping he would make the connection.

It took a moment to register, but when it did it was quickly visible on his face. His hand slammed down on the tabletop and he leaped to his feet.

"Jocelyn, you didn't. Tell me you didn't," he roared.

Jocelyn took one step back and winced.

"Yes and no. Please hear me out before you explode.

Tom had begun pacing the floor, mumbling incoherently and waving his arms about in frustrated gestures.

"Tom," she yelled, "just listen."

He leaned against the countertop and dropped his head in one hand.

"Yes I went to see Nichole McCallister. I didn't tell her who I was and certain unforeseen circumstances prevented me from ever mentioning Michael."

"How did you find her?" he asked. "What did you say to her?"

Jocelyn relayed the story of finding Nichole on the internet. She spoke briefly about the restaurant she had opened and the conversation that ensued and aside from the present migraine and chest pains Tom was experiencing due to Jocelyn's impromptu confession he was silently relieved to know that Nichole was doing well.

Tom had always liked Nichole although he had only met her several times. It was he who had inadvertently unearthed her secret horror. He had been as equally repulsed by the savagery done to her, as he was enchanted by the woman she had become in spite of it. Something in him had known early on that if any woman could ever tame the feral ways of Michael Collier, she would be the one to do it.

"What stopped you from mentioning Mike?"

Jocelyn stilled, staring at the floor she drew in a deep breath and sighed.

"Tom." She struggled for the words. "Did Michael ever mention anything to you about Nichole being pregnant when they were together?"

Tom Hogan's brow knit together. No, he could never have forgotten a detail such as that.

"No. Why do you ask?"

"Because as sure as I'm standing here in front of you, there lives and breathes a little girl in Williamsburg, Virginia whose father is Michael Collier."

His jaw dropped. He searched his mind for something, anything he might have missed. It was years ago, the memories were clouded now yet despite the time that had passed he would have never forgotten something such as this. Michael? A father?

"Jocelyn, if you never mentioned Michael how do you know for sure."

"She looks exactly like him, Tom. She came running up to Nichole while we were talking and it took everything I had to keep it together. She has Nichole's eyes, but the rest is Michael. And Nichole said she was almost two years old. You do the math."

Tom's head was spinning. His wife was not a woman quick to jump to conclusions and the numbers did add up.

"Do you think Michael knows and never told you?" she asked.

Tom vehemently shook his head.

"No. There's no way. Mike has done his share of shitty things in his life, but he would never abandon his own child even if he didn't love the mother and we both know he's still in love with Nichole to this day. Not to mention that deep down Mike wants a family more than anything else in the world. He'd never admit it of course."

Coffee. He needed coffee; he needed to be able to think clearly. Tom knew he should be furious with his wife, but how could he under the circumstances. He helped himself to a cup in silence. They both felt the impact of Jocelyn's discovery. Now, what to do about it?

If this was Michael's daughter, a child he knew nothing of, then he deserved to know. Michael had never made empty promises to any woman, never offered more than he intended to give. Tom knew if he had been given the time Michael would have offered Nichole the world. He was guilty only of hiding the truth to protect her, the rest lay at the feet of Caroline Collier. Yet it appeared he would be content to punish himself throughout eternity in his silent form of penance.

Michael would have sooner given up his life than intentionally caused Nichole such pain. Underneath his hardened exterior beat a heart of gold that had been buried by years of torment. Tom had no doubt that Michael would be an amazing father and he knew without pause that Michael Collier needed his little girl, as much as she needed him.

The weight of it all settled suddenly on Tom's shoulders. The anger replaced by concern. My God, this changed everything.

"What's her name?" he asked studying the steady flow of steam rising from his cup.

"Hanna and she's beautiful."

"With those two as parents, no doubt," he said flatly.

Jocelyn asked the question Tom had been avoiding himself.

"How are you going to tell him?"

Tom looked up from his cup. His body was in the room, his mind was somewhere else, running through every plausible scenario, every possible reaction from Michael, every fated ending to the story.

"Well here's the hard truth of the matter," he said. "Since Nichole never volunteered the identity of her child's father and we have no real proof that she is his, I can't walk in and tell him he has a child he knows nothing of."

"But Tom," Jocelyn tried to argue. Tom waved a dismissive hand.

"Jocelyn, hear me out. I cannot get his hopes up like that if there exists the slightest doubt and nothing short of a confirmation from Nichole or a DNA test can prove otherwise. It would destroy him if it turned out this little girl wasn't his."

Jocelyn was so certain that Hanna McCallister was truly Michael's daughter she hadn't stopped to consider the fallout had she been wrong. The instant she laid eyes on that sweet face she knew, she needed no further proof but the truth of the matter was that they were playing God with peoples' lives and she agreed it was best to stay on the side of caution.

"All right," she said, "but is there any possible way you could arrange for Michael and Nichole to meet without either of them knowing. I know that despite the restaurant, despite her new role as a mother she's as miserable without him as his is without her. We spoke for almost an hour. I could see it in her eyes Tom. It's the same sadness, same distant look of torment that Michael carries in his eyes."

Tom thought on that for a moment. For all his wife's matchmaking, interfering ways she may be on to something. Again he paced the floor.

"You know," he said, "it's easy for Mike to resist contacting Nichole from here in Texas. There's over fifteen-hundred miles of safety net between them . . . but_if I were to arrange a crisis at the Collier Center in Virginia he'd have to go himself."

The smile on Jocelyn's face was unmistakable. Finally after all these years of marriage her husband was beginning to think like her. That was a small victory in itself.

"And you think," she said enthusiastically, "that once he's there close to her he won't be able to resist any longer."

"It's possible," he agreed. "Are there any signs advertising her restaurant, billboards, fliers in the hotel?"

"They're everywhere. Hell, there is a sign in the baggage claim of the airport with McCallister's written in big bold letters." She paused, suddenly knowing this was no ordinary man they were dealing with. Michael could be exceedingly stubborn. "What if you're wrong? What if he still refuses to contact her?"

Tom spoke, he words staggered with trepidation.

"If I'm wrong . . . If I'm wrong, then we have no choice. We'll have to tell him our suspicions when he gets back."

Chapter 28

IT HAD PROVED TO be a daunting task. Tom Hogan had struggled for months attempting to create a crisis where none existed. To develop such a scheme and have it prove convincing enough to demand Michael's personal attention required manipulating funds, erasing documents and constructing a façade of chaos which would inevitably result in someone or many losing their well-earned jobs.

No matter how desperate he was for Michael to learn about the child that bore his face, but not his name, Tom could not justify making victims of innocent people as a means to an end. Three weeks of fruitless attempts of devising a convincing charade had passed when nature stepped in to lend a hand.

The call came during the early morning hours, the sun yet to make an appearance in the Texas sky. Tom struggled to consciousness, his outstretched arm fumbling along his nightstand in an attempt to squelch the incessant chirping of his cell phone.

Still half asleep, he listened to the voice on the other end, each word registering slowly in his mind. Hampton Roads had been hit by a Nor Easter, the strongest one to date with flooding and gale force winds to rival that of any hurricane in the past twenty years. Power to half the city was still out, trees were down, and several people had lost their lives. Tom's sleepy haze quickly dissipated and was replaced by a sense of urgency.

"Mr. Hogan," said the voice on the other end, "Collier Center suffered significant structural damage. Either you or Mr. Collier need to come out here as soon as possible."

Tom sat up quickly in bed nearly waking Jocelyn asleep beside him. The answer he desperately sought, delivered by fate herself.

"Okay Al, not a problem. I'll have Mike on a plane first thing this morning."

Never in his life had Tom been grateful for a natural disaster. He knew the situation being what it was demanded Michael's attention. He may go grudgingly with a bit of coaxing on Tom's part, but go he would.

Later that morning Michael stood undaunted at Tom's request.

"What time's my flight?" he asked without the slightest him of opposition.

A look of total surprise washed over tom. The battle had been fought and won before it had begun.

"You'll go then?" he asked, incredulous of Michael's easy acceptance at the prospect of returning to Virginia. "Just like that? No argument?"

Michael stood and took his itinerary from Tom's hands. He quickly scanned the first page.

"No, no argument," he said flatly.

Not only was he not going to argue the subject, Michael was eager to be on his way. He had seen the reports on the early morning news. Southeast Virginia had been hit hard overnight. Scenes of the flooding and devastation flashed across the screen before him. Homes had been destroyed, trees upturned. Everywhere rescue attempts still in progress for those victims in areas of flash flooding. Many had been injured and several lives lost, yet no names were given.

Michael's chest tightened, all color draining from his face as he watched in horror the images of entire families waiting in fear on rooftops for rescue boats to pass their way. Cars floated haphazardly through flooded roadways, trees toppled smashing through houses.

The storm had been expected to move quickly through the area yet stalled during the late hours of the night trapping many residents unaware. Michael's blood ran cold, a barrage of unanswered questions assaulting his troubled mind. This changed everything.

"Dear God, let her be okay," he said aloud.

He needed to hear her voice. He needed to know something, anything. Michael dialed Nichole's number having no idea what he would say should she answer. His pulse raced, the implications of each unanswered ring increasing his anxiety, his stomach turning in knots. Finally, he was greeted with an automated message that service to the area was unavailable. Michael hurled first a curse and then his phone, its casing shattering at his feet into broken pieces of plastic and metal.

Michael's self-imposed exile from the life of Nichole McCallister was at an end. He resolved to fly the company jet to Virginia himself if need be, but he needed to see with his own eyes that she lived and breathed. He would not intrude upon her life uncertain if the hurt he had caused still lingered within her as it had him. For now he would be content to merely gaze upon her from a distance, yet the whirl of emotions coursing through him at the mere thought of seeing her again suggested otherwise.

He had lost precious time punishing himself, wallowing in his own misery when all the while he should have done whatever necessary to earn back Nichole's trust. To have her by his side each night as he slept, to wake each morning with the warm effervescence of her smile to great him and to know that beyond a shadow of a doubt that she was safe and protected, those were the things that mattered most.

Years wasted on women who were as cold and empty inside as he was, women who had given their bodies eagerly, in the end to be denied the love they desperately sought. Only one woman was capable of stirring emotions in him that were intense, raw and uncontainable. Michael had never loved any woman before Nichole and he believed himself incapable of ever loving another in her stead. To continue to deny the truth was nothing short of insanity.

"No Tom," he said with a sly, confident air, "no argument at all. As a matter of fact, I would say this trip was long overdue."

Though the storm had showed no mercy, McCallister's had come through unscathed. Having withstood two hundred years of downpours, droughts and blustering winds, its foundation was sound, constructed of brick and stone it had literally stood the test of time.

Nichole had been born and raised in Hampton Roads. She knew well to never underestimate the fickle disposition of Mother Nature in her part of the world. The moment she became aware that they were in the projected path of the storm she closed for business and in turn opened the restaurant's doors as a shelter to friends and family, employees, and any passerby in need of refuge.

It was behind sturdy walls, with ample food, free flowing drink and a warm fire they all passed the hours as the stinging rains mercilessly pelted the world around them.

"She looks like an angel when she sleeps," Max said as he spread his blanket on the floor next to Nichole and a soundly sleeping Hanna.

Nichole nodded in agreement. "Yet how easily her wings give way to horns once those eyes open."

"Your father says she's a miniature version of you when you were her age."

Nichole let loose a muffled laugh, the flames of the fire warming her face as she looked down at her daughter.

"She may have my temperament," she agreed, "and my eyes, but the rest . . . the rest is Michael. Her voice was shadowed with sadness.

Max crossed his legs in front of him and took Nichole by the hand.

"You still miss him," he said as more fact than question. "After all this time you still love him don't you, Nikki?"

Nichole winced as if his words had pierced an open wound. She turned her face to the window, gazing out into the night with a far off look. It had proven less difficult than she had thought, to conceal her true feelings from those around her. The restaurant, Hanna's heart condition, the endless task of being a single mother all proved to be successful temporary distractions, yet did nothing to ease the pain or curb her longing for the touch of the one man capable of reaching her and pulling her out from the clutches of her tormented past.

Single-handedly he had erased the terror that hung heavy in her eyes, yet placed a haunting sadness in its wake. In spite of it all Nichole knew within her heart that she would do it all again without hesitation. Despite the ever-present aching need inside her, Michael Collier had brought about her metamorphosis from a frightened young girl to a proud determined woman. She swallowed hard and fought back against the sting of tears.

"Yes, I still love him. And I honestly believe that I will go to my grave loving him silently, from a distance, but I have accepted my fate and made peace with it if you will." Her face softened as she admitted her secret truth, her gaze distant and a subtle smile played upon her lips as if she were locked away within some precious memory.

Max reached out and gently grasped her chin, turning her delicate face in his direction.

"Nikki, it doesn't have to be this way. You know that."

"Oh Maxie, I love you dearly, but you're wrong. I never told Michael I was carrying his baby, I've kept her hidden from him for two years. He'd never forgive me for that. Not to mention the fact that in that time I've probably been replaced a dozen times over at least."

Max shook his head and quickly waved a dismissive hand.

"Honey you underestimate yourself," he said sincerely. "I don't believe that for one minute. I saw the way that man looked at you Nik. He studied your every move when you were in the room almost as if he couldn't believe you were real or as if he were afraid you would disappear into the clouds with the other angels."

Nichole leaned in to kiss Max on the cheek. If only she were as certain, she might have put an end to this madness a long time ago. Not a day had passed since the moment she had met Michael Collier that he hadn't dominated her thoughts. Each time she closed her eyes he was there holding her, making love to her, rescuing her again and again from her past, from herself.

She knew she was blessed to have true friends and a devoted family at her side and she was grateful, but it was the memory of Michael's touch that warmed her on cold nights such as this. To have known love and passion so completely indefinable, all consuming and then have fate rip it from your grasp was a form of inner torment that was impossible to break free of.

Max retrieved a bottle of Nichole's favorite wine from behind the bar and a plate of steaming hot appetizers from the kitchen. She had been busy all evening taking care of everyone else's needs and seeing to the safety and comfort of those around her that, as oftentimes happened, Nichole neglected to take care of herself, the storm, yet another element of surprise in an already chaotic life. She needed a warm meal and rest. That Max could see to himself. But what she needed most was peace of mind.

Nichole picked at her plate and graciously accepted the wine. It felt warm and soothing going down and helped to relax her troubled mind. They spoke of Hanna's impending exam. In the worst of weather, the Children's Hospital never closed its doors. She would have to make her way through back roads and detour flooded streets, but she would be there bright and early. If all went well this time around she would not have to return for a full year. She would be free to be a child, to laugh and play and be free of the ties that bound her closely to the adult world of hospitals and endless arrays of testing. Despite Max's reassurance, Nichole's stomach turned in knots each time she thought about it. How desperately she yearned for this phase of life's lessons to be over.

As the winds faded to a whisper and the fury from the sky moved out to sea, finally she slept a rather peaceful sleep, her daughter nestled at her side. Nichole and those around her passed the storm tranquil and unaware of the true tempest about to blow into town.

Chapter 29

BY THE TIME HIS plane had landed, Michael had already abandoned his plan to seek out Nichole inconspicuously. Throughout the flight reports filtered through via the pilot concerning flooded areas of highway, roads blocked due to fallen trees and the availability of the few hotels that remained fully intact.

For a terrifying moment, he sat frozen in his seat. If harm had come to her, if somewhere she lay hurt and frightened, victim to the storm he would never forgive himself. He needed to be close to her, to see life in those eyes that had captivated him time and again. It was pure selfishness on his part and he knew that well, but certain as he was that his soul was already damned to hell he had nothing left to lose.

Nichole had given him the only true moments of happiness he had ever known. A single smile perched on her full, supple lips or an inviting glance of her hypnotic stare cast playfully in his direction and suddenly all was right with the world.

Time had done nothing to erase her memory that had been seared into his being. The sound of her laughter still lingered in his ears when the world around his was quiet, images of their bodies pressed together in throws of passion still fired his blood. They were a perfect fit as if her body had been molded by the angels especially for him.

Michael had made his peace with the knowledge that he was to expend the rest of his days with nothing but his memories to sustain him. He could live his life in some form of contentment knowing that somewhere Nichole McCallister lived and breathed and God willing had found happiness in spite of him, but he could not begin to fathom the prospect of living in a world without her in it. The mere thought of it horrified him and he quickly pushed it from his mind.

She would think he had gone mad at best, showing up without a word after all this time, slap him perhaps, and storm off without a word. A fate which he knew he richly deserved. Regardless he would find her. To know she was alive, safe, and unharmed would have to be enough.

He made his way through the airport terminal with long determined strides eager to retrieve his belongings and be on his way. Yet as soon as he stepped foot into the baggage claim area he was stopped in his tracks. Jocelyn's words rang true. The display advertising McCallister's Restaurant could not be missed.

Dominating the wall before him it stood five feet tall by three feet wide, the letters that made up her name written in bold letters of gold foil against a darkened background. A clear photo of the building itself surrounded by smaller photos of the interior filled with smiling, joyful guests, and plates of steaming delicacies before them.

Michael walked toward the wall as if in a trance oblivious to the stream of travelers in his path. Frantically he scanned each face in the photos desperate to find Nichole among them, his fingers tracing the surface of the protective glass covering to no avail. A disappointed sigh escaped his lips; the only face he longed to see was missing. However, there was a complete address and phone number listed among the information given, an acceptable consolation prize for the time being.

Quickly he jotted down the address on the back of the plane ticket he held in his hand. When he glanced up a second time to retrieve the phone listing he saw it there, a small subtle line near the bottom of the display; *Proprietors Nichole McCallister and Maxwell Porter.*

He drove in brooding silence to the Landmark Hotel where Tom had a room waiting for him. Though he was momentarily consoled by the knowledge that Nichole was doing well for herself in the aftermath of the destruction wrought by his ex-wife, one thought tormented him, Max Porter.

Max had been responsible for saving Nichole's life, she beamed whenever the man entered a room and had admitted herself that he was her closest friend. Max was there the night of the Grand Opening turned Grand Disaster and undoubtedly remained to help her put back together the pieces of her life that Michael himself was responsible for shattering. How could Nichole help but to fall in love with such a man and who would blame her.

Michael ground his jaw, the muscles of his face twitching. His expression darkened at the thought of any man's hands upon her. Never in his life had he envied another man, yet when he thought of Max Porter, his emotions betrayed him. Nevertheless, it was a situation of his making and Michael was never a man to shrink from facing his fate.

He made his way to his hotel room shortly after eleven and once in the solitude of the walls that surrounded him he quickly dialed the number he had jotted down.

"McCallister's, this is David how can I help you?" a voice answered.

Finally Michael thought, a human voice and not some damned recording. At least that was a good sign. They had power and phone service and were open despite the storm. Michael cleared his throat before speaking. His emotions were all over the place. He needed to know if Nichole was safe and he needed to know now, reduced to questioning the teenage host of a restaurant.

"I need to speak with the owner," he demanded, "is she in?"

"No sir. Mr. Porter is available if you'd like to speak with him?"

"No thank you," Michael replied, sounding increasingly irritated. "I need to speak with Nichole McCallister, is she due in today?"

"Yes sir, later this afternoon around two I think.

Michael swallowed hard and closed his eyes. This kid better know what he's talking about he thought to himself. He questioned further.

"She's all right then, she wasn't hurt in the storm?"

The voice on the other end faltered for a moment not expecting the current line of questioning.

"No sir . . . she's fine I spoke with her myself this morning. Can I leave her a message?"

"No. No message," Michael said quickly and hung up the phone.

His chin fell to his chest and the air escaped his lungs in a giant whoosh. Relief washed over him like warm rays of sunshine in the dead of winter. Nichole was safe and for the moment that was all that mattered. She wasn't due in until two. It was best this way. Had she known he was in town she may have never have agreed to see him, arriving unannounced gave her little choice in the matter. Michael looked down at his watch. He had three hours to shower, dress, and prepare for what would be the most important meeting of his life.

The area of Settlers Cove surrounding McCallister's revealed no evidence of the crippling, destructive force of nature that had thrashed Hampton Roads the night before. Dark, threatening clouds made way for a brilliant clear sky, golden rays of sunlight penetrated a thick canopy of leaves overhead, and the winds remained still, nary a breeze to be found for miles.

Michael stepped from his vehicle a menacing figure, his hair black as night falling slightly across his brow with a hint of fatigue splayed across his rugged, perfectly chiseled features. He paused momentarily to eye the structure before him when a slow smile of admiration crept upon his lips. The scene that unfolded around him echoed the Nichole he had grown to know and love. The beauty of nature pure and untamed blending with the strength of rising pillars and towering oaks, powerfully alluring like the lady herself. Michael had never doubted her ability to forge ahead no matter what the circumstance but with this wonder she had outdone herself and he stood admiring her conquest with pride.

As he stalked his way toward the entrance the broadness of his shoulders and physique cast shadows on the still damp ground before him. His heart was in his throat and he winced at the knowledge that for the first time in his life he was actually nervous at the prospect of approaching a woman.

It wasn't the idea of approaching her as much as it was about the reception he was sure to receive. She had every right to toss him out on his ass without as much as a hello. In the blissful months they had spent together, night after glorious night of lovemaking he had said the words I_love you only once and that he had saved for when his head was on the chopping block. What reason did she have to believe him now?

Once inside, he had requested a discrete booth neatly tucked away in a distant corner, invisible from the curious glances of any wandering eyes, practically invisible to Nichole herself should she happen to pass through unaware. He made his way through the crowd unnoticed and breathed a small sigh of relief. Longing for a tall brandy to steel his nerves he opted for black coffee instead knowing well his mind needed to be clear for the line of questioning sure to ensue.

Dear God, no woman had ever wielded such power over him, but no woman had ever opened herself up to him as Nichole had. The beauty, the courage, the passion that made up this unique creature he had never seen the likes of before. To carry such darkness and bear it before him alone served to free not only herself but Michael as well from the bonds of the past. She was hope and light and she was his, but for only a short time and now he was hell-bent on doing whatever possible to win back what he had carelessly lost.

Ten minutes had passed and his anticipation grew. The space he had chosen provided privacy yet offered little in terms of room to move his cramped and tired body. His shelter of anonymity proved to be all too fleeting when an old familiar face spied him from beyond the kitchen doors. Max Porter was stunned to a halt mid-step among a throng of wait staff sending the entrees of several soon to be disappointed patrons to the floor with a resounding crash. The moment of truth had arrived.

Chapter 30

"NIKKI . . . Nichole."

The voice grew louder with each word yet the sound of her name being called aloud failed to register in Nichole's troubled mind. The slight touch of a cool hand on her shoulder caused her to flinch and recoil unexpectedly from such a simple gesture.

"Good Lord child," Estelle Peterman said aloud. "What on earth has you wound so tight?"

Nervously twisting the thin band of pearls that accented her neck, Nichole quickly regained her composure at the welcomed sight of concern emanating from the stoic old woman before her.

"Oh damn," Nichole said, clasping Estelle's soft wrinkled hand, "I'm sorry, Estelle. I'm a bit distracted at the moment."

Estelle stepped back to survey the situation. Nichole's face was flushed and wrought with worry, her hands slightly trembling.

Paling slightly herself, she questioned almost frantically, "It's not Hanna? Tell me nothing is wrong with the baby."

Nichole quickly threw her hands up in protest, her eyes widening.

"No, no, nothing like that. Hanna's fine. She's in the office with Maxie."

"Well, what is it, honey?" Estelle asked. "You look like you've seen a ghost."

Nichole brushed back a strand of long dark hair from her face and swallowed hard.

"It's Michael. He's here and he's waiting to see me."

This time it was Estelle's eyes that widened. Quickly she shuffled her way to the arch that separated the hostess station from the main dining room and spied him immediately, his devilish good looks standing out in the crowd from the secluded corner in which he sat.

"Well it's about damned time," the feisty gray-haired woman muttered to herself.

Despite what had happened between the two Estelle had always believed in her heart that Michael truly loved Nichole, as did everyone else who had ever witnessed the two together, save Nichole. Yes, he had made a mistake, screwed up in royal fashion to use the old woman's words, but his feelings for Nichole were undeniably etched in his expression whenever she was in the room, a possessive hand placed upon her whenever she was within reach, his gaze quietly in search of her whenever she was beyond his view. When he left Virginia and Nichole without a fight Estelle had berated him silently for months, but knew in her heart that a time would come someday in the future that he would stop listening to his head and follow his heart back to her. Little did he know of all that awaited him.

"Poor boy doesn't stand a chance," she uttered before returning to Nichole.

She slipped a thin arm around Nichole's shoulder and looked at her with compassion.

"This is a long time coming don't you think?" she said.

Nichole nodded. "I know, but I need a few moments to gather up the courage to go over there and face him."

"Bah," Estelle roared. "You need courage? Nichole McCallister look at you. Look around you. By the age of twenty-one, you survived the darkest life had to offer. With a heart in tatters and a swollen belly you built all of this," she said, making a sweeping gesture with her arms, "and made one hell of a name for yourself. You brought a sick baby to health and raised her every day of her life on your own and you're going to sit there and tell me you need to search for courage.

Nonsense."

Nichole smiled sheepishly, thankful for the boundless wisdom and impeccable timing of such a great lady and friend.

"Now you listen to me," Estelle continued, "you march your butt over there with your head held high. He is on your territory this time and that man only has as much power over you as you give him."

Warmed by her words Nichole smiled in earnest.

"How did you get to be so smart, Estelle?" she asked.

"Oh honey, you don't get to live as long as I have by being stupid," she replied.

Estelle had agreed to fetch Hanna from the office, slip out the back door and watch her until Nichole returned home. She also let it be known with a wink that it would be quite all right for Hanna to spend the night if Nichole found it necessary to not to return home until the following morning. That, Nichole assured her, was not a remote possibility.

Nichole stood and squared her shoulders. Looking down she gave herself one last surveying glance. The dress she wore was form fitting yet sophisticated, pearls dangled from her ears and hung around her neck, her sable hair long and flowing.

As she walked the length of the dining room to the booth where Michael sat waiting, several hands reached out to her from frequent visitors among the crowd. She forced an amiable smile and kind welcome to each and every one all the while her heart banged violently against her chest. Every nerve in her body felt as if it were on fire and inches from his table she prepared herself for one of the greatest performances of her life.

Michael sat unaware, staring into his cup completely lost in his thoughts. When a familiar voice echoed his name, his head snapped in her direction. For several moments of stunned silence, their eyes locked rendering them both mute, the world around them suddenly seeming quiet and still.

Nichole was the first to look away, her attempt at appearing cool and detached failing miserably the moment the ice-blue eyes of Michael Collier fell upon her. Instantly he stood and motioned to the empty seat across from him.

"Please, Nichole," he said softly, "have a seat."

The next few minutes seemed to drag on endlessly in awkward silence, neither knowing what to say. Michael's expression was somber and tinged with sadness. He held no pretenses, his emotions laid bare for all the world to see. Inwardly it felt as if a dagger had pierced his heart, to be this close after all this time and still be unable to simply reach out and touch the one woman that not only had the ability to warm his blood and fire his passion but bend his will and redefine his existence. It was brutal agony.

"You are still amazingly beautiful," he spoke finally.

The words rolled off his tongue slowly, the tone of his voice velvety and soothing. Nichole gave a half smile. This was quickly becoming a slow form of torment for her as well. His mere presence had an intoxicating effect upon her, confusing her senses and dizzying her mind.

Nichole bit at her bottom lip not quite certain what to say. She wanted to scream and yell, to let him know how badly he had hurt her, make him brutally aware of all that she was left to struggle with. She wanted to cry because of the child that she carried and had raised alone, the endless nights spent at the side of a helpless infant plied with plastic tubes and steel machines in a cold and sterile hospital and she wanted to laugh at the irony of it all. Now he had come, when the greatest of battles declared won.

"Michael, why are you here?" she questioned plainly in a last ditch effort to maintain some control of the situation.

He visibly winced. Now that was the reception he had expected and yet was surprised at how much her words stung. He clasped his hands together in front of him and looked her in the eye hoping for mercy, knowing he deserved none.

"Angel, I know I have no right to show up here unannounced. I would be the most presumptuous bastard that ever lived to expect that you'd be remotely happy about my presence here. When I turned on the television this morning and saw news of the storm that swept through Tidewater I . . . I needed to know that you were safe. I needed to know that you weren't out there somewhere hurt and afraid."

Michael's eyes revealed that the words he spoke were true, looking at Nichole yet through her, his darkening orbs gave warning of a smoldering storm under the surface of his cool exterior.

Nichole was moved yet still skeptical. She wanted desperately to believe that despite the past and the time spent apart that it was true concern for her that spurred his inexplicable return, yet with Michael Collier she had learned that fact and fiction had a tendency to blur and she would need to proceed wearily for the sake of her sanity.

"So," she questioned hesitantly, "you decided to hop on a plane and fly over a thousand miles instead of merely picking up the phone and calling?"

"I tried calling you, angel, many times but all I got was an irritating automated message that service was unavailable due to the storm. You know me . . ."

"Do I?" Nichole cut him off sharply. "I thought I did once, but that was a long time ago," she said her melancholy tone quickly giving way to the raw pain still simmering beneath her skin. "At one time Michael, I truly believed I knew you better than any other person that walked this Earth, but there were a few major details about yourself that you neglected to share. I honestly have no idea who you are."

Michael scanned the wall behind her, searching his mind for the magical words to right this wrong. So much time had passed and yet the emotions were still raw and biting. How could this one woman be both heaven and hell to him? The essence of her perfume surrounded him, tormenting him. How many mornings had he woken to the scent of her lingering in his bed after making love to her the whole night through? She had seared herself into his thoughts; she would forever be a part of him.

Michael took a deep breath and sighed as Nichole quietly studied him. He was still damned dangerously enticing, his shoulders broad and strong, his powerful presence, and his all too familiar dark, brooding good looks. He was unchanged, yet she could not deny the worried look that darkened his eyes.

Taking advantage of the silence, he took Nichole's small hand in both of his and held tightly. To his surprise, she did not resist. She sat still, as if stunned and stared at the strong warm hands encircling her. He had anticipated anger and bitterness, but in her expression she wore only signs of pain and sadness. The wake of all the damage he had caused etched on her delicate features. A wave of regret washed over him that was crippling.

He tilted his head to meet her and without blinking met her gaze.

"Please. Nichole. Hear me out. Give me a chance to explain," he said softly.

Nichole sat quietly trying to think, an uncertain look upon her face, her heart betraying her mind.

"Why now Michael?" she asked. "Why now after all this time has passed?"

He tightened his grasp on her hand ever so slightly.

"Nikki, I tried to explain that night all hell broke loose. I wanted to tell you everything, but the look in your eyes . . . I knew that no matter how good my intentions, selfish though they were, the damage had been done. What Caroline did, what I did by not telling you about her, it was unforgivable. I left hoping that in time you might forgive me, try to contact me, but fear and regret kept me away."

He reached up and brushed away a lock of sable hair that danced across her cheek, a slight touch of hand, yet enough to cause Nichole's pulse to quicken. She uttered a slight sound and looked away into nothingness. He mind was spinning in all directions at once. Who coveted the most unforgiveable secret now? Who told the most damaging lie she thought to herself? Or were they ever lies at all? Sins of omission perhaps or simply words not spoken?

How could she punish him from hiding a wife he was trying to divorce while she sat here keeping his child her treasured secret? Right and wrong suddenly began to blur. There was no black, there was no white, it was all gray.

In truth her anger had faded years ago, it was the pain that lingered fueling her coolness toward him. Despite the gnawing fear of reliving the old hurts once again, Nichole knew all too well that there was much more than her heart to consider. She owed it to her daughter, their daughter to at least hear him out. Her stare rose to meet his and a subtle smile of submission gave rise to her lips.

"Okay, Michael, I'll listen to what you have to say, but not here."

Inside Michael breathed a sigh of relief and the tension eased from his expression. Being this close to Nichole after endless days and nights without her was bittersweet torment. The sight of her set his body on fire, holding her hand while his arms remained empty, longing for her to fill them. She belonged to him, they belonged to each other and he was hell-bent on making her realize it as well. For now she was willing to listen and he would push no further, at least not yet.

Chapter 31

NICHOLE MADE HER WAY through rush hour traffic in a daze, a myriad of thoughts running through her mind. Fortune and fate, wielding their power once again in her life in such a cruel and beautiful way. Michael Collier was back in Virginia and from all appearances wanted her back in his life. For now that is, until he learned the truth, the truth that was likely to turn whatever love he still held for her into loathing and disdain. Damaged pride and a wounded heart all seemed trivial now. Hanna was what mattered most now, her future, her happiness, her right to know her father.

Walking through the threshold of the sanctuary that she called home, Nichole was greeted by the sounds of splashing and laughter. Despite all that weighed on her there was no sound more soothing to her soul than the hearty belly laugh of her baby girl. Kicking off her shoes she followed the scents of bubble bath and baby shampoo down the winding hallway and smiled brightly at the sight before her.

"Is there a baby somewhere underneath all of those bubbles?"

At the sound of her mother's voice, Hanna's tiny hands flew into the air sending soapsuds across the room.

"Bubbles mama," she exclaimed with the innocent awe that only a child possess.

“I see that baby, lots of bubbles.”

The bathtub filled to nearly overflowing, a white sparkling foam covering Hanna from head to toe, Nichole sent a questioning glance to Estelle.

“Any chance you may have overdone it a bit, Estelle?” Nichole asked, trying to suppress her laughter.

“Hanna made me do it,” the old woman replied in mock defense.

“Hanna is two years old she can’t make you do anything.”

Towel in hand, Nichole plucked her squirming, giggling daughter from the water.

“Nichole McCallister that is a bold faced lie and you know it, “she retorted, “that little girl of yours has unknowingly dictated the moods and movements of everyone she

has come in contact with since the day she was born.”

Nichole surveyed the babe in her arms; the dark silky hair, a tiny button of a nose, eyes bright and hopeful. To know Hanna was to love her. She was a magical being, precious and sacred, sent from a place far greater than Earth. To Nichole, she was life itself. To those lucky enough to fall under the spell of her tiny beaming smile, she was hope.

“I see your point Estelle. Let’s hope she has the same effect on her father.”

“You told him, well thank God.”

“No, not yet, but I’m going to. I couldn’t tell him there in the middle of the restaurant, I have no idea how he’s going to react. He’s supposed to call later this evening. We’ll set a time and place to meet tomorrow. I’ll tell him then.”

“He’ll be thrilled, I know it.”

“He’ll be furious . . . or worse,” she paused a sinking feeling in her stomach, “completely indifferent.”

“You know, Nikki, you never gave Michael enough credit. Now, I know he hurt you and I’m not trying to justify what he did to you, but I believe with all my heart that boy has loved you from the moment he laid eyes on you, I’ll bet the bank he still does and he doesn’t stand a chance against that angel in your lap.”

“What if he hates me for not telling him? What if he doesn’t want

Hanna? In the time we were together he never mentioned anything about wanting children."

"Bah, have faith child, for once in your life let down your defenses. You can never see the view clearly from behind guarded walls."

The sun had almost set, the faintest glimpse of a purple hue barely visible on the horizon, Hanna was sleeping, tucked safely in her bed blissfully unaware of how her world was about to change in such a monumental way and still there was no call from Michael. Estelle had left well over an hour ago and unable to relax Nichole paced the floor rehearsing in her mind the conversation she both dreaded and eagerly anticipated. She startled at the sound of the front door opening.

"Honey, I'm home," Maxie announced as he entered, overnight bag in one hand, bottle of wine in the other.

"I don't need a babysitter, you do know that right?"

"Of course you don't, that's why you've almost worn a path through the carpet with your pacing."

Placing a kiss on her forehead he deposited his bag in the guest room, then retrieved two wine glasses from the kitchen. Making his way to the sofa he patted the space beside him, "Sit," he commanded and poured the chilled Pino. "Now drink."

Nichole did as she was told. There was no point in arguing with Maxie, at times it seemed he knew her better than she knew herself. He knew she would be obsessing, driving herself insane and as always he showed up without asking, exactly when she needed him most.

"Did you tell your parents?"

"No," she choked out, almost spilling her wine. "The last thing I need to deal with right now is my father beating his chest and my mother's nervous breakdown. Tonight I'm entitled to a nervous breakdown of my own."

"You're not going to have a nervous breakdown," he said putting an arm around her.

Nichole leaned into him, her back snug against his chest and sighed.

"I promise one of these days you can have a crisis of your own and I'll be there to pick up the pieces."

"I have no doubt and this isn't a crisis, Nikki. I'm with Estelle on this one. I think it's a good thing. It will all work out, you'll see," he reassured her.

"I'm glad you're gay, Maxie."

"Excuse me," he laughed aloud.

"No, I'm serious . . ."

"Exactly how much wine have you had," he interrupted.

She playfully punched his arm. "Will you listen to me?"

"I'm sorry, please continue."

"When a woman has a gay man as a best friend she knows for a fact that he is truly her friend. There are no ulterior motives; he's not trying to take advantage of any crappy situation she's in to get into her pants. She knows he loves her for her. It's rare and its special and I love you for it."

Maxie couldn't help but smile. He'd never thought of it that way. "I love you to Nikki."

The sound of her phone chirping to life rendered them both silent. They looked at each other, then at the phone on the table in front of them. Nichole sat frozen unable to move, staring at the piece of plastic and metal as if it were a lethal creature ready to strike. Max snatched it from its resting place and deposited it firmly in her hand.

"Answer it," he said, standing, "I'll give you some privacy. I have a few calls I need to make myself."

Nichole hit the answer button and spoke softly trying to conceal from her voice the shaking she felt inside.

"Hello."

"Hello, angel."

She closed her eyes and dropped her head to her chest. With several glasses of wine working their way through her bloodstream, the mere sound of his husky voice using his pet name for her melted her defenses.

"I'm sorry I called so late," he continued, "I've spent the last few hours dealing with the storm damage at the art center."

Of course, it hadn't occurred to her that he might be here on business, leaving her as a mere afterthought. The realization stung causing her to visibly wince.

"The center . . . the storm, that's why you're here." Her voice was no longer able to hide her true feelings and Michael quickly picked up on her change in her demeanor.

"No Nichole that's not why I'm here. I won't lie, the center is the excuse I fed myself to get my ass on the plane should you have refused to see me, but make no mistake about it, you are the real reason I'm here. You and you alone." His tone had a severity to it she could not ignore. "Now please tell me you haven't changed your mind about meeting me tomorrow. There are many things that I need to explain to you."

Not half as much as I need to explain to you, she thought to herself.

"No, Michael, I haven't changed my mind."

He breathed and audible sigh of relief. "Thank you, angel."

"Don't thank me yet," she mumbled, not intending for him to hear.

"What's that?" he asked.

"Huh . . . oh nothing . . . where would you like to meet?"

By the time the conversation had ended Nichole was surprised to find that her shaking hands had steadied. The weight of carrying her secret for so long was finally about to be lifted and she found peace in the realization that she was in fact making the right decision for everyone involved no matter the outcome. Secrets had that way about them, no matter how desperately the bearer fought to keep them banished to the darkness, they always managed to work their way into the light to be known, for better or worse.

She lay in bed that night thinking back to the day they had met. He was an imposing figure, oozing charm and good looks, gruff yet tender. They had shared a mutual unspoken attraction for months, tiptoeing around each other with a stolen glance here, a sly innuendo there. In no time at all he had broken down her walls and she ended up in his arms and his bed. She mused at how right things were with the illustrious Michael Collier, how passionate and intense, right up until the moment it all fell apart. Now almost three years later he was back to sit down with Nichole, to right the wrongs of the past and unbeknownst to him, to meet the child he never knew he had.

Michael sat on the sofa in his hotel suite, feet propped up on the table in front of him. He left the balcony doors open wide ensuring he could hear the rush of the ocean, smell salt air. Losing his tie he dropped it to the floor in front of him and raked a hand through his thick black hair.

The conversation with Nichole had gone as well as could be expected considering the circumstances, yet he was left with wanting much more. That was always the problem where she was concerned, from the moment he had laid eyes on her he wanted to touch her, from the moment he touched her it fueled a need to possess her. When it came to Nichole McCallister, he could never have his fill.

Their time apart had proved the cruel truth to him day after day, night after endless night. He had hoped that time would fade the feeling he had for her, wash away the memory of the magic in her touch. Weeks turned into months, months into years and she still dominated his thoughts with every rising sun. Filling the hole she had left in his life was pointless. He was a self-destructive hollow shell before her and reverted back to the same soulless, empty creature without her. However, now she was here, within arm's reach and made a silent vow to take back what was his.

He absentmindedly flipped through the call list on his phone. Tom had called four times throughout the day, but Michael had been either too distracted or too busy to take his call. Now was as good a time as any. He dialed the number and Tom answered on the first ring.

"Mike what the hell," his voice bellowed through the receiver.

"Simmer down there slugger, what's with the urgency?"

Tom paused, he had to proceed with caution. This was a delicate situation he was supposed to know nothing of.

"I was concerned is all, Collier Center, the storm, the damage. How bad is it?"

"It's a mess, but a manageable mess," he said "I have crews working through the night to get things up and running as soon as possible."

"Okay sounds good," Tom replied. "Anything else? How was the flight? See any old faces?"

It wasn't like Tom to make small talk, he was always a straight to the point kind of guy. Michael smiled to himself. Leave it to the Hogan's to take a natural disaster and turn it into a matchmaking opportunity. This has Jocelyn written all over it. He chuckled aloud and decided to put his best friend out of his hen-pecked misery.

"Tom I saw Nichole if that is what you and that lovely wife of yours are getting at."

"You did," his voice boomed through the receiver sounding oddly relieved. "Well, how is she? What did she have to say?"

"Hogan you really need to start spending a little less time at home."

"Answer the damn question Mike."

"Nichole is fine. She's actually doing quite well for herself. She has her own restaurant in Williamsburg, the storm barely touched that area of Tidewater, but the good news is she didn't throw hot coffee in my face when she saw me."

Tom forced a laugh, yet inside he was conflicted. What about the baby he thought over and over unable to say a word about the child was driving him half-mad.

"Well that's progress," he replied. "Did she have anyone with her?"

"Anyone with her? Tom, what the hell are getting at? You mean like a man?"

"No, it's nothing, forget I asked. Are you going to see her again?"

Michael dismissed Tom's bizarre inquiry. It had to be Jocelyn. Her mission in life the past few years seemed to be single-handedly procuring Michael his happily ever after.

"To say the least she was a bit surprised to see me and we didn't talk for long but she's agreed to meet me tomorrow morning. I'm not going to lie, man. I'm going to do whatever it takes to win her back. I can't say for sure when I'll return to Houston.

Tom Hogan was finally appeased. If Mike was determined to win Nichole back then he would go through hell and high water to make it happen and in the process he was bound to learn the truth.

"All right, Mike, I've got things covered here. Get some sleep and give me a call tomorrow let me know how it all works out. Good luck."

Michael threw back his head and rolled his eyes.

"Thanks, man. I'm going to need it."

Chapter 32

NICHOLE HAD INSISTED ON a semi-private place for their meeting point. She had witnessed Michaels temper in the past and although it had never actually been directed at her, she had no desire to be in a crowded public space should he decided to blow. Nor did she want the seclusion of his hotel suite. It was brutally evident from their brief meeting at McCallister's that the intense chemistry between them was still as powerful as ever. She had done her best to hide it, but it was there pulling at her chest. The desire to touch him and be touched by him was too great, best not to risk the temptation.

In the end, they had agreed upon the walking trails at First Landing State Park. Located near the Chesapeake Bay in Virginia Beach it was a nature lover's oasis smack dab in the middle of a busy city teaming with people. Almost three thousand acres of botanical beauty, it was a perfect setting to escape the outside world. Families walked their dogs along the paths of the maritime forests, lovers passing hand in hand, it was a peaceful place, tranquil and serene. Nichole hoped that the beauty of their surroundings would help to soften the impact of the secret she was about to reveal.

She chose a pair of tan shorts that flattered her derriere without being too tight and tawdry, an off the shoulder pale green sweater embellished with gold thread, strappy sandals on her feet and good hoops adorned her ears.

She arrived at the Ranger's Station where they were to meet a full half hour before Michael was to arrive. She had always loved the tranquility of the place, yet her visits were far too few. The hectic schedule she kept did not often allow for woodland getaways. She walked a short distance into the Bald Cypress Trail, took a deep breath, and sighed. Cypress trees grew out of the marshes around her reaching thirty, forty feet into the sky, the hanging moss that clung to their branches blowing in the breeze, lending a haunting quality to her surroundings.

Nichole closed her eyes and fought to steady the growing anxiety inside her. She did not hear his approach, yet when his hand landed gently on her shoulder she stood stoic with her back to him, unflinching.

"Hello, Michael," she said turning to face him.

"Hello, angel." He mouthed the words more than spoke them.

He wore tight-fitting jeans and a snug fitting black shirt that accentuated the muscles in his arms and chest. Nichole felt a flutter low in her stomach. Michael was always firm and muscular, but it was apparent that he had been spending a lot of quality time in the weight room during their time apart.

He reached out and placed a hand on her cheek, silently thrilled when instead of turning away from his touch she rolled her head into it.

"It's been far too long Nichole, I've missed you."

She nodded in agreement. Words escaped her. His touch had lingered too long. She stepped back breaking the spell he was weaving in her direction and let his hand fall to his side.

"Let's walk," she suggested.

He fell in step with her and they rambled mostly about things that were completely inconsequential to them both, the Art Center, her restaurant, trying to break the ice, attempting to avoid the awkwardness, failing miserably at both. The idle chitchat was driving him mad. After years of making love to her in his mind from thousands of miles away she was close enough to touch, close enough to taste and he desperately longed to do both.

Michael studied her as she spoke, the exotic green eyes that cast a spell on him the first time he dared to look into them, the full red lips that knew every inch of his body intimately, and swell of her breasts from beneath her sweater taunted him. Crossing a wooden bridge he spied and iron bench nestled between two moss-covered trees. He grasped her firmly by both wrists, led her to it, and pulled her down next to him.

"Angel, please, let's drop the bullshit," he demanded. "I didn't come here to talk about work. We can't spend all day doing this tap dance around our issues. We need to talk about what happened. We need to talk about us. There are many things that I need to explain to you . . ."

"Michael, please," she interrupted, "there is something that you need to know."

She had to tell him now before she lost her nerve, before he poured out his soul to a woman who had deceived him in the worst possible way.

"I don't know if there is a right way to say this,"

"Shhh." He silenced her with a finger placed softly against her lips. "I'll let you have your say when I've finished."

Nichole groaned, she knew she could simply blurt out the truth about their daughter, yet a huge part of her wanted to hear what he had to say, needed to understand the reasoning for his betrayal and shattering her heart into a million, jagged, tiny pieces.

"When I first came to Hampton Roads," he continued, "the last thing that I expected was that a beautiful, emerald eye, spitfire would walk into my life and turn my whole world upside down. It's no secret that my sins are many, but I have never once mislead a woman into believing that I cared more for them than I actually did. I never promised them anything or hinted toward the inclination of a future together. It may sound crass I know, but the point I'm trying to make is that I never believed I was capable, of truly caring about anyone other than myself. I never once lied to you about my feelings for you. I told you the morning after we first made love that you were different than any woman that I had ever met and the night of the grand opening when I told you that I loved you I meant it. I was not some desperate attempt to hold on to you."

Nichole grew agitated, she was being assaulted by a myriad of emotions and seemed unable to processes one from the other. That night held for her such horrific memories and anytime her mind was forced back to it the emotions were still painfully raw.

"You know, Michael, what I don't understand is that if you cared about me that much, shared in my pain and trusted me with the truth about your childhood, how is that you forgot to mention the fact that you are married?"

"Was married," he retorted, "the divorce is final."

Nichole rolled her eyes toward the sky and silently asked god to give her strength.

"Fine," she said, facing him. "Was married. But at the time we were together, during the moments you made love to me you were in fact married."

Michael tensed and raked his fingers through his hair, "On paper only. Angel, by the time I had met you I had been separated from that bitch for many years. She drug out the divorce for the sole purpose of making my life a living hell. Caroline is poison plain and simple. I'm a coward okay; I didn't want to risk losing you. I didn't want the mere idea of her to taint anything we shared."

Nichole could see the pained expression on his face. He was obviously telling the truth. The look of pure disgust in his eyes at the mention of Caroline's name was no act for her benefit. He wholly despised this woman, the truth of which left Nichole with more questions than answers.

"Michael, you were married to the woman. You must have loved her at some point."

"Loved her." Michael laughed out loud, a cruel cutting sound. He stood to pace the ground as he spoke, his focus far away, distant and cold. "Caroline and I met when we were both young, both greedy and both focused on climbing the ranks among the obnoxiously wealthy. I wanted her political connections, she wanted my money. It was a shallow business arrangement that worked for us for a while. When she found out about my past she was repulsed by the fact that I had come from a poor, abusive, alcoholic father." He turned to look at her, the storm in his eyes pulling at her soul. "Jesus Christ Nikki, the woman never told me she was pregnant and went out and aborted my child because children were not in her plans. How in the hell could I ever love that."

Nichole stared in stunned silence, all color draining from her cheeks. She stood to face him struggling for words, but ultimately rendered mute by the harsh reality suddenly thrust upon her. Her hands flew to her mouth in an effort to suppress the need to wretch. When she was finally able to speak, her words were shaky and broken. "Please tell me, tell me that's a sick metaphor for something else . . . she didn't . . ."

There was sadness in Michael's eyes she had never seen before, a hauntingly painful gaze that looked more through her than at her. "Yes, yes she did. Caroline never wanted children. When she discovered she was pregnant, she told no one and scheduled the procedure out of town. I found out by accident months after the fact. I don't know how far along she was, have no idea if I would have had a son or a daughter. I only know that for a small space in time I was almost someone's father."

Chapter 33

NICHOLE STEPPED BACK HORRIFIED, her heart beating frantically. She tried to breathe. "Oh Michael," she spoke, wild-eyed and shaking nervously. "Oh dear God, Michael I'm sorry."

Tears began to spill down her cheeks, the breeze around her suddenly cold and biting.

Michael knew the story he had spun was not a pretty one, yet he hadn't expected it to illicit this type of reaction. He closed the space between then in two long strides and took her face in the palm of his hands, kissing away each tear before they had the chance to spill from her face and hit the ground.

"It was a long time ago, angel, and I am a man not worthy of your tears."

Nichole broke free from his tender grasp, her hands splayed nervously through her hair, her eyes wild with emotion. She walked off the trail and further into the trees, hoping to disappear completely. Michael followed more confused than ever. Once they were far out of earshot of any passerby she turned to look at him, her face stained with tears, "Michael you don't understand, it's what I've been trying to tell you since we arrived. I'm so very sorry."

He grabbed her by the wrists in an attempt to steady her shaking and hoping to make some sense out of this sudden tirade of emotion. "What is it, Nikki? What do you have to be sorry for? You did nothing."

She looked up at him her eyes wild, swallowing hard she managed to speak as coherently as possible. "You have a daughter, Michael."

He looked at her with an equal amount of confusion and concern. "Angel, there is no way you could know that. It's been over ten years since Caroline had the abortion. No one could know that."

Nichole was becoming frustrated and emotionally exhausted. She managed to steady her nerves and looked him directly in the eye. "Michael, listen to me. You have a daughter. We have a daughter. Her name is Hanna. She's two years old. Three weeks after you left I found out that I was pregnant. I was hurt, afraid, and incredibly confused, but I knew one thing for certain I wanted our baby."

Michael stood stone-faced, her words were almost too surreal to be true, and yet he knew in his heart his entire life had changed in a matter of seconds. He took Nichole by the hand and pulled her beside him on a patch of grass and wildflowers. They sat, Nichole continued speaking nervously twisting a blade a grass between her fingers.

"I desperately wanted to tell you. Part of me was afraid you would try to take her from me and she was all I had left of you. I had no idea how Caroline truly fit in your life, but I knew for certain I did not want her anywhere near my daughter." She paused to catch her breath, to slow her beating heart, the weight she had carried for so long finally being released in the secrets she revealed.

Michael stilled her trembling hands by grasping them between his own, the warmth of his touch welcomed yet surprised her. For the first time since she had begun speaking she stopped to read his expression and to her surprised he was smiling, his eyes ice blue, and not the stormy gray she had expected.

"Why are you smiling? You have to hate me right now."

He picked a blue Bellflower and handed it to her. "Are you ready to calm down now, my angel?"

She looked at him and nodded like an exhausted child at the end of a tantrum, eyes stinging, through a mantel of wet lashes.

"I could never hate you Nichole, not ever. You are everything I dared to dream existed, but thought for certain I'd never have. Now you're telling me we share a daughter. A little miracle we created together. How could I hate you?"

"Because I kept her from you hidden from you, you've missed out on her first steps and her first words all because of me," she said, looking at the ground as she spoke. "I know it was a horrible thing to do. I was afraid of losing her and . . ."

"Stop and look at me," he said, raising her chin, forcing her to look at him. "I was mesmerized by you the moment I saw you. I fought my feelings for you for weeks, but I was in love with you long before I ever made love to you. There may have been space and time between us, but my feelings never changed. You have been a part of me every waking moment since the god-awful night of the opening and I've hated myself for hurting you ever since. I understand why you did what you did, angel. Please tell me now that you will allow me to be in our daughter's life. Tell me you still want me in your life."

An hour had passed, possibly two. The entire conversation seemed surreal, suspended in time. Nichole felt as if she were almost outside her body watching it all take place as mere spectator. But it was real, Michael was real and he was here beside her, surrounded by the beauty of nature as she confessed her sins to the man she loved and God above. A chill had settled in the air piercing her skin and the sun lowering in the distance cast a golden hue on her surroundings; the scene itself enchanting if it weren't all emotionally exhausting.

Nichole smiled for the first time since their conversation began and removed a picture of Hanna from her pocket. "Yes . . . I want you in my life and I want our daughter to know her father, but I need to be sure you plan on staying in our lives. If not mine then most definitely hers, you have to be certain beyond all doubt that you want the role as her father. I can't let you break her heart, Michael," she said, handing him the photo.

He cradled the image in the palm of his hand as if it were the rarest gem on Earth. In silence he studied every tiny nuance of the cherub staring back at him; ebony hair exactly like his, the bright beaming emerald eyes of her mother and smile to melt the coldest of hearts. He was mesmerized by her button of a nose, the shape of her fingers and her chubby little toes.

With a an expression of pure awe he turned to Nichole, the mother of his child, the woman who had turned his entire world upside down yet again, grabbed her face and planted a fierce, passion filled kiss upon her lips. “I have never wanted anything more in my life do you understand me?” he commanded.

Nichole, lightheaded from the sudden rush to her senses merely nodded. “You, Nichole McCallister, belong to me, you have always belonged to me.” His voice was filled with passion and pride, a man claiming possession of what was rightfully his. “And this magnificent creature that we created she needs both of us. Don’t you agree?”

Nichole managed another nod and then erupted in joy-filled laughter. The dream she never dared to dream was finally coming true. Michael wanted them, both of them and when Michael Collier truly wanted something nothing could stand in his way.

“Would you like to go meet your daughter?”

“Try and stop me.”

Chapter 34

As they made their way across the Chesapeake Bay, Nichole filled Michael in on the complete tragic account of everything their daughter had been through, the endless days and nights of testing, the surgery to close the hole in her heart and another full year of gut-wrenching anticipation while they charted her progress. He said next to nothing through the telling of the tale, but a single tear that trailed the form of his face told Nichole all she needed to know.

Night had settled in by the time they pulled into the drive. Michael cut off the engine and sat in silence enveloped by the darkness around them. A whirl of emotions coursed through him yet he sat perfectly still as if he were made of stone. A moment such as this he had never dreamed imaginable and it left him feeling equally eager and apprehensive.

Searching out his expression in the blackness of the night it was if Nichole could read his unspoken thoughts. Gently reaching over she took his hand in hers and squeezed, "Michael, she's going to love you. I have no doubts and neither should you." He let loose a heavy sigh, pulled her hand to his lips and kissed each finger lightly.

Several of the lights in the house were on and two other cars lined the driveway. The first he immediately recognized as Estelle Peterman's. He was sure to get a ration of shit from her. Glancing to the other vehicle he questioned, "Whose Beamer?"

“Estelle and Maxie are inside for moral support. No one was sure how this day would play out. Now come on,” she urged, “let’s go meet your daughter.”

The door swung open before Nichole had a chance to put her key in the lock. Behind it stood the silver-haired powerhouse that was Estelle Peterman with her ever present *I told you so* grin.

“Do I need to say it?” she asked Nichole.

“Please don’t. You were right. You’re always right and I promise to never doubt a word you say for the rest of my life,” Nichole playfully replied, as she bet down to kiss the soft wrinkled cheek.

“Make sure you explain that to George in the morning. We’ve been married for half a century and he has yet to figure that out. And as for you,” she said, pointing a finger at Michael as he entered warily fully expecting the berating he was about to receive. ”I have a thing or two to say to you, Michael Collier.”

“Yes ma’am,” he replied, sounding like a chided child though he couldn’t help but smile. He missed Estelle and her willful ways more than he had realized. Though he never truly knew a home, this place felt like home, these people were his home.

Estelle approached him with her hands on her hips and looked him over thoroughly, a steely expression upon her face. For several prolonged moments she stood in silence wearing her housecoat and slippers and silently critiqued every last detail of his visage. Finally after what seemed like a small eternity of studied silence she threw her arms open wide and hugged him tight. “What the hell took you so long, son?”

Michael had never known his mother, had never had any form of a mother figure in his life yet he couldn’t imagine any person on the planet more suited for the role, than the wise old woman in his arms. She took to him the instant they met, scolded him whenever she saw fit and gave no inclination that she was neither impressed nor intimidated by his money or his power. She saw him for him from the start. He lifted her off her feet and held her tight. Delighted when she squealed and her worn slippers fell from her feet to the ground.

She playfully punched at his shoulder. “Put me down you rascal, what will the neighbors think?"

He placed her bare feet gently on the carpet. "I've missed you too Estelle."

Maxie entered from the kitchen. He approached Michael and extended a hand in greeting. "Max Porter," he said. "I don't think we've ever formally been introduced. I've sure heard a hell of a lot about you."

Michael smiled, he had never expected such a warm reception to his arrival. It was clear these people loved Nichole deeply and supported whatever choices she made and for that he was grateful. "Michael Collier, it's a pleasure to finally meet the man that literally saved the life of the woman I love. I can never thank you enough for all you've done for her and my . . . my daughter."

"Still getting used to the idea I see."

Michael nodded. "It's a lot to wrap your mind around in one day."

Max looked at Nichole. "She's asleep in her room. You should let Michael get a good look at her before she wakes up and the horns push away her halo," he said. "Estelle why don't you come in the kitchen and help me open a bottle of wine."

Estelle looked confused yet followed him anyway as Michael and Nichole made their way down the hall. "Since when do you need my help opening a bottle of wine? I wanted to see Michael's face when he saw the baby for the first . . ."She stopped cold when she eyed the look of dread in Maxie's expression. "What's wrong?" she demanded.

He placed his back against the kitchen counter, placing a hand on either side of him as if attempting to conceal what was stacked behind him, his fingers grasping tightly as if trying to crush the granite beneath them. Swallowing hard he spoke, "You were here all day correct?"

"Yes, why do you ask?"

"Where you here when the mail was delivered? Did you see anyone put anything in the mailbox?"

Estelle was becoming agitated. This line of questioning made no sense to her. "I suppose I was here when the mail was delivered. It usually comes around three o'clock, but I didn't spend the day watching the mailbox. I was watching Hanna. That's a fulltime job in and of itself. Maxie what the hell is this . . ."

He hesitantly produced an envelope from behind him, a red ribbon the color of blood attached to its surface, the sight of which immediately set the old woman's hands to trembling.

"No," was the only word she could manage.

When he pulled out the contents of the envelope she knew it had to be true. At only one other period in her life had she seen that familiar antique parchment, with the message it held hidden carefully scripted in calligraphy and it was a dark time indeed.

"No," she repeated, now visibly shaking all over. "It's not possible. He's not allowed to send mail through the prison without it being read first. They'd never allow him to send her anything," she protested.

Maxie held the envelope in front of him, displaying its entire surface for her to see. "That's the scary part. There is no postage on this thing. It had to be hand delivered and placed in her mailbox. I found it tucked between some magazines like it was hidden there on purpose."

Estelle tilted her head back and looked to the sky as if silently asking for strength. "What does it say?" she asked, certain she did not want to know.

With pure disgust hanging on every syllable, he read the words aloud.

"*When all appears certain in an uncertain world, faith will be tested fury unfurled.*"

Michael Collier sat on the living room sofa, babe in arms and bathed in bliss. Hanna had opened her eyes the moment they entered her room, sat up and smiled at her mother and the man who stood beside her. She studied him curiously for a moment, pushed away the covers, and toddled over to place a hand on his cheek. In that moment, Michael's heart melted away. As if by instinct Hanna threw up her arms, wrapped them around his neck and laid her head on his chest. He scooped her up without hesitation and was certain from this point on he would never let her go.

Nichole lingered by the fireplace utterly dazzled by the sight before her. She had dreamed of moments like this, but nothing could have prepared her for the intensity of this brief time in space. It was magical and it was surreal. Michael's strong solid frame seemed to dwarf the child in his arms. Hanna was two now and toddler hell-bent on taking over the world, but asleep in Michael's tender embrace she looked small and fragile. This is how it was always meant to be she thought to herself, the three of them together . . . a family.

Maxie entered from the kitchen with a tray of wine filled crystal glasses. He handed one to Michael and then to Nichole and took one for himself downing the entire glass in one sudden gulp.

Nichole spied him suspiciously. "Thirsty?" she questioned accusingly.

"Something like that," he replied.

Estelle followed soon after and struggled to maintain her composure. She held her glass with both hands in an attempt to disguise the trembling she felt inside and took her usual seat in the recliner at the edge of the sofa. This was the moment Nichole had waited for since the day Michael left town. Three years of heartache and torment and now all that she had ever wanted was right here in this room. How could they break this news to her now? Shatter her safety and solace? Yet if all she suspected was true how could they not? If that monster of a man was somehow free, watching them, waiting for them. She had to know the truth one way or another.

Michael was oblivious to all that was transpiring around him. He was lost in the angelic presence he held close to his heart, but Nichole was immediately aware that something was not right. She eyed Estelle and knew the woman's fake smile in an instant, then immediately looked to Maxie.

"What is it," she demanded. "What's wrong?"

Maxie stood beside her and filled her glass to almost overflowing. "Take a drink."

"I don't want to take a drink. Now will you two tell me what the hell is going on?"

"Take a drink, Nikki and then I'll tell you."

Broken from his trance Michael reluctantly handed the sleeping child over to Estelle and stood. Nichole downed half of a full glass of wine in one swift gulp.

"Now tell me whatever it is you don't want to tell me," she demanded.

Maxie raked a hand through his hair, looked to Michael and then to Nichole.

"Did you receive any calls today?"

"What do you mean?" Nichole asked, silently starting to panic.

"Have you checked your cell phone at all today, Nikki? Any calls out of the ordinary?

She paused and thought for a moment. The entire day was such a blur, a whirlwind of emotions. "I turned the ringer off before I got out of the car to meet Michael. It's still in my purse. Why?"

"Would you get it please?" Maxie asked, his voice plain and flat. Not like Maxie at all.

Growing frustrated and increasingly impatient, Nichole retreated to Hanna's room to retrieve her purse. In her absence, Michael cast Max a disapproving glare. "What the hell is going on," he mumbled barely above a whisper.

"Maybe nothing," he replied, "but if it is what I think it is I'm damn glad you're here."

Nichole returned with her purse and fumbled through its contents searching for her cell phone. She spied the metallic case and snatched it from the bag, its surface displaying five missed calls in bright red lights that assaulted her eyes. She looked up at the two men before her, her eyes wide and frightened. All the calls were from the same number. A number she hadn't seen in over a decade.

Reaching for her glass of wine she quickly downed the remaining contents and held it out to Maxie. "Fill it," she demanded.

Michael quickly tiring from what appeared to be a twisted mental mind game between the woman he loved and her so-called best friend began demanding answers. "Will one of you tell me what the fuck is going on here?"

Nichole looked down at her phone fighting to steady her hands and then at Michael. "I have five missed calls from the Virginia State Police."

It took a moment for Michael to grasp the severity of the words she spoke, but when he did he became enraged. "Give me the phone, I'll listen to the messages."

"No, I have to do this," she said, her fingers struggling to press the right buttons on the screen to grant her access her voice mail.

Nichole lifted the phone to her ear as her whole body began to shake. She closed her eyes to forcibly hold back the tears, but they flowed silently down her cheek. Her mind suddenly filled with horrific images of mayhem and madness, she became dizzy and she struggled to breathe. The wineglass slipped from her grasp, shattering at her feet in an array of broken crystal shimmering in the fire's light and at the same moment the front of her home, her place of safety and solitude was illuminated by red and blue flashing lights. Denton Walsh had escaped from prison and he was coming for her.

End

Acknowledgements

To my family for their endless support and poking and prodding, I thank you. In answer to your questions my darling daughters, "yes I am finally going to finish my book."

Author and dear friend P.D. Stevens, thank you for your encouragement and guidance in helping me to achieve my dream. I'm not certain I would have gone all the way with this if it weren't for you. Much Love.

To Robin Harper from Wicked by Design thank you for making my vision a reality. It is truly beautiful.

To my editor, Kerry Genova of Writer's Resource Inc., thank you for your hard work and patience in working with this first timer. Just so you know, I promise not to use just so, so much, in the future.

To the Great Spirit in the sky who guides us, thank you for your presence in my life. I know I'm not an easy one to watch over. Blessed Be.

Made in the USA
Charleston, SC
08 June 2015